Strange Sensations

"I feel it is a bit warm in here, don't you?" asked Celia.

Severly sat down next to her. "No, but I would expect you to. How many cups of punch have you had?"

Celia looked around the room vaguely. "Two or three, I believe. Everyone has been fetching me cups." She turned to the duke and gazed at him quite boldly, noting how handsome he looked. A hazy glow seemed to surround the duke. The blood pounded in her wrists and temples and Celia wondered why she felt so muzzy.

"More like four or five," the duke said archly.

"Four or five what?" Celia asked, her eyes fixed on the scar on his cheek, thinking that it was most attractive.

"Cups of punch, Miss Langston," he explained patiently.

"Oh, yes, cups." Celia had no idea what he was talking about and continued to gaze at his face. Celia reached out a gentle hand and lightly touched the scar on his cheek. The duke was suddenly still.

"I feel very strange," she said faintly, unable to look away. She wanted to feel his lips on hers. Ever since the day she had rebuffed Squire Marchman's fumbling attempt to kiss her, she had often wondered how it would feel to kiss someone she wanted to kiss.

Telling himself there was no harm in one kiss, Severly leaned and gently took her lips with his. As the warmth of his mouth held hers, the world stopped for Celia. Everything became part of this moment—the sunlight filtering in from the window behind them, the scent of tuberoses and lilies, all became part of this, her first kiss. . . .

A Spinster's Luck

Rhonda Woodward

A SIGNET BOOK

SIGNET
Published by New American Library, a division of
Penguin Putnam Inc., 375 Hudson Street,
New York, New York 10014, U.S.A.
Penguin Books Ltd, 80 Strand,
London WC2R 0RL, England
Penguin Books Australia Ltd, Ringwood,
Victoria, Australia
Penguin Books Canada Ltd, 10 Alcorn Avenue,
Toronto, Ontario, Canada M4V 3B2
Penguin Books (N.Z.) Ltd, 182–190 Wairau Road,
Auckland 10, New Zealand

Penguin Books Ltd, Registered Offices:
Harmondsworth, Middlesex, England

First published by Signet, an imprint of New American Library,
a division of Penguin Putnam Inc.

First Printing, December 2002
10 9 8 7 6 5 4 3 2 1

REGISTERED TRADEMARK—MARCA REGISTRADA

Printed in the United States of America

Prologue

1806

Silence reigned throughout the cavernous darkness as the thin young girl slowly descended the great oak staircase. Again, sleep's gentle touch eluded her, and she hoped a mug of milk might aid her to slumber. As she reached the first landing, she paused. Could someone be there? Tilting her head to the side she listened intently, trying to probe the dense blackness. Her breath expelled in her relief. The sinister noise was only the *swish, click, swish, click* of the massive pendulum clock a few feet away.

Stopping at the bottom of the staircase, she extended one hand searchingly before her. Vaguely, she recalled the kitchen being located down a long passage to her left. Cautiously, she proceeded, unnerved in the dark and eerily quiet house.

"Drake, my dear brother, you cannot be so heartless! Celia's parents have been dead for just a week." The girl froze upon hearing her name and the anger in the Duchess of Harbrooke's usually gentle voice.

"Be reasonable, Imy; the chit is little more than a child," came the irritated reply. Realizing the voices were coming from the library, Celia moved silently and tentatively toward the door that was slightly ajar. She recognized the deeper voice as belonging to her grace's brother, the Duke of Severly.

"As you know, before he died, Philip gave me half guardianship over your sons," he said. "I take this responsibility seriously, and I do not like the idea of a child having charge over my nephews." The duke's tone was emphatic. Celia's breath suddenly felt trapped in her body. With trembling fingers she clutched the edge of a hall table to steady her legs.

"Celia is sixteen, Drake, which is not infantile. Her father was the vicar of Harford, and when my dear husband died, he and his wife were of great comfort to me. Celia is a good and intelligent girl. I like her, and so do the boys. Celia is an orphan now. Having her live with me and the boys is the best arrangement for us all." The duchess's voice sounded stubborn.

"Sixteen? I hesitate to give a child so much responsibility. Can you not find someone like our old nanny, Crawfie, to care for the boys? Someone more mature, more trustworthy?" His deep voice portrayed intolerance and impatience.

Terror filled Celia's heart as she suppressed an anguished gasp with a clutched hand pressed to her mouth. They were going to send her away! Where could she go? Would she end up in a workhouse? *Oh, Mama, Papa, why did you leave me?* Celia restrained herself from crying out in her fear and loneliness.

Standing petrified, she listened to the argumentative tones, oblivious to the faint chill seeping into her skin from the cold stone floor.

"Drake, you know Crawfie is too old to take full charge of the boys, but she will still be here to help. Besides, I have no desire to be away and leave them under the supervision of someone else. Do you think I will go back into Society just because my year of mourning will soon be completed? No, I am very content to stay here at Harbrooke."

"I can see that you are determined in this, Imy, but if I ever feel the girl is not doing a proper job of caring for Henry and Peter, I shall press the issue."

"Everything will be fine; you will see. Let us not argue on this any longer," Imogene said wearily.

"Of course, dear sister, get some rest. I shall stay and read a little longer."

Celia heard her grace's steps coming toward the door. With a quick turn, she lifted the skirt of her bed gown and fled back down the hall, her bare feet barely making a sound on the cold stone. She did not slow her flight until reaching the sanctuary of her little room on the second floor.

"Why does he hate me?" Celia wondered aloud in anguish, clutching the bedpost as if someone were trying to wrench her from it. "What have I done?" Tears rolled down her thin face. How the duke terrified her with his mean, hawklike face. At this moment she believed he could be the devil himself. Celia crawled into her feather bed and buried herself under the covers. Squeezing her eyes shut, she prayed fervently that the duke would leave Harbrooke very soon and never return.

Chapter One

1816

A chilling wind pierced the air, but the day was bright
and there was the sparkle of moisture from a recent rain on the expansive parkland surrounding Harbrooke Hall. This proved an irresistible lure to Drake,
the fifth Duke of Severly, and his steed, Blackwind. The
duke decided he was enjoying his visit to Harbrooke
Hall, his sister's residence in Kent. Or to be more accurate, it was the home that now belonged to his young
nephew, Henry.

Harbrooke Hall brought to his mind many happy
childhood associations. Indeed, this very stretch of field,
leading to a wooded area to the east, reminded him of
when he and Philip Harbrooke used to slay dragons and
challenge highwaymen with stick swords. With a quick
movement of his heels, he guided Blackwind across the
field into the copse of wood, a nostalgic smile touching
his handsome face.

Many years ago, before death and war had invaded
his peaceful life, Drake and his family had often visited
Harbrooke. One particular holiday—a lifetime ago, it
seemed—stood out in his mind.

On an exceptionally fine spring day, he and his friend
Philip had swaggered about the estate in their doeskin
breeches and spurs. They had been drinking themselves
silly and making absurd wagers with all the cockiness only
young men on term break from Oxford could display.

Imogene had been just a slip of a thing, but already showing signs of great beauty. Philip, to Drake's disgust, had been casting sheep eyes to the girl who would soon become his wife. During luncheon, to their mothers' mutual horror, Philip challenged Drake to a steeplechase. Knowing the challenge was intended to impress Imy, Drake, willing to help his friend show off, had accepted with alacrity.

Drake would never forget that wild ride through the cool gloom of the evening, hearing the thudding of the horses' hooves and feeling the wind whip his cheeks.

Philip, several yards ahead, had thundered into this very wood, hoping for a shortcut. Drake could still see his fair head and hear his whoops of excitement. Drake reined in his horse, cautious for not knowing the terrain as well as his friend. Philip's horse fairly flew over the hill, leaving Drake well behind.

A moment later Drake heard a loud noise and Philip's distressed cry. He shouted Philip's name, terrified that his friend had broken his fool neck. As he crested the ridge, his horse stumbling in its haste, Drake came upon Philip up to his neck in a duck pond. Then Drake's horse, not being fond of water, had pulled up abruptly, pitching its rider over his head. Drake had landed quite near Philip, sailing face-first into the shallow murkiness.

After righting himself, he brushed a lily pad from his shoulder. Drake gave Philip a disgusted look. "I am certain this is not the way in which you intended to impress my sister," Drake said to his soaked and muddy friend.

Their fathers had roared with laughter, and even Imogene had hidden a few sniggers behind her hand when they had sloshed back to Harbrooke Hall. A pained smile now touched the duke's face at the bittersweet memories. He mused at the ironic fact that all their wealth and address had not protected him or Imogene or even poor Philip from fate's cruel stab.

Philip's father had died only a short time after the duck pond incident. Philip passed only a few years later from a lung ailment, leaving Imogene a young widow with two small boys. Drake still missed Philip, especially on a day like this. With thoughts shifting to his parents, Drake experienced a faint yet nagging sense of guilt. He had been away on his grand tour, living in a rather disreputable manner, when his mother and father had been struck down by the pox. Now his family consisted only of his sister, Imogene, and her sons, Henry and Peter.

Not that life did not have its compensations. The duke was proud of his family seat in Derbyshire, a beautiful mansion in the Georgian fashion. Recently, he had gone to some expense in modernizing the huge place, even installing water closets in a number of the bedchambers and gas lighting in the staterooms. An invitation to Severly Park in the winter was a much-sought-after favor.

He tried to visit his sister and nephews two or three times a year, but his days were occupied with the running of his vast estates and other manly pursuits in which he so excelled. Though the duke would not admit it to anyone, it was a source of personal pride that he was becoming a respected speaker in the House of Lords. He also took care to ensure that no one could say that he had not added to the already immense family coffers. All in all, he was a man contented with his lot.

As the duke continued to gallop, he crested a knoll and decided to let Blackwind drink from a nearby pond so he could see how the terrain had changed in the last few years.

Upon hearing childish voices and splashing water, he pulled the horse to a slow walk. From a vantage point protected by an ancient oak tree and a dense thicket at the edge of the wood, the duke looked for the source of the voices. Soon he saw his nephews and their governess skipping stones on the recently thawed pond a little distance away.

"Is this a good stone, Celly?" Peter asked in his high little-boy voice.

The young woman bent to examine the stone.

"That should do very well, Peter," she responded seriously.

Peter turned and threw the stone at the pond. It sank without skipping once. Henry, the older of his nephews, and already showing signs of being tall like his father and uncle, had a better understanding of it and threw his stone with more expertise.

"One . . . two . . . three!" the dark-haired Henry counted the skips excitedly.

"Why don't my rocks skip?" Peter kicked a clod of dirt, dejected, as little brothers often are when an older brother can outdo them.

"Well, let's see what we can do," said the governess as she stooped to look for more rocks, lifting her skirts almost above her ankle to avoid the mud around the pond. "Ah, here is one. Now Peter, hold the stone so. Very good. Now hold your arm like this. Crook your elbow. That's it. Hold it out sideways. When you throw, throw it sharply from the wrist, thusly." She made the proper wrist movement to demonstrate.

With a deep breath Peter braced his sturdy legs, and, doing his best to follow instructions, he gave a flick of his wrist, forearm, and elbow.

"One . . . two . . ." Peter grinned with delight as Henry and the governess praised his effort.

The duke, sheltered by the trees, enjoyed watching his nephews' youthful fun. He decided not to disturb them because he had noticed a tendency for them to become rather self-conscious in his presence. Bending down to pat his restive horse's neck, Drake let his curious gaze drift to the governess. From this distance he judged her to be slim and fairly tall, with an elegant way of carrying herself. He noted her golden brown hair but could not recall any specific details of her face. In fact, he could recollect addressing the young woman only two or three times in the last ten years. He remembered fussing a bit when Imogene had engaged her, because the girl had been so young, but the boys had seemed to thrive, so he hadn't given it much thought since then. His curiosity grew. His nephews were luckier than he had been, he thought with some chagrin. The duke's own governess had been quite plump and would never have dreamed of skipping stones with him.

"Come, we must return to the hall now," directed the governess.

The boys protested this loudly.

"You are both filthy," Celia chided gently, "and if you are to get cleaned up before you have tea with your uncle, we must go now."

"Please, just a little longer, Celly?" Peter pleaded.

Henry scrambled around the edge of the pond for a suitable rock. With a triumphant cry he held up a beautifully flat, round stone to his governess. "Here, Celly, you skip this one," he encouraged.

"All right, but just this last one," she warned. Taking the stone from him, she crooked her elbow, and with an expert flick of the wrist she sent the stone skimming across the water.

"One . . . two . . . three . . . four . . . five . . . six!" the boys counted in unison, and Peter jumped about in excitement.

"That was the best ever," said Henry. Both boys turned to their governess, awestruck, as little boys often are when they discover that someone is proficient at skipping stones. The governess dusted off her hands, shook her skirts, and picked up her reticule from a nearby rock.

"Let us go; we do not wish to be late," she said calmly, and turned toward the house.

The duke watched the retreating figures for a few moments with a slightly bemused smile on his face before steering Blackwind back toward Harbrooke Hall. He had no desire to be late for tea.

On the third floor, in the cheery nursery that faced the back garden, Celia was trying to comb Peter's hair. With his face contorted into a severe grimace, he was resisting her ministrations when Imogene, the Duchess of Harbrooke, swept into the room with the smell of lilacs surrounding her.

With her coffee-colored hair and hazel eyes, the duchess greatly resembled her brother, Drake, in countenance, though she appeared petite and almost fragile in her lavender tea gown compared to her brother's large-boned masculinity.

"I can see you two are almost presentable," Imogene observed with a smile, approaching her eldest son and straightening his lapel fondly.

"Mother, why doesn't Celly have tea with us when Uncle Drake is here?" Henry queried. This subject had been on his mind of late, and Henry's brow furrowed from concern. He felt Celly was one of the family, and it did not seem right to him that she did not come to any of the meals when Uncle Drake was visiting.

The duchess gave Celia a disconcerted look. She knew Celia felt uncomfortable around Drake and took measures to avoid him during his stays. But how could the boys be made to understand this?

As she gave a last flick of the brush to Peter's hair, Celia flashed a helpless smile back to Imogene. The boys had been questioning Celia since returning from the pond, and she felt at a loss as to what to tell them.

A mischievous smile raised a dimple at the corner of Celia's mouth. She tried to imagine how they would respond if she said, "I have no tolerance for your arrogant and heartless uncle. And even if I did, he would raise a disgusted brow if a mere governess were so familiar as to join him for tea." No, that would not do, she thought with a mental shake of her head. Especially with Henry. He would never stop asking questions until he was satisfied with the answers. Celia knew something had to be said, and since Imogene didn't seem inclined to offer a response, the job was left to her.

"I am sure your uncle would like to spend some time with the two of you without me tagging along." It was as good a response as any to offer, she thought as she put away the hairbrush.

Henry gave Celia a level gaze with his surprisingly mature blue eyes. "Mother is always there at mealtimes when Uncle Drake visits," he pointed out logically.

What could she say to that? Celia wondered in dismay, looking around the cozy nursery for a clue. At thirteen, Henry would not easily be fobbed off with evasions. Imogene, Henry, and Peter stood in the middle of the room, staring at her expectantly.

With an inward sigh, Celia decided to be straightforward with her charges. "Henry," she began carefully, "it just would not be seemly for me to join you and your uncle at mealtimes. After all, I am not a member of the family, and your uncle is the Duke of Sev—"

"Yes you are too family!" interrupted eleven-year-old Peter. He looked at his mother and older brother with wide brown eyes, not understanding how Celly could say such a thing.

"*I* am the Duke of Harbrooke," Henry said, and for the first time in his young life he sounded like it. "Mother and Grandmama are both duchesses. You *always* eat with us unless Uncle Drake is here."

"Such a fuss over nothing." Imogene, seeing this conversation was not progressing well, stepped forward. "Celia just means that she does not know Uncle Drake, and he, of course, does not know her. Really, we can't expect him to love Celly as we do. Besides, the only time Celly gets a chance to read or sew is when you two are otherwise occupied. My goodness, I did not realize how selfish you two have become! Uncle Drake is waiting for you. Now run along, and I shall be down presently."

This seemed to satisfy Peter, but Henry still frowned, though neither one said anything as they left the room. Both women sighed in relief as the door shut behind them.

"My, you've been having a time of it, haven't you?" Imogene observed as she seated herself before the fireplace and watched Celia pick up the boys' discarded clothing.

"Yes, rather." Celia laughed, a lovely, trilling laugh that usually elicited an answering smile from those who heard it.

Celia looked at the duchess, her expression changing to chagrin. "My goodness, Henry sounded like a barrister! Can you imagine what the duke would say if Henry had dragged me to tea?"

Celia envisioned the duke sneering down his perfect, aristocratic nose and ordering her from the room for being so presumptuous. Not that she had any desire to be included. In fact, for the last ten years she had been successful at avoiding any contact with the duke on his visits to Harbrooke. She had paid close attention to his habits, when he rose and retired, which parts of the house he rarely visited, all so that she could avoid the imposing man. Granted, Napoleon had aided her, for the duke had been much away because of the war, but it was still disquieting when he did arrive. The whole house became unsettled. The maids and footmen bustled about nervously. Even the cantankerous cook strove for unusual perfection in the normally delicious meals she served.

"I cannot imagine that Drake would say anything," the duchess replied. "This is my home, and Drake is too well mannered to censure me for who sits at my table. Besides, Celia, you are my dear friend and it would be natural for you to dine with me."

Imogene had never understood Celia's marked aversion to her brother. She always suspected that Celia knew that years ago Drake had been critical of so young a girl caring for the boys. Even so, she never pressed Celia on the subject, out of respect for the sensitive girl's feelings.

"What a dear you are!" Celia exclaimed, crossing the room to sit next to the duchess. "It is just that we are all so familiar and used to one another here at Harbrooke that we forget that the duke is used to town manners. I am sure it would offend his grace's sensibilities to be forced to dine with the governess," she reasoned.

"Oh, twaddle! You aren't really the governess anymore; you are more of a companion to me. As for Drake's sensibilities, I believe he gave those up long ago," Imogene opined dryly.

Celia made no response, and the duchess could see that she was not going to budge. She never had. And it was unlikely that she would now.

Changing the subject, she told Celia, "Jarvis rode over today. Edna has taken a bad turn and he is hoping that you will go over to Harford Abbey and sit with her. Evidently she is giving Jarvis and the servants fits again."

Celia's eyes flashed to the duchess in surprised concern. Harford Abbey was a musty old manor house built on the ruin of an ancient abbey some three miles away. Edna Forbisher was the local eccentric, a recluse who had not left her house for over thirty years. Local gossips liked to claim that old Miss Forbisher had been crossed in love in her youth and had never recovered from her broken heart.

There was some truth to that supposition, but Celia felt she knew the full reason: Edna Forbisher could not stand the company of most people. She was headstrong, intolerant, and in bad health. It had just been easier for the woman to grow old staying at home alone than to deal with the local populace.

Celia's mother had taken her to visit Edna many years ago. At first, the odd old woman had rejected the kindness of the good vicar's wife. Slowly, though, Celia's mother had won her over, and Edna became grudgingly grateful for the company.

Celia made her first visit alone to the frightening old woman's home a few months after her parents' deaths. Somehow it made her feel closer to her mother to continue to do something they had shared. After a while, she came to enjoy her visits with the peculiar woman and the dark, faded beauty of Harford Abbey.

"I had planned to visit her the day after tomorrow, but of course I will go in the morning if Jarvis thinks she's that poorly," Celia said, a concerned frown on her brow. Edna must be ill if her butler came all the way to Harbrooke to see if Celia would visit.

"I don't know how you can abide that gloomy place. It would fair give me the shivers, even in the light of day," Imogene said, emphasizing her point with a good shudder.

"It's not so bad when you've been there a few times. The house reminds me of an old woman who was once a great beauty. You can still see vestiges of her loveliness in unexpected ways," she said thoughtfully, sadness touching her lovely eyes.

Imogene looked at her friend with some surprise.

"You really are fond of the place and old Miss Forbisher, aren't you? It's not just a duty to you."

"Oh, no, I look forward to my time with Edna. She wasn't always this way. Once, she led an interesting life."

And it was sad—sad to be old and lonely with no family. Knowing that her friend would strongly disagree, Celia did not tell Imogene that she felt an affinity with Edna Forbisher. Celia knew she could very easily end up the same way as the old woman.

That evening, Celia had her dinner on a tray in her room, her usual practice during the duke's visits. After several hours of unaccustomed inactivity, Celia soon tired of her pretty cream and blue room. Setting aside a pair of stockings she was darning, Celia rose from the chair by the fire, deciding to seek a book from the library before retiring.

Avoiding the duke had never proved a difficulty. She would just take the servants' stairs and ask one of the maids for the duke's whereabouts. If he was not in the library, she would dash in, choose a book, and be back in her room in a trice.

All went according to plan until she stepped from the library, holding the prized book.

"Ah, just the person I was hoping to see," came a deep voice from down the hall.

Celia froze in terror, feeling as if she had been caught trying to steal the crown jewels. Why did she always have this reaction to him? she wondered, annoyed at herself for reacting so. It was as if she were ten years younger and he still had the power to throw her out.

She took a deep, steadying breath. "Yes, your grace?" she asked, turning toward him with a quick curtsy. Celia was a tall girl, but she still had to look up to see his face. She saw that he was dressed for dinner in a coat of Spanish blue superfine, well molded to his broad shoulders. His waistcoat was a cream-colored brocade picked out in blue thread, and his beige trousers hugged his muscular, well-defined legs all the way to the ankles. He wore his dark hair slightly long and styled in the fashionable windswept mode. She could not help perceiving that he evidenced the epitome of manly elegance.

Celia always found the duke's appearance a bit jolting, for his face proved a masculine version of his sister's countenance. She noted a square jaw with a slightly cleft chin, a straight, aristocratic nose, and darkly fringed hazel eyes. A small, jagged scar marred the high plain of his right cheekbone, but she thought it suited the rakish air that surrounded him. His smile was dashing, she knew, for she had noticed it once when she had chanced to see him playing with his nephews in the garden.

Despite the languidness of his stance, Celia sensed something assessing in his eyes. It occurred to her that beneath his polished and urbane exterior, his grace was a formidable man.

"May we speak in the library?" He gestured toward the room, pleased that coincidence finally presented him with the opportunity to take a closer look at the young figure that had intrigued him earlier in the day.

"Of course." She stepped past him to stand in the middle of the library, feeling curiosity surface through her fear. Why in the world would he wish to speak to her?

The duke walked to the fireplace and stood with his back to it, facing her. He scrutinized the young woman before him. Her gown was a dark gray-blue and very plain, without even a ribbon to relieve its severity, but the color showed to advantage her very pale, ivory complexion.

Earlier, at the pond, he had thought her quite slim, but now he noticed her subtly voluptuous figure. His lazy gaze traveled up to her faintly flushed cheeks. He saw the perfect oval of her face, and her cheekbones, high and smooth. She was beautiful. But her eyes were what made the breath catch in the duke's chest.

They were the most arresting eyes he had ever seen, and he was a man who had looked into the eyes of many beautiful women. They were large, dark-lashed, brownish, and slightly aslant at the corners. Even in the poor light of the fire he could see green flecks in the irises.

He wondered how he had ever missed this lovely creature. How had half the men in Kent? *And what the devil was I going to say to her?* he asked himself vexedly.

Staring down at the book in her hands, Celia struggled to quell the nervous trembling of her fingers while waiting for the duke to speak.

After a moment, as the duke still had not spoken, she glanced up and met the full force of those hazel eyes and instantly found it difficult to breathe correctly. It suddenly occurred to her that she had never been alone with a man in the whole of her life, nonetheless one as imposing as the Duke of Severly.

This was all rather daunting for Celia, because even in quiet Harford, the duke's reputation was well known. She had heard it said that all of London proclaimed him a famous whip for having beaten Lord Alvanly's record from London to Windsor with his matched grays. Rumor had it that Gentleman Jackson considered the duke his best pupil, and that if he had not been a duke, his grace would have made an imposing pugilist. Even his own sister said that he casually wagered enormous sums of money on the turn of a card, and won more often than not.

Imogene and her mother-in-law, the Dowager Duchess of Harbrooke, discussed in hushed tones, and with much concerned shaking of heads, the duke's reputation for having broken more than his fair share of hearts.

Celia knew that someone as sophisticated as the duke could only find her the dowdiest of bumpkins, and decided that that must be why he looked at her so oddly. Gazing at him expectantly, she waited politely for him to speak as she sought to hide her trembling.

Recalling himself, the duke began, "Er . . . Miss . . . Ahh?" *Oh, famous,* he thought, *I can't even recall the dashed girl's name.* He could not very well call her Celly, as the boys did.

A hint of a dimple appeared in the left corner of Celia's mouth. "My name is Celia Langston, your grace," she supplied quietly, her lashes lowered to her cheeks.

"My apologies, Miss Langston. How remiss of me not

to recall the name of my nephews' governess," he said, giving her the slightest bow of atonement, accompanied by a smile that had set more than one lady's heart aflutter.

To Celia, who had long been accustomed to thinking of the duke as a monster, the smile appeared menacing. Her skittishness increased, and she glanced at the double doors, desperately hoping someone would enter.

The duke noticed her distress and wondered at it. He couldn't positively recall ever speaking to the girl, nonetheless giving her a distaste of him. He frowned. In truth, he could not recall giving *any* female a distaste of him.

Walking over to one of the bookshelves, he said, "I wish to discuss Henry and Peter." He noticed the frown that instantly marred her delightfully arched eyebrows. "They are getting older and I am concerned. I want to know if you feel they do as well as they should in their studies."

In her surprise at his words, Celia forgot her nervousness. He did not know if his nephews, of whom he was guardian, were prepared for school or not? Celia thought he should be ashamed for not taking a better interest.

"Yes, your grace, it is my opinion that Henry and Peter are doing very well. They are both intelligent boys with a desire to learn, and a curiosity about the world around them. Their tutor, Mr. Drummond, is quite pleased. You have no reason to worry about them academically." She stood very straight and her tone was defensive, as if he had implied an insult.

The duke, who had been a successful strategist during the war, knew when it was wise to retreat. Somehow he had gotten off on the wrong foot with the lovely Miss Langston. He could not explain her abrupt manner toward him, but he did know when to cut his losses.

"Thank you, Miss Langston; that is my opinion also. I did want to confirm it with you, as you are their governess and are with them regularly."

Celia's ire immediately deflated. To give him his due, he had always taken great interest in everything concern-

ing the boys. Maybe he just needed reassuring, she reasoned. Either way, the encounter had not been so horrid,
and it appeared she would be able to escape
momentarily.

"I understand, your grace," she said quickly with a
curtsy. She waited for his dismissal and looked at the
scar on his cheek, since she found it impossible to meet
his unsettling gaze.

With a slight inclination of his head he wished her
good-night, and Celia hoped she did not appear rude in
her haste to leave.

Chapter Two

The next morning, after the boys ran off to the stables with lumps of sugar for Blackwind, Celia entered the breakfast room a little later than was her habit. Knowing the duke normally broke his fast early, she wanted to be certain that she would not encounter him again.

She stopped short as she entered the breakfast room. For there sat the duke, leisurely reading the *Times* across the table from Imogene, who looked up and gave Celia an I'm-just-as-surprised-as-you-are look and shrugged.

This is the outside of enough, Celia thought in frustration, forcing the frown from her face with difficulty. How vexing to come across him twice in as many days. She had weathered every one of his previous visits to Harbrooke without having to say so much as a good-morning to him.

When the duke glanced up from his paper, he saw Celia standing just inside the room. He rose from his chair politely, his gaze surveying the dove-gray gown she wore. It was as severe as her gown of last evening, but again, its sobriety could not detract from her beauty. He thought her remarkably pretty with the morning sunlight beaming in from the French windows, picking out deep golden highlights in her brown hair.

She curtsied deeply, but not before the duke noticed her discomfiture.

"Good morning, Miss Langston," he offered with a slight smile and an arched brow.

"Hello, Celia. Come have your toast," directed the

duchess quickly, for she knew Celly would turn and flee
if not prevented.

Lifting her chin, Celia said, "Good morning, your
grace, Imogene," and allowed Grimes, the butler, to
seat her.

The duke noticed that Celia had not greeted the duchess formally. Now, as he watched them enjoying their
toast and hothouse fruit, a suspicion grew.

He noted the casual way Imogene chattered to Celia
about domestic affairs and the way Miss Langston responded just as naturally. This was all very curious, he
thought with a frown. He had visited his sister as often
as the war and his own affairs had allowed and had never
come across the girl, except in passing. But here they
sat, conversing as if they were the best of confidantes. If
this was so, his thoughts concluded, how had he never
come to hear of it?

As he watched Miss Langston's graceful form, he could
not help observing that she seemed uncomfortable in his
presence. It was obvious in the way she refused to look
at him. Could it be possible that she had been purposely
avoiding him all these years? His first inclination was to
dismiss this thought as absurd. He turned his attention
to their conversation.

"Are you sure you will not take the carriage, Celly?
It's almost three miles to Harford Abbey, and the days
are still chilly," said the duchess.

"Thank you, but I always enjoy the walk. If I may,
though, I would appreciate the carriage tomorrow when
I go into the village," Celia requested as she spooned
strawberry preserves onto a slice of toast.

"Of course. Shopping or the lending library?" the
duchess questioned after taking a sip of hot chocolate.

"Both. My quarterly arrived, and I believe Finchley's
has some new fabric. Is there anything I may get for you
while I am there, Imogene?" Celia was very relieved that
the duke was reading his paper, so she would not be
forced to converse with him. He must be a slow reader,
she thought in passing, noting that he had not turned a
page since she sat down.

"If Finchley's has the latest edition of the *Lady's Magazine,* I would like to have a look at that," the duchess responded. Imogene loved looking at the latest fashions and saw no reason why she should not dress fashionably even if she did live quietly in the country. Besides, the villagers expected it of her.

"Have Cook make up a basket for you to take with you, Celly. I know that Edna will keep you all day and not even offer you a decent meal," Imogene chided. Glancing at her brother, she saw that he had laid aside his paper to lounge back in his chair and openly attend to their conversation.

"You've heard me speak of Edna Forbisher, haven't you, Drake? She is our local oddity. Why, the only one allowed in that dank old house of hers, besides a servant or two, is Celia," she revealed with an impish smile to her friend.

"Yes," Severly replied, thinking Celia was even lovelier this morning than she had been last evening in the library. "I know of your local eccentric. Philip and I used to try to sneak up to the house, but her old butler always chased us off. Philip said she was quite mad," the duke commented.

Celia's head snapped up at his last comment. She was forced to look at him because she could not let this assumption pass.

"Oh, no, Edna is not mad at all," she exclaimed, turning to address the scar on his cheek. "It's just that when she was young and making her come-out in London, she liked a certain gentleman very much, but he preferred someone else. I believe he kept Edna on a string, so to speak, until he had secured the affections of this other young lady. Edna has never been in robust health, always wheezing at the slightest exertion, and her possessing a lofty temperament added to the shame of it all. When she returned home she just could not bear the pitying faces, the questions, and all the fuss and bother. So she stayed home and read her books," Celia explained with an expressive shrug, feeling that this was a weak clarification of Edna's state of sanity. She wondered if someone like the duke could understand Edna's behavior.

Severly nodded and crossed his arms over his broad chest. "Yes, I can see why someone with a surfeit of pride and weak lungs would find the humiliation intolerable. Especially in the country, where a sad love affair would be gossip fodder for years."

Celia gave him a surprised smile, startled at the duke's understanding, "Yes. That is exactly the situation. Edna is far too sensitive and proud, but one can understand her feelings."

"Quite," Severly replied, irritated with himself for feeling so pleased with the dazzling smile she had bestowed upon him.

After a moment, Celia excused herself, promising Imogene she would speak to Cook about the basket to take along with her. She then dropped a quick curtsy before swiftly taking her leave.

Severly rose and watched her slim figure as she left the room. After reseating himself, Severly cast an accusing eye to his sister. "The two of you are bosom bows," he charged.

The duchess looked at him with startled eyes very much like his own. "Rather," she admitted. "We have so much in common, you know."

"No, I didn't know," he pointed out dryly.

Imogene frowned in agreement. "It is odd, but she has always disappeared whenever you come to Harbrooke. The boys were just commenting on it yesterday."

"Why?" demanded her affronted brother. "I don't recall exchanging a word with the girl."

Imogene shrugged and placed the delicate cup back in its saucer. "Celia is a bit shy. To a simple country lass, someone such as you might be too formidable."

The duke frowned, ill-pleased with her answer. He bit into a peach as his sister picked up his discarded paper.

"What did she mean when she said her quarterly had arrived?" he asked after recalling the comment.

"Oh, that." Imogene waved the paper dismissively. "She receives a stipend from the vicarage for being an orphan. It affords her enough to buy the occasional book and fabric for a new gown. Celia is too proud to take anything from me, and says food and shelter are more than enough. Of course, the money would cease if she ever married."

"Is that likely to happen?" Severly quizzed.

"Well, Celia is almost six and twenty, which is pretty well on the shelf," she stated as a matter of fact. "But Squire Marchman has been calf-eyed over her for years. Stares at the back of her head the whole while we're at church every Sunday," she offered helpfully.

Severly recalled a bovine farmer living a few miles east of Harbrooke and immediately felt offended for Celia. He shook his head, disgusted that such a ham-fist had the effrontery to aspire to someone like her.

"I believe I shall give Blackwind some exercise." He rose and gave his sister a kiss on the cheek. "Willow is a lovely shade on you, my dear."

Imogene watched her brother with a perplexed expression as he strode from the room.

As she trudged through yet another sodden field, Celia wondered if she had made the wisest choice in declining Imy's offer of the carriage.

A recent thaw had caused the ground to run muddy in places. Celia grimaced at the muck splattering on the hem of her gown with every step, knowing Edna would be quite irked if she arrived in this state. The old lady had little tolerance for anything she considered unladylike.

Stopping at the top of a knoll, Celia set her basket down on the stump of a tree and turned back to look at Harbrooke Hall. A picturesque view of sloping farmland, parkland, and extensive gardens met her gaze. With her heart swelling at the sight of the struggling late-winter sun shining on the hall's mellow golden spires, Celia found it difficult to comprehend that she actually lived in such a lovely place.

She was fully aware of how fortunate she was, and never ceased to give thanks. Within days of the horrible tragedy that had caused her parents' deaths, Imogene, the recently widowed Duchess of Harbrooke, had rolled up to the vicarage in her smart carriage and asked Celia to stay at Harbrooke Hall and help take care of her little boys.

Through this beginning and the tragic deaths of their loved ones, a deep bond developed between the two young women that transcended the difference in their ages and stations in life.

It would have been more than enough to have a roof over her head, but Celia had also been accepted as one of the family. Life was very good, and she dearly loved Imogene and the boys. The only fly in the ointment was a very small one indeed: the occasional visits by the insufferable Duke of Severly. *How could someone as sweet as Imy have such an odious brother?* Celia wondered with a bemused shake of her head.

Frowning, she recalled her encounter last night with the duke. She must somehow have been careless, she decided, for never before had she been caught so unexpectedly by him. And also at breakfast this morning. Never before had he lingered so long at the morning meal. She would have to be more careful in the future.

Resuming her walk, Celia continued to contemplate her life. Of late, she had been having thoughts that made her feel ashamed of herself. It wasn't that she was discontent, but sometimes she could not help wondering what it would be like to be married and to have her own family and home.

Elizabeth Tichley, the miller's daughter and a friend of Celia's, had been married last fall. Celia and Elizabeth often spoke after church services, and Celia found herself becoming wistful after listening to Elizabeth's accounts of domestic bliss.

Recalling how happy her parents had been made this avenue of thought even more painful. Once, when Celia was about twelve years old, her mother said, "One day you will fall in love, and if he is as wonderful as your papa you will be blessed indeed."

There is little chance of that happening. I am firmly on the shelf now, she thought wryly. There was always Squire Marchman, she reluctantly conceded, but he thought of nothing but farming and read only the almanacs.

Pushing back her shoulders and lifting her chin, Celia scolded herself: "You ungrateful wretch," she spoke aloud. "Here you are, crying for the moon when you have the most wonderful friends and are living in one of the most beautiful homes in all of England. For shame!" She nodded her head sharply, as if to put a stop to her wayward thoughts, and continued on.

Moments later, a small, gentle voice seemed to whisper to her heart that there really was nothing wrong with wondering what it was like to love and be loved. Giving in with a shrug, she allowed herself to daydream about Sir Galahad. As she walked on, dodging the mud as best she could, the light morning breeze teased golden brown tendrils from her neat bun.

Jarvis must have been watching out one of the grimy windows for her because the door stood open as she came up the overgrown drive a little while later.

"Oh, Miss Celia!" The old man seemed unusually distressed, and Celia hurried up the drive, a shock of fear coursing through her body. Edna must be in a bad way for Jarvis to be so discomposed.

"She is very poorly, miss. The doctor be with her now. She 'as been asking for ye all morn," he told her as he ushered her into the dismal foyer and took her cloak and basket.

"May I go to her?" she asked, moving swiftly toward the staircase.

"Yes, miss. They be waiting for ye."

Celia raced up the dusty, creaking staircase to Edna's rooms. The door stood ajar, and she could hear the low voice of Dr. Rayburn. Old Miss Forbisher was lying in a very large four-poster bed, its moth-eaten canopy long since discarded. A vase of dogwood sat on her bedside table, evidencing the fact that Edna's rooms were the only ones in the house that received any kind of attention.

"Where can she be? I'm sure she should have been here by now," came Edna's voice, a hoarse and distressed whisper. Celia felt a stab of guilt. If she had taken the carriage she would have arrived much sooner. Celia pushed the door open. The old lady looked ghastly, withered and pale. Celia could hear her labored breathing from where she stood.

"I am here, Edna. I'm so sorry I am late," she said sincerely as she approached the bed. Edna appeared to have lost even more weight in the few days since Celia had last visited her.

"There you are, Celia!" A gnarled hand reached out. Celia took it in hers and turned concerned and questioning eyes to the doctor. He gave her a slight frown with his faded blue eyes.

"Now, Edna, the tonic I gave you will help you rest. Miss Langston has arrived and I wish to have a word with her," he said in his benign bedside manner.

"You may as well speak in front of me. You will not say anything that will jolt me. I know I am dying." Her voice was clear despite its weakness.

"Do not say that, Edna! You will soon feel better." Celia squeezed the old woman's hand and looked to the doctor to confirm her words. He hesitated, gathering up his medical items and placing them in his black leather bag before answering her unspoken question.

"Who is to say? All are in the Lord's care. Miss Forbisher may have a week, a month, or years. She is dying, but I cannot speculate as to when."

Strangely, the words comforted Celia. It was not hopeless. She would not lose her friend this day.

"I will see you out, Dr. Rayburn. I will be only a moment, Edna. Please rest." She gave her friend a reassuring smile.

"Don't be long," the old woman ordered imperiously.

Celia followed the doctor out of the room to the top of the staircase.

"No need to come any further, Miss Langston. I will see myself out," he said kindly.

"Is there anything I should do, any instructions that need to be followed?" she asked in a troubled voice. An anxious frown creased her forehead.

"Matthews, her maid, has all the instructions. Her lungs are bad. The best thing for her is rest and quiet."

Celia nodded and thanked the doctor for coming such a long way. He would be back the day after tomorrow to check on Edna. If she should take another bad turn Celia should send Jarvis for him, he instructed as he pulled on a pair of gloves. Celia thanked him again and he took his leave.

By midafternoon, Celia realized that she would have to stay the night with Edna. She was much too ill for Matthews, her elderly maid, to care for by herself. Edna did not help the already difficult situation by being irritable. It had been almost impossible to persuade her to have some soup and the few drops of laudanum the doctor had prescribed.

"That doctor is a charlatan. He has never helped me," she had pronounced unfairly, and not for the first time. Her wrinkled face screwed up in defiance as she turned away from the offending spoon. The two women finally cajoled her into taking half a dosage of the laudanum.

Celia then went downstairs to ask Jarvis if he would ride over to Harbrooke and explain the situation to the duchess and return with a small satchel of necessities.

Celia stayed with Edna as the old lady tried to rest. After some time, Jarvis returned with the bag and gave Celia a note from the duchess expressing her concern and sympathy. She encouraged Celia to stay as long as need be and to send Jarvis if the duchess could be of any help. Celia admitted to herself that though she was deeply concerned for Edna, it would be a relief to be free of the duke's unexpected presence.

Edna napped a few hours in the late afternoon, but by evening she began making demands and ordering everyone about.

"Matthews, you may retire. Miss Celia shall sit with me."

"Very good, ma'am." Matthews gave Celia a look that said, *Good luck,* and left the room after stoking the fire.

"So, Celia, tell me of the goings-on at Harbrooke."

The invalid felt restless and bored and wished for Celia to entertain her.

Celia told her of some of the silly pranks the boys had been up to, trying to make the intrigues as lively as possible to divert Edna's attention away from her misery. She told her of Imogene's plans to drain the south field, and how the Dowager Duchess of Harbrooke was expected to visit soon.

Edna paid close attention and asked many questions, but Celia had been saving the best for last. When she had run out of domestic topics to prattle on about, she stated casually, "Oh, and the Duke of Severly has been visiting. The boys have been excessively excited about it."

The old woman propped herself further up on her pillows and looked at Celia with a keen eye.

"Does the duke bring any news from London?" Even though she hadn't left her own yard in more than thirty years, Edna still found gossip, especially of London, distracting.

"A little. The poor king is still quite mad. And the regent, it is rumored, is in enormous debt and does not care a fig."

Celia paused to refill her cup with weak tea and settle more comfortably in her chair before continuing with her news. Edna's face wore an avid expression as she waited impatiently for Celia to go on.

"It has been announced that Princess Charlotte will indeed marry Prince Leopold. There is some surprise because the Chapel Royal at St. James will not be used for the nuptials. Everyone in the *ton* is having eruptions from worry lest they are not invited to the grand reception the regent is giving."

"Where will the wedding take place then?" Edna demanded to know, all agog at the abundant news Celia had brought with her.

"The duke told Imogene it is to take place at Carlton House sometime in May. Isn't it exciting to have a royal wedding after so many years of the horrible war?"

"Yes, indeed. And it's also very important that the old

king's grandchild should marry. The regent isn't likely to have another child, and we need a male heir," Edna opined.

They continued in this fashion until Edna began to nod off. After carefully pulling another blanket over the frail old woman, Celia tiptoed to the little dressing room next door to prepare for bed. Matthews had thoughtfully provided a pitcher of water and a basin. But the room was so chilly Celia shivered. The only source of heat was the meager fire in Edna's room. Hastily, she bathed, then donned her old flannel nightgown and jumped into the little bed before her toes could get too cold.

She lay there for a while, listening to the night sounds of the timeworn house, watching the strange shadows that lurked in the corners, and worrying about Edna. Edna was Celia's last link to her past. Some of her dearest memories were of visiting Harford Abbey as a small girl with her mother. And, despite Edna's ill temper, Celia had grown extremely fond of the old woman. Before she drifted off into slumber she sent up a fervent prayer that Edna would feel better soon.

When Celia entered Edna's room the next morning she found the old woman much improved. She had eaten all her breakfast, Matthews told her proudly, and was up, bathed, and seated in a chair by the fireplace in a faded yellow dressing gown and tattered mobcap. She had even allowed Matthews to open the threadbare drapery and let the feeble sun shine in on all the dust and deterioration. Still, Celia frowned at how much weight her friend had lost.

"I trust you slept well, Celia," Edna said. It was evident to Celia that the old lady's breathing had greatly improved since yesterday.

"Very, Miss Edna. I'm pleased to see you looking so well this morning," she stated as Matthews set a tray of tea and toast before her. Princess Charlotte's wedding still occupied Edna's thoughts. Celia was glad Imogene had relayed the information, since it seemed to put Edna in better spirits.

"Did the duke say what her wedding robes will look like?"

"No." Celia laughed. "I'm sure that is not something the duke would be interested in. Imy would have informed me if he had mentioned anything about her trousseau." Celia smiled to herself at the thought of anyone so masculine as the Duke of Severly conversing about what Princess Charlotte would wear to her wedding.

"Shall the Princess of Wales be at the nuptials?" Edna queried.

"No, the duke does not believe so." Even Edna had heard of the estrangement between the regent and his vitriolic wife.

Edna continued to speculate on the wedding clothes and the food at the receptions and balls that would be given in celebration of the happy event. After a few moments, she began a new train of thought.

"Have you ever given any thought to marriage?" she asked Celia pointedly, a keen look in her sharp old eyes.

Almost choking on a sip of bitter tea, Celia squeaked, "Me?" With a laugh she said, "I'm well past all that. I'm quite on the shelf, you know." Celia thought this was an unusual subject for Edna to introduce, considering she was a spinster herself.

"Stuff and nonsense! You are a child! And a beautiful one at that. Believe one who has been old a very long time. It is too bad that we are so rural here. You should have a few young men to look over," she said, pointing her bony finger at Celia for emphasis.

Celia threw her beautiful head of brown-gold hair back and gave in to deep, bubbling laughter.

"Even if Kent were teeming with eligible young men, why would anyone of them look at a spinster like me? I don't even have a dowry to tempt the least discerning man."

Edna gave Celia an odd look and her bright blue eyes became troubled.

"You must listen to me, Celia," she began earnestly, leaning forward in her chair, the ribbons of her mobcap swinging, the faint odor of mothballs surrounding her.

"I am old and have not long to live. Learn from me,

my dear. I have been too proud, too unwilling to forgive. You are young, beautiful, and have a warm and generous heart. Soon you will have many choices to make. Life will not always be this way for you. I was young once too, but spoiled and rather silly. I gave my heart to someone who was not worthy. If I had had any sense I would have had a good cry, then gotten angry and gone on with my life. But it took me many years to realize what a ninny I had been. By then, it was too late."

The old woman sat back in her chair, exhausted by the unaccustomed emotions. Her eyes met Celia's, who sat motionless, listening to the sad voice of her old friend.

"You have a natural grace and good manners, but most important you are intelligent and have a virtuousness that will guide you even in the most difficult circumstances. You can bless your parents for that." She nodded wisely, and Celia wondered why she was saying these things. It was unlike Edna to speak in riddles.

"Celia"—her tone was grave—"do not make the foolish mistakes I have made. Do not run from life, child. Do not run even from pain. I found out much too late that even through the worst pain, one can find a deeper joy."

Celia still did not fully understand Edna's meaning, but she could see that this was most important to the old woman. Leaving her chair, she knelt by Edna and took her gnarled, blue-veined hand in hers. Celia's lovely brownish green eyes were unsettled, and her sweetly defined mouth trembled.

"You will remember what I have said, won't you, Celia?" Edna asked, looking down with affectionate eyes at her young friend.

"Yes, I will, always." Her voice was choked, and for the first time in their long association they embraced.

Chapter Three

The Duke of Severly lounged back with his long legs stretched comfortably before him in one of the over-stuffed chairs in the library. Moments earlier, Grimes had brought him a stack of mail. He had sifted through most of the invitations and letters of business when a missive addressed by a familiar hand caught his eye.

After he'd read the note, a pleased expression crossed his face. He rose and went to the door, calling to his sister. Imogene entered the room a few seconds later. "My goodness, what has you in such a taking?" she questioned with a curious look.

"You will not believe who has tracked me down," he said with an uncommon smile.

Imogene could not remember the last time she had seen Drake looking so pleased. Usually he wore an expression of disdain or, at the very least, boredom. Imogene felt she understood why her brother always seemed so ill-content. Drake was so handsome, wealthy, and had had so much excitement and danger during the war, regular life must be a bit tedious for him. Even as a little boy he had treasured only what had been most difficult to obtain.

"Well, who then?" she asked impatiently.

"David Rotham! He is back from Scotland, where he saw Westlake and asked him for my direction. From what I read in this letter, he shall be in Harford the day after tomorrow," he informed her, glancing down at the letter again. "He apologizes to you in advance, Imy, for descending upon us with so little notice, but I know you won't mind."

The duchess, looking charming in a cream-colored morning gown, stared up at her brother in mild alarm. She knew Major David Rotham was one of her brother's closest friends. They had served together during the war, but more important to Imogene was the fact that fifteen years ago she had quite broken his heart.

Imogene had met him during the thrill and fuss of her first and only London Season. Even though she had been in love with her darling Philip for years, she and her parents had wanted her Season to be wonderful.

Her come-out had proved a wild success, and her father had received many offers for her. But David Rotham had been the most determined of her admirers. She admitted to herself now that she had been deeply flattered by his attention and had even encouraged him.

She remembered him as a tall, fair young man with an engaging grin and a confident manner. He was from a very good family, being the nephew of the Earl of Rotham. It was his confidence, though, that had both attracted her and made her a little unsure of herself.

He had been positive that he could win her affections, even when she had confessed to him her feelings for Philip. He had laughed and said it was just because she had known Philip all her life that she *thought* she loved him. That had made her angry, very angry, because for one swift, heart-rending moment she had wondered if he could be right.

So she had refused to see him. But after the announcement of her engagement had appeared in the newspapers, David had confronted her in an anteroom at Chesterfield House on the night of her last ball of the Season.

"I will never forget you, Imogene Severly"—his blue eyes were blazing and his voice was raw—"and you shall never forget me." With that he left the room and she had not seen him since.

And even though Imogene had never regretted a moment with her darling Philip, she never had forgotten

David. Now her brother was saying that Major David Rotham would arrive at her home the day after tomorrow.

"Thursday?" she said faintly, grabbing the back of a
red leather couch. "There is so much to do. Goodness, I
don't know where to begin. Is Major Rotham married?"

"No, he hasn't been leg-shackled yet," her brother
stated with a quizzical glance to his sister's flushed
cheeks. What the devil was wrong with her? he wondered
with a frown. His sister was the most competent woman
of his acquaintance. He could see nothing about one
guest that would give her the vapors.

"Thank goodness Celia is returning this morning," she
stated in a distracted manner.

"So the old woman is improved then?"

"Celia says so in the note she sent over yesterday,"
his sister confirmed.

"Fine, then the numbers shall be even when we dine
Thursday," the duke said emphatically.

Imogene turned to stare at her brother in surprise,
completely taken aback by this statement.

"Drake, Celia will never agree to dine with us! Why,
she would have my head if I even suggested it."

"I don't see why." Severly raised a dark brow in query. "I
understand from the boys that Miss Langston always dines
with you. Even when your mother-in-law is staying."

"Well, yes, that is true," Imy admitted reluctantly,
"but I know she won't agree. Drake, there is something
about you she doesn't like."

"Yes, I had noticed," he said dryly, "and I'm quite
curious to know why."

"So that explains this sudden interest in Celia!" she
accused with narrowed eyes, placing her hands on her
hips. "You are bored, and now you want to upset poor
Celly. Well, I won't have it, Drake. Celia is not one of
your worldly London ladies, you know."

"Don't get yourself in such a state, Imy," he soothed.
"I merely see no cause for the girl's aversion to me and
am curious to know the cause. Besides, you need not
change your normal mode of doing things just because I
am here."

"Just so long as that's all," she warned, her expression still suspicious.

He gave her the same smile that as children he had used to obtain her allegiance when he had gotten into a scrape.

"Of course that's all. Dash it, Imy. She's the governess," came his innocent reply.

Henry and Peter ran down the garden steps when they espied Celia returning to Harbrooke later that morning.

"You've been gone four days," Henry chastised as if she were a truant child.

Celia laughed and gave him a hug. Peter held on to her skirts and vied for her attention.

"We have missed you so much!" Peter was so mournful she felt as if she had been gone for a year.

She pulled them both to a nearby bench and listened as they told her of all they had been doing while she had been at Harford Abbey. Celia could not help smiling as they talked over themselves in their excitement. After four days of solemnity at Harford Abbey, the boys' exuberance was delightful.

"There you are, Celly!" Imogene called from the drawing room's French doors as she saw Celia in the garden. "I am so glad that you are home. Now I must speak to you privately. Children, run along and play. You can see Celly later," she said, waving them off.

Celia looked at her friend in surprise. Imogene rarely allowed herself to become ruffled. Celia actually began to worry as Imogene tugged her into the house by the wrist.

Closing the French doors of the drawing room behind her, Imogene pulled Celia to a blue damask–covered settee.

"Celia, Major David Rotham is coming here the day after tomorrow!"

Evidently, by the look in Imogene's eyes, this caused much more than the distress of feeling unprepared for another guest, Celia concluded.

"Why are you upset, Imy? Is this Major Rotham a horrible person?"

pleasant

"Oh, no, he is very ~~nice.~~ At least he was fifteen years ago. He is one of Drake's greatest friends. They served together. But I knew him also, years ago, during my come-out in London."

Imogene looked away from her friend and bit her lip, feeling a little self-conscious at what she was going to say.

"You see, David was one of my admirers."

Still somewhat confused, but trying to allay whatever fears Imy seemed to have, Celia said, "I'm sure you had legions of them, Imy."

"He wasn't just a suitor, Celly. David was one of my particular beaux, and . . . well . . . you see, I believe it quite hurt him when I married Philip."

Imogene's eyes looked to Celia's for understanding. Because of their years of friendship, Celia knew that Imogene must have cared for this man if the thought of hurting him still distressed her after so many years. Imogene had previously recounted her wonderful time in London and tales of her many beaux. She had even shown Celia some of the more flowery epistles she had received from admiring swains. But the descriptions had all been lighthearted, and Celia could not recall Imogene ever mentioning a David Rotham.

"I see," she said with empathy. "You must feel rather awkward. One never knows how to handle these situations with urbanity. Surely, the years must have assuaged any pain he may have felt?"

"I'm sure you are right, and I know I'm being a silly goose. He has probably completely forgotten my existence by now."

"I very much doubt that. But by now, he probably has forgiven you for marrying the man you loved," Celia said reassuringly.

"I hope so." She proceeded to tell Celia the whole story, ending with the scene at Chesterfield House.

Celia, who was very romantic underneath her veil of practicality, was enthralled by the tale. It sounded so heart-rending and exciting that her heart fairly broke for both of them. Secretly, she had never found Imogene's account of her romance with Philip very romantic. Of course, she would never say so to Imy, and truly, Imy had loved Philip deeply.

They discussed plans for Major Rotham's arrival, and Celia told her of her stay at Harford Abbey.

"I would like to renew my plans to go to the village tomorrow, if you wouldn't mind," Celia declared.

"Go right ahead, my dear. I'm sure you would like a little time of your own after spending the last few days in that gloomy house. Now I must go speak to Cook."

As she walked from the village of Harford's only lending library to Finchley's shop, Celia felt a sense of well-being that had not been present for some days now. She also felt quite pleased with herself. Edna was better, the day was fine, and she had been able to completely avoid the duke yesterday. It had been easy too, she thought, allowing herself a satisfied smile.

March had arrived and the days were already becoming warmer. The ground was muddy only in low spots, so Celia had decided to walk from Harbrooke instead of taking the carriage to the village. Many people spoke to her as she meandered along the sidewalk, looking into shop windows.

Plump Mrs. Adelforth stopped to ask after everyone at Harbrooke, and as Celia responded, a black phaeton with scarlet wheel spokes caught her attention as it turned down the lane. From the corner of her eye, Celia watched the vehicle pass with a sinking heart, hoping the duke would not see her and stop.

After the phaeton reached the end of the lane, Celia sighed in relief and took her leave of Mrs. Adelforth. She would choose her fabric and leave the village quickly, lest she encounter the duke.

Severly had indeed noticed Celia's slim figure as she stood on the sidewalk. After a moment, he decided that the girl would probably have given him the cut direct if he had stopped and tried to address her. His finely shaped mouth firmed in a line of irritation as he tooled his horse down the lane. He was annoyed with himself for being so curious about his nephews' governess and irritated with the chit for being so elusive. It was just his pride, he knew, that made him so interested in the girl.

After all, since reaching his majority, he had grown accustomed to the most beautiful women in London fawning over him. All things considered, he was not a vain man. It was just the way life had been for him. So for a governess to snub him was rather lowering to his address. Besides, he really could see no reason for it. On the rare occasions that he had ever spoken to Celia, he had been nothing but polite. It was dashed queer in his opinion, and he'd never been able to resist a challenge.

Pulling his horses to a stop and turning the reins over to Johnny, his tiger, he leaped with agility from the conveyance, and turned back in the direction he had seen Celia walk.

The humble villagers were soon agog at seeing the redoubtable Duke of Severly walking the quaint streets of Harford. The attention did not faze the duke's urbanity. Accustomed to causing a stir wherever he went, he strolled along the village street, nodding to those who had the temerity to address him.

As he passed the mantua maker's shop, he paused to take a pinch of snuff. He glanced in the window and saw Celia, her lovely hair covered by a plain and rather bedraggled poke bonnet, stroking a bolt of violet-blue velvet. The proprietor lifted the bolt for her closer inspection. Celia pulled her hand away and smilingly shook her head and said something to the man. He put the bolt of velvet back and produced a bolt of dark green muslin.

The duke continued on, entering the next shop to purchase a new tin of snuff. Emerging shortly thereafter, he signaled Johnny to bring the phaeton around. Stepping into the conveyance, he glanced back at the mantua maker's shop before urging the horses to a light canter.

A half an hour later, laden with her green muslin, Imogene's magazine, and books from the lending library, Celia left the shop with a last, longing glance at the beautiful violet-blue velvet. It had felt as soft as rabbit fur, she observed wistfully. Finchley's rarely carried such exquisite fabric, but it was far beyond Celia's touch.

Walking down the lane, Celia crossed Highstreet to enter the road that led home. A phaeton pulled up alongside her, and she quickly stepped off the road to let it pass.

"Good afternoon, Miss Langston. I see you've been shopping. May I convey you home?" a deep voice asked, and lazy hazel eyes smiled down at her.

Celia was speechless for a moment, completely startled by the duke's abrupt appearance.

"No, thank you very much, your grace, I enjoy walking." She curtsied quickly and lifted her skirt slightly to aid her quick escape.

The duke stepped from the phaeton and gave his tiger a few instructions, then turned toward Celia as the phaeton left at a fast clip.

Staring dumbfounded at the retreating vehicle, Celia wondered if the duke had taken leave of his senses. Glancing warily at his sparkling black Hessian boots and Skeffington brown coat, she wondered how he planned to get home.

Giving her astonished face a devilish grin, he offered her his arm.

"I too would enjoy a walk."

Celia almost broke out into a chorus of hallelujahs when the welcoming porticoes of Harbrooke Hall finally came into sight. The last half an hour had been agony for Celia, leaving her confused and even a little frightened.

When the duke had offered her his arm and taken her packages, she had seen nothing else for it but to go with him. As they strolled along the road, the duke spoke to her in a deep, almost teasing voice. He asked after her purchases, and offered in a tone of old friendship that he hoped she had not spent all her money on fripperies. He examined with great interest her books from the lending library.

"What, no gothics? I was under the impression that all young ladies read gothics voraciously," he bantered, gazing down at her with an engaging smile.

To each of these inroads, Celia had been as stoical

and brief in her responses as possible. She wished he would go away and not look at her as if he found her amusing.

On his part, if Severly had not seen her behave in such a lively fashion with the boys and his sister, he would now be questioning her verbal capabilities.

After a few more fruitless attempts at furthering the conversation, they fell silent for a time. The only sound was their shoes crunching along the path. The duke wondered, with some exasperation, what to say next. And Celia prayed that he would walk faster.

"I am sure Imogene has told you that my friend, Major Rotham, will be arriving tomorrow?" Severly tried again.

"Yes, your grace."

"We were in France and Spain together during the war. He took a lead ball in the leg and now walks with a bit of a limp. But for all that, no one rides to the hounds better than David."

"He is very fortunate."

"The last time I saw David was at his hunting box in Norfolk, over a year ago. Do you ever hunt or ride, Miss Langston?"

"No, your grace."

"I see . . . er . . . well, I particularly wished to speak to you about Major Rotham's visit. I would be most appreciative if you would dine with us for the duration of his stay. It would save Imogene from being stuck with two bachelors, you understand."

Celia almost choked. Desperately, she searched for a way to decline. She could think of few worse situations than being forced to dine with the duke. Glancing up at him quickly, she saw that he was waiting for her answer. To her great disappointment, she could think of no excuse to give him.

"Of course, your grace."

The duke gave the conversation one more try.

"Thank you. May I ask how Miss Forbisher is recovering?"

"Very well, your grace."

The duke stopped dead in the path. A momentary but

awesome anger flashed in his hazel eyes, making Celia catch her breath.

"Pray tell me, Miss Langston, have I offended you in some way? I find your behavior toward me quite odd and I cannot account for it. I have been trying to converse with you this past half hour and you are making it dashed—and purposely, I believe—difficult."

Celia stepped back, shocked by this sudden attack. How dared he speak to her in this way, towering over her in that imperious manner? A latent but fierce temper made the blood pound in her ears, and the green in her brown eyes caught fire.

"I beg your pardon, your grace. I have been as civil as anyone could expect, considering that you have practically forced your presence upon me this afternoon." Her voice was icy and her chin went up. For the first time she looked him in the eye.

The anger completely left the duke as he watched this transformation take place. A moment ago she had been placid to the point of blandness. Now he wouldn't be caught off guard if she took her packages back and threw them at him.

With throaty laughter and raised hands, Severly said, "Cry truce, Miss Langston. You are perfectly right. I did force my rude self upon your walk. But how else could I speak to you about dining with us?"

Suddenly, Celia was horrified by what she had just said. How had she dared ring such a peal over him? Her slightly unsteady hand attempted to cover the blush coming over her throat. It must be due to the familiar situation at Harbrooke Hill, she owned. Being as one of the family had given her too much assurance.

He did not appear incensed with her effrontery, Celia observed with relief. To her great surprise, amusement definitely glimmered in his lazy eyes.

Celia suddenly became acutely aware of the attractive cleft in his square chin, as they stood alone on the quiet country lane.

For the first time, Celia could see how the duke had gotten the reputation for being a heartbreaker. That smile could almost make her forget what a selfish libertine he really was. Almost.

She didn't know where to look, and her heart began to beat a little faster. Suddenly, she recalled a tale she had heard many years ago about some poor woman making a cake of herself in public over the duke. It had been a nine-days' wonder, and Imogene had been much concerned that her brother was becoming a rogue.

And no wonder, thought Celia, giving the duke a quick, cautious glance. He was obviously a practiced flirt and intimidatingly handsome. Who could blame a silly woman for becoming twitterpated over him? she thought honestly.

But I am not a silly woman. I am an old maid, and the duke must be bored with country life, she thought cynically as she looked at the scar on his cheek.

"Forgive my shrewish tongue, your grace. I can't think why I was so rude. I will be happy to make up the numbers at dinner," she said in a quiet tone, avoiding his pointed question.

"Not at all, Miss Langston. As I said, I rudely forced my presence upon you," the duke said gallantly, liking Miss Langston better when she was indignant rather than subdued.

As they resumed their walk, Celia had to prevent herself from picking up her skirts and running the rest of the way to Harbrooke Hall.

Chapter Four

*T*he ladies of the house lingered patiently in the blue drawing room while waiting for the arrival of Major Rotham. That particular room's chief appeal was that it afforded a view of the front drive.

Celia, observing Imogene sitting calmly on the settee, could not help but notice that she had taken great pains with her appearance. The duchess appeared exceptionally pretty in a lovely blush-colored tea gown with cream lace at the neck and hem and a cream ribbon threaded through her coffee-colored curls.

Imogene chanced to look up at that moment and catch her friend's appraising eye, causing a flush to rise to her cheeks.

"Well, I don't wish him to think I have completely lost my looks over the years," Imogene said defensively.

"Indeed he won't, my dear Imy," Celia soothed, knowing the duchess was feeling nervous in spite of her outward serenity.

"Oh, dear." The duchess sighed with a shake of her head. "What does one say to an old beau in a situation like this?"

Having never had a beau, old or otherwise, Celia did not know what she could say to ease Imogene's discomfort.

The duke strode into the room at that moment and greeted the ladies. "I see David has not arrived yet," he observed, pulling a watch from his pocket to check the time.

"No, not yet," his sister said with a casual air, glancing out the window as if she had almost forgotten they were expecting a guest.

The duke sat down in an overstuffed chair opposite Celia. Again, she wore the dark blue gown in which he had first noticed her by the pond. Her hair was covered with a little lace mobcap that the duke thought looked quite absurd, considering how young and beautiful she was.

Feeling his eyes upon her, Celia refused to look up from her needlepoint. She still felt self-conscious after their encounter yesterday and did not know exactly how to behave with him.

"It will be good to see old David again. Imy, didn't you make his acquaintance during your Season? I'm sure I heard him mention it once or twice," Severly asked his sister, who dropped her tatting at that moment.

"I . . . ah . . . we did meet in London. We met several times at different balls and soirees and such. I believe him to be a fine figure of a man." The flush in her cheeks had become a definite blush, and Celia stared at her with raised eyebrows. *A fine figure of a man, indeed.* Imy was really doing the thing much too brown in Celia's opinion.

Suddenly, Grimes entered the room and announced the awaited guest. Only Celia heard Imogene's small squeak of trepidation.

As their guest walked past the butler, the duke crossed the room and the two men clasped hands firmly. "David! Good to see you," the duke exclaimed.

Celia took that moment to look over the much-anticipated Major Rotham. He was near the same height as the duke, but of a lighter build. His complexion was a ruddy tan, his hair the color of wheat. His features were angular and engaging. He did possess a slight limp, but it did not seem to affect him unduly. Noticeably, he and the duke were of the same ilk. Both were athletically built men of sophisticated taste. There was an air about the two of them that told the observer that they had experienced much of what life had to offer.

Celia thought the major quite handsome and glanced to her friend to see her reaction to her old beau.

"You remember my sister, don't you, David?"

"Of course, how could I ever forget someone so lovely? Your grace." Major Rotham bowed over Imy's hand, and Celia wondered how the polite smile on her friend's face remained so placid.

"How very nice to see you again, Major Rotham. May I acquaint you with my dear friend Miss Celia Langston?"

So that was going to be the way of it, thought Celia as she curtsied to the bowing major. Imogene was going to act the cool and distant duchess.

After Imogene rang for tea and they all took their seats, the men caught up on the goings-on since they last met. Celia gave Imogene a reassuring smile, and Imogene appeared relieved that the initial meeting was over.

When Grimes entered with the tea tray, followed by a maid carrying a silver tray laden with various cakes and sandwiches, Imogene asked him to make sure the major's luggage was taken to the green room.

"I have no luggage, your grace. I reside at the Staff and Cleaver," Major Rotham said in a surprised tone before Grimes could respond. "When Westlake told me that Severly was staying at Harbrooke, I thought it was a great opportunity to see my old friend, as I have business in Harford. I never expected to foist myself upon your household." His manner was so engaging and cavalier that Celia hoped he would stay.

"Nonsense, David, we'll send a man for your things. We wouldn't stand having you stay anywhere else, would we, Imy?"

Imogene rarely argued with her autocratic brother, and, being an excellent hostess, she did not in this instance either.

"Of course you must stay at Harbrooke, Major. We are quite counting on it." She smiled in her most benevolent duchesslike manner and instructed Grimes to see to collecting the major's things. The major protested that it wasn't necessary, but he was no match for the duke and his sister and, in the end, he thanked Imogene handsomely.

Celia had little to offer the general conversation, but she was rapt in her attention to the reminiscing of the two gentlemen. Sometimes it was hard for Celia to realize the duke had been a soldier during the horrible war with France. He was so lofty and sophisticated that she couldn't picture it. But listening to them talk, it appeared that there were two heroes in the room.

As each man related stories about the other, Imogene and Celia exchanged looks of amazement.

"You never told me this, Drake," accused his sister when the major told them how the duke had saved several of their comrades after a surprise attack on the Peninsula.

"I had forgotten. It really was not as colorful as Rotham is making it sound." Severly dismissed the tale and reached for another scone.

"You mean to say that you never showed your sister the medal you received for that?" the major asked his friend, who was becoming uncomfortable with the notice he was receiving.

"Give over, Rotham, what about the time you went charging up that hill when we were hemmed in on all sides? You took out a half dozen frogs, at least, before they stopped you by putting that ball in your leg."

"I remember it well," he said, patting the leg in question, "and I also remember that you were right behind me."

"Of course, I wanted to be sure you didn't stick your spoon in the wall before you could give me the money I had won off you the night before."

Even Celia laughed at that. The duke turned to look at her, arrested by the beauty of her laughter.

Celia met his gaze and quickly turned her eyes to her teacup. Sometimes he had the oddest expression when he looked at her. He probably thought she was much too forward for laughing at his banter so heartily. Her face sobered and she sipped her tea, vowing not to be so forthcoming in the future.

The rest of the afternoon passed quickly. Imogene introduced her sons to the new guest, and he remarked on their striking resemblance to their father, which made Imogene blush with pleasure. Evidently there was to be no awkwardness about their past romance, and Imogene appeared to be completely at ease by the time she excused herself to prepare for dinner.

Celia was not so blessed. As she slowly climbed the stairs, she pondered her dread of the evening. First of all, she was quite dispirited about her clothing. She owned absolutely nothing she could feel comfortable wearing to dinner, which was always a formal occasion at Harbrooke. She barely noticed when it was just Imy or the dowager duchess, but it was very lowering to be so dowdy when two men of fashion were present.

The only possibility was an old gown that had belonged to her mother. A year ago, she had taken it apart and tried to resew the whole thing, using a plate from *La Belle Assemblée* as a model. Taking it from the armoire, she held the gown against herself and stared with critical eyes at her reflection in the mirror, twisting this way and that, hoping for some flattering angle to present itself.

The dress was sadly out-of-date, but it was of a good silk, and she felt the color, a deep greenish blue, was flattering to the green flecks in her eyes. Laying the gown across her bed, she sighed dejectedly, knowing she really had no other choice. Seating herself at her dressing table, she proceeded to pile her hair on top of her head in an unfashionable, yet becoming twist. She grimaced at the mirror. *They will think I'm an antidote,* she thought, wondering if she could feign illness. She dismissed the thought, as she had already agreed to dine with them, and she never dissembled.

The other problem that put a crease in her smooth brow was the thought of trying to make conversation. She had lived in the country all of her life, and though she was intelligent and well-read, she knew it would be difficult to converse on any subject that the major or the duke would find interesting. She had never had the chance to develop the fine art of chatting.

After putting the final pin in her hair, Celia left her

room with one last critical glance at the mirror and made her way to the salon to await the appearance of the new guest. She found the duke and Imogene already there, sipping champagne and conversing quietly. Dressed in a stunning cranberry silk evening gown, Imogene had rarely been in better looks. Celia, who did not possess a jealous bone, for the first time in her life came close to envy.

Compared to the magnificent beauty of Imogene's Empire-style gown, Celia felt even drabber, if that were possible. A stab of anger toward the duke pierced her; she blamed him for her present state of discomfiture. If he hadn't been so odiously insistent on her dining with them she would not now be looking like such a frump, Celia thought with an uncharacteristic flash of churlishness.

The duke, of course, appeared the pinnacle of elegance, she noticed resentfully. His black coat and snowy white waistcoat fit to perfection, a large diamond stickpin sparkled in his intricately tied cravat, and his lean, chiseled face wore a slight frown as he observed her standing uncertainly in the doorway.

"There you are, Celly; don't you look pretty," Imogene called across the room, her tone overly cheerful. For the first time in their acquaintance, Imogene felt uneasy with her friend. She couldn't even hazard a guess as to what Drake had said to persuade Celly to dine with them.

Knowing Celia as she did, she could see that despite her composed expression, her friend was mortified at having to appear in her mother's old, redone gown. Imogene was at a complete loss as to what to say to her and even began to feel guilty for dressing in her loveliest gown, since Celia's gown looked even worse in comparison. To hide her discomfort she prattled on in a slightly shrill tone and busied herself with directing Grimes to pour Celia a glass of champagne.

On his part, the duke felt an unexplainable anger. How was he to know that she would have nothing presentable to wear? And Imy should not have shown her up so obviously, either, he thought, frowning slightly at his sister's elegant attire. But what he felt most was guilt. He had virtually forced her to dine with them when she had made it clear that she had no desire to do so, and now his manipulating had embarrassed her terribly.

His knowledgeable eye continued to assess Celia. The gown was outdated and noticeably old. But what Imy said was true: Celia did look lovely. The color of the gown suited her well, and her upswept hair showed her long neck to advantage.

The expression on her face did something strange to his chest as he stood by the fireplace sipping his glass of champagne. A momentary glitter of anger had flashed in her extraordinary eyes when Imogene had called her pretty. She had turned her brown-green eyes to him and, with her chin up, defied him to laugh. Instead of sneering, as he somehow thought she expected him to do, he had raised his champagne glass slightly, as if in salute. Surprise touched her face for a moment. Then she turned away with a flush rising to her cheeks.

"Excuse me, I hope you haven't been waiting for me. I confess I got a bit lost." Everyone in the room turned eagerly to the major, grateful for the diversion.

"How remiss of me. I should have sent one of the maids to direct you. Let's go in, shall we? Grimes, you may serve now," Imogene said in a nervous tone with a too-bright smile.

Since the party was so small, Imogene had decided not to use the grand dining room, but a smaller room the family commonly used. The table was round instead of the usual rectangle, and the room was decorated in royal blue, white, and gold. A cheery fire blazed in the grate, as the evenings were still cold, and this combined with the smaller proportions of the room resulted in a more intimate atmosphere.

Grimes, a stolid and unflappable man, took in Miss Celia's distress and filled her wineglass to the brim. In Grimes's wise opinion, there were few uncomfortable situations a good glass of wine could not cure.

It may have been the unusual amount of wine, or the

fact that the duke and the major set out to be as felici-
tous as they were able, but the evening proved less arduous than Celia had anticipated.

Being seated between the two men had, at first, been
so daunting Celia felt unable to say anything, or even to
look up from her plate very often. After the first course
or two, with the wine and the easy conversation, Celia
forgot her shame somewhat, and behaved more naturally.
Imogene had even been able to draw Celia out enough
for her to recount an amusing story about the boys. To
her abashment, Celia noticed the duke's glittering hazel
gaze often on her. She assumed he was chastising himself
for insisting that such a dowd dine with them. *Serves him
right,* she thought defiantly, vowing to herself not to look
in his direction again.

After a dessert of hothouse fruit and fresh cream was
served, the talk eventually came around to the forthcoming Season. The major asked the duke when he would
sojourn in London.

"Most likely the beginning of April. I am hoping to
convince Imogene to join me this year. I believe she will
enjoy herself very much, what with Princess Charlotte's
wedding and all."

"Indeed she would," Major Rotham agreed, turning
eagerly to the duchess. "The town is already in a fever
over it. All the great hostesses are planning celebrations
that will long be remembered for their gaiety," he said,
watching Imogene for any signs of enthusiasm.

"Indeed, the way you and Drake describe it makes it
sound enticing, and I own that some dancing would set
me up quite well, but there is so much to do here."
Imogene was just waiting to be talked into it. She looked
at her brother and the major with shining eyes, already
anticipating the wonders of a London Season.

The men each took turns cajoling her and describing
the incomparable merriment she would enjoy.

"All right, all right, we shall go. Oh, Celly, won't it be
lovely?" Imogene asked her friend excitedly.

Imogene was young, beautiful, and a duchess. Celia
knew London was the place for her.

"You will have a wonderful time." She smiled encouragingly, already imagining all the delicious gossip she would be able to share with Edna when Imy wrote to her from London.

"But of course you are going too, Celia," Imogene said in wide-eyed surprise. "Where else would you be?"

Celia did not know where to look, such was her shock at her friend's words. She could imagine few things more horrid than being forced to reside in the duke's home, even if only for a month or two.

"My sister could not do without you, Miss Langston," said the duke when Celia began to protest. Their eyes met, and Celia felt a little breathless at the expression in his. What a peculiar man he was, she thought. One moment he was rebuking her on the road to Harbrooke, and the next he was gazing at her quite kindly.

"I just didn't think—" she began uncertainly until Imogene interrupted her.

"Don't be a goose, Celly. You will come to London. The boys will be visiting my mother-in-law, so you needn't worry on that score. Besides, I wouldn't enjoy myself half so much if you weren't there." Her eyes pleaded with Celia not to protest.

Celia observed her friend's anxious face. That niggling feeling of resentment that had plagued her all evening vanished. *What is wrong with me?* Celia wondered to herself. *Why am I suddenly so beset by the blue devils? I must stop thinking this way,* she chided, hating the feeling of dissatisfaction that had invaded her thoughts of late.

"Of course I will go, if you want me to. Thank you very much." Once she became familiar with the duke's London habits, Celia mused, it would be just as easy to avoid him there as it was at Harbrooke. Actually, when she thought about it for a moment, London would be a rare treat, duke or not.

"Wonderful!" Imogene clapped her hands together in delight. "Heavens! There is so much to do! We shall be leaving in a week and I am not prepared for anything."

"You will have time to spare, Imogene. I will send a

note to town tomorrow and let Porter know I will have two guests for the Season. The servants can take care of everything else." The Duke of Severly leaned back in his chair and sipped his wine with an air of satisfaction.

Chapter Five

*T*he charming Major Rotham had stayed at Harbrooke Hall two more days before departing with the promise of seeing them all in London. On the morning of his departure, Celia noticed the major give a last warm look to Imogene. Smiling to herself, Celia wondered if her friend was open to receiving his attentions.

The duke stayed at Harbrooke Hall until a few days before his sister and Celia were set to leave, giving instructions and making all the arrangements for the trip that would take a full day. Celia was extremely careful to avoid him, finding his company even more unsettling since their walk home from the village. Being in his presence had proved unavoidable though, on the day he set off for London.

She stood on the steps with the boys and Imogene as they said their good-byes. As much as she tried to deny it, she had to admit to herself that he cut an extremely dashing figure. This new opinion confused her because she had always thought he looked like the devil. Had her opinion changed because she was about to receive the unimaginable treat of going to London? She rebuked herself for having such nonsensical ruminations, but couldn't help noticing how his shoulders appeared even broader in his many-caped coat.

After dislodging himself from Peter and Henry, the duke kissed his sister's cheek. "Do not worry, Imy. Everything is arranged. I shall see you in a few days."

He ruffled Peter's hair and gave a salute to a curtsying

Celia before jumping into his phaeton and departing, the perfectly matched chestnuts prancing a little as they turned the drive. Celia stayed on the steps as he drove off, a confused frown touching her brow.

A few days before they were to leave for London, Celia walked over to Harford Abbey to say farewell to Edna Forbisher.

Upon her arrival, Matthews led her into a salon that overlooked the overgrown front garden. Celia was very pleased to find Edna sitting up in a chair, instead of lying on the settee in her usual mode. After greeting her friend, Celia decided that Edna appeared more robust than she had in months.

"So you are off to London to stay in the duke's fine town house. Are you excited?" Edna asked.

"Yes, I am. I have never been beyond our village," Celia said after making herself as comfortable as she could in a sagging chair.

"I know you have not. That is why you must endeavor not to behave like a country bumpkin," Edna stated bluntly, casting a beady eye over Celia.

"I will do my best," Celia responded with a seriousness that belied her amusement at Edna's manner.

"You must not gape and gawk at the sights you will see. I have been to London, so I know of what I speak."

Celia continued to struggle with her laughter. She knew it had been at least forty years since the old lady had been to town. Even so, Celia was touched and gratified by Edna's concern.

"I will try not to be overset by the wonders of London," Celia reassured her.

"Good." The old lady nodded her approval.

The salon room door opened and Matthews entered. She carried a tray bearing a battered old tea service and a chipped plate with two scones.

"You play mother," Edna said to Celia, as she waved Matthews from the room. "Since you will be in such superior company at the duke's residence, you might find yourself in the company of some young gentlemen," she continued with a hint in her tone.

Celia concentrated on preparing the tea. This was not the first time Edna had broached this subject. Celia knew how dogged her friend could be when she found a subject she liked.

After handing Edna a cup of sweet tea and a scone, Celia settled back in her chair and looked at Edna's wizened face.

"Even if I am thrown into the path of a dozen gentlemen, it would serve no purpose. I am a spinster."

Edna snorted her objection to this statement.

"Besides, Miss Forbisher, I could not be more content with my life as it is," Celia asserted firmly.

"Don't be silly. You are not quite a spinster. You just need a little luck."

Not wanting to overly excite her friend, Celia conceded her point with a delicate shrug. She then tried to coax Edna into eating the second scone. Celia rewarded Edna with a smile when she accepted half of the treat.

The two women sat quietly for a bit, enjoying their tea. Celia's eyes wandered around the dark and dusty room. Accustomed to Harbrooke Hall, Celia wondered how Edna could abide this depressing atmosphere. It could not be good for one's health, she thought.

Leaning forward, Celia said hesitantly, "Miss Forbisher, may I call Matthews? It is a lovely spring day. We will remove the holland covers from the furniture. Dust the mantel. Maybe even clean the windows."

Edna's wrinkled face hardened into mutinous objection. "No, I would not dream of having you clean my house."

Celia did not think that Edna's tone was as emphatic as it could be. Jumping up, she went to the door, saying, "Please, Miss Forbisher, I would so enjoy sweeping away the last bit of winter."

Edna continued to protest, but more mildly, as Celia called to Matthews. When the sturdy maid came in, Celia relayed her plan enthusiastically.

"Praise be," she said under her breath. "I've been trying to get to that room for years."

Celia continued to calm Edna's protests as Matthews

headed back to the pantry for cleaning supplies. When she returned, burdened with dustpans, rags, and aprons, the two women set about immediately putting the room in good order.

They worked steadily all afternoon. Edna grumbled and barked orders occasionally, but Celia was sure she was pleased when they had thrown open the curtains to reveal sparkling-clean windows.

By the time Celia took off the large apron Matthews had provided, she was pleasantly worn out and very satisfied. Ever since coming to Harford Abbey as a child, Celia had thought this room could be made charming if given a little attention.

"You really needn't have troubled yourself," Edna said to Celia. "Though I own that the room looks much better."

Celia smiled, knowing how difficult it was for the old lady to thank her. Celia walked over to where Edna was seated, wrapped in her threadbare robe. Bending down, Celia kissed her friend on the cheek affectionately.

"Think nothing of it. I shall be able to go to London happy, knowing that you can enjoy yourself in this lovely room."

"Well"—Edna sniffed—"you must write to me often while you are away."

Celia promised that she would.

"I shall miss you, Miss Forbisher," Celia said gently.

"For goodness' sake. You will only be gone a couple of months," the old lady said gruffly. "You won't have time to miss me."

With amused resignation, Celia shook her head over Edna's cantankerous ways. She said a breezy farewell, for she knew Edna hated any sentimentality, and left the salon.

"I shall write you as soon as I reach London," Celia called from the foyer.

"See that you do," Edna called back.

As the well-sprung carriage turned up the long flower- and tree-lined drive, Celia was convinced she must be dreaming. Her first glimpse of the Duke of Severly's town house, from the carriage window, made her gasp in astonishment. Never had she seen anything so magnificent, yet so imposing.

Severly House was enormous and perfectly proportioned, with wide marble steps that led to the huge front doors. As the carriage pulled to a stop, a footman liveried in vermilion and gold opened the door and helped Imogene alight. Celia adjusted her bonnet, took a deep breath, and followed unassisted.

Pulling off her gloves and surveying the house's impressive facade, Imogene said with pleasure, "Well, we are here, Celia."

Celia couldn't quite make herself believe that she was actually in London and would be staying at the duke's London home. Just a few days ago they were in a flurry of fittings and packing and listening to the boys' protests. And now, suddenly, they were in London. She felt excitement flutter through her veins.

The only thing that had put a damper on Celia's anticipation was the sad state of her wardrobe. She knew it would have been a hopeless task to have tried to make even one gown before they were to depart, so she had just determined to make the best of it. But Imogene had come to the rescue by insisting on making a gift of a few gowns.

"I won't hear a word on it, Celly. We have been friends for far too long for there to be any strain between us. You need some new gowns and I want to give them to you," she had pressed in an unusually stern voice.

So Celia had gone to Mrs. Miniver, the village of Harford's most reputable modiste, and explained her predicament and the need for urgency. Mrs. Miniver had been quite obliging, and within the week Celia had four new gowns, all very simple, yet far superior to anything she possessed. Celia hugged Imogene effusively when the finished articles had arrived and spent an extra hour before bedtime trying them on and carefully packing them.

Now she was in London, being admitted into the most beautiful house she had ever seen.

The duke, dressed for riding, was descending the wide, curving oak staircase as Celia and Imogene were being admitted into the splendid foyer. He appeared very much in his element, Celia thought, the lord of the manor.

Celia knew that the first Duke of Severly had received the title after the battle of Agincourt, and the succeeding seven dukes had improved upon the holdings. Evidently this duke was not the exception.

Everywhere Celia looked she saw magnificent treasures. She knew that the Duke of Severly was one of the wealthiest men in the kingdom. The wealth of his family had been built upon from generation to generation. But still, the unexpected beauty of Severly House was very overwhelming.

After kissing his sister, the duke asked after their journey. Even though Celia tried to stay in the background, the duke's expression included her in his inquiry.

"We've had a wonderful time! Oh, Drake, do you realize the last time I stayed here, Mama and Papa were alive and it was my first Season?" Moisture welled in her hazel eyes and she searched her reticule for a hankie. The duke offered her his.

"Yes, that was a very happy time for us all. You have been away much too long, Imy." Severly gazed down at his sister tenderly, and Celia found herself amazed by his gentleness. She was so used to seeing him with that bored and worldly expression, she could almost like him when he behaved this way.

The duke looked up at that moment and caught Celia's speculative gaze upon him. His countenance became closed and once again he wore an expression of cynicism.

"I hope you did not find the trip too arduous, Miss Langston."

"No, indeed, your grace, we were very comfortable," she said, then continued in a hesitant tone, "I wish to thank your grace. . . ."

He languidly waved off her thanks. "I believe this is your first time in London?"

"Yes, it is, your grace."

"Perhaps we can show you some of the more famous sights while you are with us."

Celia could only stare at him with incredulous eyes.

"That would be marvelous, Drake! We shall have so much fun! Celia, just you wait," said the duchess after recovering from her attack of nostalgia.

Celia agreed that they would, but was still shocked that the duke would suggest such a thing. She reasoned that his unexpected kindness was because he realized that she and his sister were good friends and he wanted to ensure that Imogene would enjoy her stay. What else could explain his attentions to a governess? she mused.

The duke's introducing a plump woman dressed in dark gray brought Celia's attention back.

"Mrs. Chambers is the chatelaine. She will show you to your rooms. I hope you will both join me for tea in an hour."

More surprises were in store as the housekeeper led a chatty Imogene and a wide-eyed Celia up the staircase. They passed remarkable pictures painted by Gainsborough and Van Dyck. The ceiling, Imogene pointed out, had been created by Thornhill. Celia would have assumed that the duke's home would seem rather cold and forbidding. This house was the farthest thing from cold. Admittedly, it was magnificent. The servants bustled about happily. The large windows allowed the struggling spring sun in, and every flat surface held fragrant bouquets of the season's earliest offerings.

They were first shown the chamber Imogene would occupy. It was a gorgeous suite decorated in varying shades of peach and cream. Mrs. Chambers and Celia left the room with Imogene's promise to see Celia in an hour's time.

Expecting Mrs. Chambers to continue to the third floor, where the servants were housed, Celia was surprised when the housekeeper led her a few doors down from the duchess's rooms.

There must be some mistake, Celia thought when they entered a sumptuous room of rose and gold. A petite blond maid skittered about, already unpacking Celia's meager belongings. A canopy bed draped with rose satin curtains stood between two long windows. A lovely little secretary and chair stood against the opposite wall. Two rose-and-gold-striped chairs were placed by a large fireplace, and a dressing room could be seen through an open door on the other side of the room.

"I'm sure there must be a mistake, Mrs. Chambers," Celia exclaimed, turning to the plump woman. "This cannot be my room."

"This is the room his grace chose for her grace's friend. I know there is no mistake, miss; his grace told me himself," Mrs. Chambers said anxiously, looking at the young lady with great concern because she looked as if she might be going to faint.

"Are you feeling well, miss? May I bring you something?"

"No . . . no, I am fine," Celia assured her, removing her small bonnet. "I just need to rest for a bit. Thank you very much."

"Very good, miss. Please ring if you need anything," the housekeeper said, indicating a bellpull near the bed. "Dora here shall attend you during your stay," she stated before exiting with the little maid following close behind.

For a long moment, Celia stood in the middle of the room, trying to absorb the serene beauty all around her. A deep flush stained her cheeks, and a queer feeling settled in the pit of her stomach. The duke had told Mrs. Chambers to put her here! It was most astounding.

She went to the window and saw that it faced the back gardens. Flowers were in early bloom, and she noticed a fountain with several benches scattered around it. With a bemused shake of her head she decided that this must truly be an enchanted place.

Celia pressed her cheek against the cool glass and realized she was in complete confusion regarding the duke. She could still remember clearly that night, many years ago, when he had rebuked Imogene for taking her in. That episode had caused Celia many years of insecurity and nervousness, lest she do something to displease him. She recalled the many stories from Imy and her mother-in-law about his escapades and scrapes. Yet here he was, being so kind. It made little sense. It must be evidence of the regard he held for his sister to treat the governess whom she had befriended so hospitably, she reasoned before turning back to the room.

Feeling much too excited to rest, she decided to bathe in the dressing room and change from her traveling apparel into a new purplish pink tea gown. Afterward, she sat down at the little desk to write a long missive to Edna. She described everything in great detail and told of her surprise at being given such a lovely room. Smiling to herself, Celia could imagine the old lady excitedly reading the letter to Matthews.

When she made her way downstairs an hour later, she placed the letter on the entry table so it could go out in the morning post. A footman directed her to the stately, oak-paneled drawing room, where Imogene and the duke were already seated. The duke rose as she entered, and Celia saw him glance at her new gown. Remembering her mother's old remade gown, Celia blushed deeply.

"Only you could look so well in that shade of amaranthus, Celly. Doesn't she look pretty, Drake?" Imogene asked her brother as she directed Celia to sit next to her.

Mortification surged through Celia. Imy had practically asked the duke to compliment her! Almost against her will, Celia glanced at the duke to see his reaction. He caught her eye and gave her a rakish grin, causing a spark of anger in Celia that did much to dispel her embarrassment.

"There are no two arguments on the subject, Imy. Miss Langston owns that particular shade," he drawled. "I trust you have everything you need, Miss Langston? If not, please don't hesitate to inform Mrs. Chambers or myself."

Celia still felt so overwhelmed and charmed by her room that she forgot to be intimidated. Leaning forward, her beautiful eyes wide, she said, "Indeed, your grace, I have more than I need. The room you appointed me is enchanting. May I ask, is that a Laguerre mural in the hall?"

"Yes, it is," Severly said in some surprise. He had not

expected her to recognize the mural or, more surprisingly, to speak more than three words to him.

"I would be happy to give you a tour of my house tomorrow, if you wouldn't find it a bore," he offered casually, reaching for another scone and watching the conflicting emotions play across her face.

Imogene looked from her brother's nonchalant visage to Celia's confused expression and took matters into her own hands.

"That would be delightful, Drake. It has been many years since I explored Severly House," the duchess offered helpfully.

"Tomorrow, then, after breakfast, shall we say?" His glance went to Celia for confirmation.

"Thank you, your grace. That would be lovely," Celia said to her teacup.

Chapter Six

The duke, as promised, gave Celia and Imogene a tour of the house the day after they had arrived. At first, Celia was so discomfited by the duke's attention she could pay little heed to her surroundings. No matter how she tried to hang back and let Imogene and the duke stay a little ahead of her, he would pause and wait for her to catch up.

It was obvious that the duke had a great pride and interest in the history of his home. The two women laughed frequently, for he was most entertaining with his urbane and amusing stories about the previous occupants of Severly House. After a little while, Celia began to relax under the duke's patient and engaging manner. The gallery had been particularly interesting to Celia, for all the portraits of the male members of the Severly family held a great resemblance to each other. Celia bit back a giggle when they came to the portrait of Severly's great-grandfather. It looked for all the world like Severly in a great powdered wig and a frilly coat with lacy cuffs.

The duke caught her struggle, quirked a brow, and said pointedly, "Shall we leave the gallery and see what other amusements we can find?"

In that week, Celia had enjoyed walks in the fragrant garden, and helped the head gardener with pruning the profuse number of rosebushes. At first, the little man had been uncomfortable with a guest of the duke's doing any kind of work, but after seeing how her pretty face glowed over an armful of flowers, he began to look forward to the congenial young lady's company.

To her relief, she found the dinners at Severly House much less intimidating than she had expected. Sometimes Major Rotham joined them, and she surprised herself by contributing to the conversation with ease. The marvelous works of art around every corner continued to delight her, and, of course, the library held a wealth of wonder. All in all, Celia was thoroughly enjoying her stay in London.

Inevitably, the *ton* got wind that the beautiful Duchess of Harbrooke had come to town for the Season. And the fact that the duke, for some curious reason, had not given one dinner party or soiree since coming to town only whetted Society's appetite more for the elusive duke's company. The unflappable butler brought in dozens of invitations daily for the duke and Imogene, most of which the duke tossed out.

After much careful consideration, the duchess decided to reenter Society by attending a musical evening hosted by Princess Esterhazy.

Celia was quite excited when the night of Imogene's "come-out," as they had come to call it, arrived. Life at Harbrooke Hall had never been so exciting. To Celia's delight, Imogene went to Celia's room to show off her gown before leaving for the evening.

"How beautiful you are, Imy!" Celia exclaimed as she viewed her friend in a new golden gown of the finest silk. The color made works of art of her hazel eyes. Diamonds dripped from her ears, neck, and wrists. The duchess promenaded about the room displaying her finery.

"I hope I don't make a cake of myself this evening. The *ton* is terribly censorious, and it has been fifteen years since I was last in Society." She stopped pacing to stare critically at her reflection in the large mirror near the rosewood wardrobe.

"You don't think I look like mutton dressed as lamb, do you?" she asked nervously, tugging up the front of her gown.

"You are a goose!" Celia laughed, stepping behind Imogene to look at her friend's reflection.

"You look absurdly young to be the mother of two growing boys. No doubt you will be the loveliest, most elegant lady present!" Celia avowed. "Every other woman will be put in the shade next to you," she predicted loyally.

Imogene looked doubtful. "At least Drake will be with me, and David." She sighed with a last glance in the mirror. "I must be off, Celia. Wish me luck," she said, and kissed Celia's cheek.

"If you wish, you can wake me when you return. I'm sure you will be bursting to tell me of your triumphs," Celia teased, and Imy brightened at the prospect.

"Wonderful! I will be able to tell you everything while it's still fresh," Imogene said excitedly.

She swept out of the room with a wave, and Celia settled into a deep, comfortable chair by the fireplace to pass the evening with a book. She wondered if there would be dancing at Princess Esterhazy's party, and what it would be like to have someone as tall as the duke to guide her around the dance floor.

Despite spending a goodly amount of time in Celia's room in the wee hours of the morning, Imogene was still full of last evening's excitement at breakfast. As Celia predicted, she had been a success. The most illustrious members of the *ton* had sought out the beautiful duchess. And Imogene tasted, again, the heady feeling of being a rage in London.

The clock read past eleven o'clock when Imogene and Celia finally made an appearance in the morning room. They found the duke lounging in his chair, reading the *Times.* He stood as they entered and bade them good morning.

By now, Celia felt comfortable enough in the duke's presence to meet his glittering gaze, at least briefly, and return his salutation with sincerity.

"What a delightful time we had last evening, Drake!" Imogene sighed in pleasure as she sipped her chocolate. "Everyone was so kind and engaging, I have never enjoyed myself so thoroughly," she expressed firmly.

An amused smile touched the duke's lips as he glanced up from his paper. "A passable evening. Imy, you have been in the country too long," he said dryly.

"Oh, you are so jaded," she admonished, and turned to Celia, who promised to listen with rapt attention.

"You should have been there, Celly. The beautiful gowns, the jewels, the music!" she rhapsodized, waving her hands expressively.

"The princess was kindness itself, and her ensemble was breathtaking. The house smelled of lilacs and roses, and when we went in to supper, I thought the tables would collapse from the amount of food," Imogene went on.

Celia's eyes were wide with interest, for it sounded very grand.

Casting a sly glance at her brother, Imogene continued, "You should have seen all the unattached ladies fawning over Drake. I feared I'd choke with laughter when Lady Marsten presented her squinty daughter." Imy laughed with delight at the memory. "Oh, Celly, you should have been there. It was a wonderful evening."

The duke looked up from his paper and frowned at his sister, thinking her quite thoughtless to say that Celia should have been at last evening's festivity. Imogene was more than aware that it would be impossible for a governess to enter society, unless of course she married a member of the *ton*.

Not that Celia displayed one whit of resentment; in fact, looking at her beautiful and attentive face, he felt confident that she was enjoying herself immensely.

Coming to a decision, the duke set his paper aside. "I had thought to go to the bookseller's today. If you both can manage to be ready within the hour, I would be delighted with your company."

Celia turned to stare at the duke in astonishment, her cup of tea poised halfway to her lips. To visit a bookstore in London would be an undreamed-of treat. She knew the duke to be a very busy man. He attended to all the business of running his various estates. He was often at his clubs, or the races, or visiting Gentleman Jackson's.

He also made speeches in the House of Lords. Escorting his sister and a governess to the bookseller's seemed too tame for the easily bored duke. But Celia was determined not to look this unexpected gift horse in the mouth and looked hopefully to Imy.

"What a famous idea, Drake, and of course we shall be ready within the hour."

In three-quarters of an hour, Celia found herself in the duke's high-perch phaeton with the red spokes. She wore a simple lavender-blue day dress and a new chip-straw bonnet. The duke had smiled at her shining, excited eyes as he handed her into the vehicle. Imogene sat between them and pointed out the sights of London to an enthralled Celia. To further the enjoyment of the outing, the duke took a meandering route to give Celia a chance to see some of the more spectacular homes of London. She had not thought there could be a house equal to Severly House, but Chesterfield House left her speechless, and moments later Holdernesse House in Park Lane caused her to gasp. London was so full of new sights and sounds, Celia feared her neck might get a crick because of twisting this way and that in an effort not to miss a thing. She thought, with awe, that London must be the most exciting and beautiful place on earth.

"Not Hatcherd's, Drake. Celia and I wish to purchase books, not watch the beau monde strutting about," Imogene said as her brother turned the horses onto Piccadilly.

The duke bowed to his sister's wish and turned the phaeton toward Colburn's, a very reputable but less fashionable establishment.

Having only ever been to the meager lending library in Harford, Celia could at first only walk through the aisles of Colburn's, amazed at the plethora of books to be had.

Imogene settled herself into a chair with a copy of *La Belle Assemblée* and declared that Celia should browse at her leisure.

Curiously, no matter which aisle she entered, the duke was close at hand. But Celia felt too excited about the outing to be disconcerted. After a moment, the duke stepped forward, pointing out the different sections and topics available. Celia thanked him, again surprised at his solicitude.

Looking into her reticule, Celia found she still possessed a little money, left over from her last allowance. Since the next quarterly was due in another week or so, Celia felt easy about buying one or two books.

As these would be books she would be keeping for the rest of her life, she made very careful selections.

"If you are interested in explorations, here is a book on the wilds of the Colonies. There are some very interesting descriptions of the natives," the duke offered after observing the books Celia seemed to find interesting.

Taking the book with some surprise, Celia glanced at its red leather cover. *How very obliging of him*, she thought. Her opinion of him had been undergoing a subtle change over the last week. Even though the duke could be autocratic and imposing, no one could say that he was not a gentleman. He never failed to be solicitous to any female, she had noticed.

The book promised to be intriguing, and Celia thanked him sincerely. After browsing a bit, she found a biography on the Plantagenets and took her treasures to the proprietor's stand to pay. Gazing around, she noticed a table with an assortment of books at reduced prices. The title *The Haunting of Henchley Manor* caught her eye. Rechecking her funds, Celia decided there would be enough left to include the book in her purchases and set it on the table to be wrapped with the others.

"Ah, here is the gothic," a teasing voice said behind her.

Celia turned to see the duke examining *The Haunting of Henchley Manor* with a raised brow.

She laughed, remembering the comment he had made the day they had walked home from the village. Celia forgot to look at the scar on his cheek and found herself smiling into his eyes. The duke held her magnificent gaze until it occurred to him that he could easily drown in their brownish green depths if he did not have a care.

Another moment passed and he decided to dismiss this unsettling notion.

"I confess to a penchant for melodrama on occasion. Miss Forbisher has me read them to her occasionally. She enjoys them so," she explained as the proprietor handed her the package of books.

Celia had never spoken of herself in so personal a manner, and the duke pressed the advantage as he took the package from her.

"What a soothing way to spend an evening. I am sure you must have needed a brace of candles at night to keep the monsters at bay," he said in his most engaging tone. They left the shop and stepped onto the busy sidewalk with Imogene trailing behind.

"Oh, no! Never leave light in the room when you are scared," she admonished as if everyone knew this. "Monsters lurk in the shadows. If the room is pitch-black and you hide your head under the covers, the ghouls can't find you," she explained sagely, stepping lightly over a puddle.

The duke could picture Celia as a charming little girl afraid of ghosts, and her mama telling her they couldn't find her in the dark. He was beginning to think that Miss Langston was not only beautiful, but also unique.

"How silly of me to think that you would be afraid of the dark." The twinkle in his eye belied his serious tone.

Celia laughed as they walked along the crowded sidewalk to the awaiting phaeton. "Once, I was reading a particularly suspenseful passage to Miss Forbisher. The ghost was about to speak to the heroine. The ghosts always turn out to be smugglers or crazed aunts, you know. Anyway, as I was about to read what the ghost had to say, a log in the fireplace gave a deafening crack and Miss Forbisher and I jumped a yard and shrieked. Matthews, her maid, ran in wielding a poker in our defense. We explained that all was well and she said, 'Well, ye look as if ye've just seen a ghost!' "

Imogene, walking behind them, observed her brother and her dearest friend. Drake's dark head was thrown back in laughter, and Celia looked so happy and relaxed. A speculative light entered her eyes.

On the way back to Severly House, the duke and his sister chatted as Celia watched the fashionable people, crested carriages, and intriguing sights of London. She tried to absorb everything so that she could write of it to Edna. *What an unexpectedly wonderful day,* she thought with a contented sigh.

Porter, the duke's very tall butler, opened the massive double doors as they walked up the steps and immediately asked for a word with her grace. With a surprised glance at Celia and Drake, Imogene obligingly stepped into the blue drawing room with the butler.

Shyly, Celia turned to the duke to thank him for the outing, but before she could begin he said, "Thank you, Miss Langston, for accompanying us today. Perhaps another day you and Imogene would be interested in one of London's fine museums."

Dumbfounded, Celia struggled with how to respond. "Why . . . thank you. How lovely . . . er . . ."

"Fine then. Now, if you will pardon me, I must attend to some business matters."

She thanked the duke for a lovely outing and with a curtsy excused herself from him before walking across the foyer.

On the entry table, Celia noticed a letter addressed to her in Edna's scrawling handwriting. Picking it up with an anticipatory smile, she started up the stairs, when Imogene emerged from the drawing room.

"Drake, will you please step in here for a moment?" she asked her brother quickly, walking toward Celia with outstretched arms. "Let us go up to your room, my dear." Imogene grasped her surprised friend's arm and ascended the stairs with her.

A horrible, frightening feeling swept over Celia. She glanced back to see the duke moving to the drawing room with his dark brows drawn together in a frown.

They reached Celia's chamber and Imogene pulled her friend down beside her on the bed. The duchess gazed sadly into Celia's wide, frightened eyes.

"There is no way to ease this blow, dear Celia." She grasped her friend's hands tightly. "I have just been informed that Miss Forbisher died the day before last. I am so very sorry, my dear," she said gently.

Celia stared a moment, then looked down at the letter in her lap. Edna could not be dead. She had just received a letter from her. It must be a mistake.

"How do you know?" she asked in a very calm voice.

"Her solicitor, a Mr. Whitely, arrived a short time ago. Porter wisely thought that I should be the one to tell you this sad news. I know how much you cared for her, Celia."

"I've just received a letter from her." She picked up the missive and clutched it to her chest.

"Are you all right, Celia, dear? Do you wish to be alone?" She noted that the color had completely drained from Celia's face, and the fingers that held the letter trembled.

"I'm quite fine. I just can't comprehend that Edna is gone. How can she be?" There was a stricken look in her eyes.

"I hate to ask it of you, dear, and I will ask Mr. Whitely to return in a few days if you aren't up to it, but he is hoping to have a word with you now."

"Why, of course, I must thank him for bringing the news." She stood, still clutching the letter from Edna.

The duke and Mr. Whitely stood in the middle of the dark-paneled room, conversing quietly as the ladies entered. Mr. Whitely, a thin, bespectacled man in a dark brown woolen suit, turned toward the ladies as they entered. Celia vaguely thought he looked just as a solicitor should.

"Celia, this is Mr. Whitely," Imogene said.

Mr. Whitely bowed deeply and looked at her with polite, yet saddened, brown eyes. "May I extend my deepest sympathy to you, Miss Langston. I sincerely apologize for imposing on you at this time. I hope you will understand after I have explained."

Celia inclined her head in understanding, not trusting her voice at the moment. It was all too real. Edna must,

indeed, be dead. Even though Dr. Rayburn had prepared
her, it still came as a shock. Celia and Imogene moved
to sit on the settee; Mr. Whitely sat opposite and the
duke stood by the fireplace, watching Celia's pallid face
closely.

"Thank you for bringing me the news, Mr. Whitely,"
Celia began, surprised that her voice sounded so clear.
"May I ask the circumstances of Edna's . . . ?" Speech
failed her then.

The duke could see that Celia was deeply shocked.
Going to the liquor cabinet, he poured Celia a snifter
of brandy. She accepted it without a word, feeling his
fingers warm upon hers for a moment. She barely noticed the heat that coursed down her throat at the
first sip.

"Matthews—her maid, I believe—entered Miss Forbisher's room on Tuesday morning. May I say that Matthews imparted to me that Miss Forbisher had a very
peaceful expression. I do not believe there was any pain
involved," he assured her kindly.

Celia looked down at her hand, still clutching Edna's
letter.

Mrs. Chambers entered with a tea tray and the duchess
offered a cup to Mr. Whitely.

"Thank you, your grace. Now, Miss Langston, there is
the matter of the will and a letter that Miss Forbisher
wished to be read immediately after her death."

He sifted through a sheaf of papers he had extracted
from a leather portfolio.

A will? Celia could think of nothing of worth that Edna
owned. Harford Abbey, Celia assumed from things Edna
had said on occasion, was entailed to a distant relative.

"Ah, here is the letter. She wished me to read it before
the will," he said, glancing at Celia over his spectacles.

"I beg your pardon. I must ask Miss Langston if she
wouldn't prefer to hear this privately," the duke interrupted quietly.

Celia lifted her head and met the duke's enigmatic
gaze.

"I would rather that you and Imy stay, please," she

said simply, refusing to examine why she did not want him to leave. The duke inclined his head and she turned her attention back to the solicitor.

Mr. Whitely cleared his voice. "The letter is dated February eighth, eighteen hundred and sixteen. It reads as follows.

"My dear Celia. It is very strange to think that when you hear this I shall be dead. It is my request that Mr. Whitely read this to you. As I am sure your friend, the Duchess of Harbrooke, will also be present, I know you will not be able to ignore what I have to say.

"First of all, I positively forbid you to wear black for me. I am not a relative and I believe the practice, except in the case of immediate family member, is unnecessary. I know, because of the friendship we have shared, that you shall grieve for me, and that is enough. Even in this, do not allow yourself to become maudlin.

"Furthermore, I wish you to purchase a complete wardrobe immediately. You may think this is silly, but clothes give a woman confidence, and confidence is important.

"Lastly, Celia, I encourage you to rely upon Mr. Whitely. I have known him for more than thirty years and have found him to be of impeccable character. I know he will be enormously helpful to you in the future.

"You have been a delight to me these past years and I ask our Lord to watch over you and keep you. Sincerely, Edna Forbisher.

"Postscript: From what I know of the duchess, I believe her to be a woman of intelligence and kindness. I feel confident that she will help guide you in the future. I regret that I never had the honor of meeting her, but if I had received the Duchess of Harbrooke, I would have had to receive the whole county. Please convey this to her grace."

Despite her shock, Celia could not help smiling at the last bit, it sounded so like Edna. Mr. Whitely folded the letter and handed it to Celia. She accepted it with trembling fingers. He then proceeded to the will. Celia absorbed only half of the words she heard as tears began to pool in her large eyes at the thought of never seeing her friend again. She sat there, slowly sipping the brandy the duke had given her, while Mr. Whitely's correct voice flowed over her.

An astonished gasp from Imogene pulled her from her reverie.

"I'm sorry, Mr. Whitely, I didn't quite catch that. Could you repeat it, please?" she apologized after glancing at Imy's wide eyes.

Mr. Whitely, after many years of reading wills and dealing with grieving people, had grown accustomed to repeating himself.

"I have just reached the main part of the will, Miss Langston. If you prefer, I shall dispense with legal terminology and explain it in lay terms."

He looked to see if this met with her approval, and continued. "Miss Forbisher has left you Harford Abbey and the forty-two acres it occupies. There is approximately thirty-five thousand pounds in capital at Coattes Bank that shall be transferred to you after I receive your signature on a few documents. There are various other stocks and investments that total approximately fifteen thousand pounds. Other real property, such as works of art and jewelry, are worth over twenty thousand pounds."

He paused to pick up a red leather box by his feet. "I have brought with me Miss Forbisher's jewelry. She wished you to have it immediately," he explained to a stunned Celia as he handed her the box. Imogene took the case as Celia made no move to take it from the gentleman.

The duke stepped forward to rescue the crystal goblet in danger of slipping from Celia's lax fingers. He frowningly scanned her pale face, fearing she was about to faint.

Mr. Whitely continued, "I will not take much more of your time, Miss Langston. If you will be so good as to sign a few papers, I will leave a duplicate of the will and various other papers for you to review. When you are felling better, I hope I may explain everything in greater detail."

"Yes, of course," Celia said faintly, finally able to move and take the papers he wished her to sign. The duke procured a quill and ink pot.

"May I say, Miss Langston, that Miss Forbisher asked me to personally convey her wish that you enter Society and not mourn her death unduly."

Celia closed her eyes. The world seemed to be whirling around her, and the piquant smell of the irises on the mantel suddenly seemed sickeningly sweet. After taking a few deep breaths, she managed to choke out a few words: "Thank you, Mr. Whitely, I am having difficulty comprehending all of this, but I'm sure I will have many questions."

"Yes, of course," Mr. Whitely said, "there is no hurry, and I am at your service."

Imogene, unable to contain herself any longer, spoke up. "I just have to ask how Miss Forbisher managed all of this, Mr. Whitely. None of us had any idea that she was anything but an eccentric old lady."

Nodding his head in agreement, Mr. Whitely stated baldly, "Miss Forbisher was a miser. She had virtually given up on life in her youth, until she discovered some property and capital left to her by her father in a codicil to his will. Over the years, I believe that one of her few pleasures was seeing her wealth grow. I came to realize that it was almost like a game. She was not interested in the wealth, just the numbers. I grew to respect her business acumen greatly."

Celia looked up at Mr. Whitely then and examined his expression closely. She realized that the quiet solicitor was grieving for Edna, too. Celia was very glad to know that Edna had had another friend in the world.

Mr. Whitely took his leave of them then, leaving his calling card for Celia. She thanked him, and the duke escorted him to the front door.

Celia sat next to Imy on the settee, the small pile of

papers in a neat stack on her lap. These and the red leather box were the only real evidence that this past half hour had not been a dream.

"Oh, Celly, what a turn the day has taken," Imogene said with a bemused shake of her head. With that, the floodgate opened and Celia burst into great, racking sobs.

Chapter Seven

$\mathcal{T}$hree days after receiving the news of Edna's death, Imogene came to an important decision. After breakfast she went in search of her brother. A footman informed her that he was in his private study, going over estate business with his secretary. She tapped on the door lightly and poked her head into the wood-paneled room, requesting a few moments of his time when he was free.

"Of course, Imy, I am just finishing now. Thank you, Hammond, that will be all for today." Severly rose from his chair, dismissing the scholarly-looking young man. The duke directed Imy to a chair, reseated himself, leaned back, and gazed at his sister's serious face.

"What is amiss, my dear?" he asked after the door closed behind Hammond.

The duchess plucked absentmindedly at the lace on the front of her morning gown as she wondered how best to approach him. Taking a deep breath, she plunged in before losing her nerve.

"It is Celia. I am much concerned about her situation," she began with a shake of her head. "I feel that I should launch her into Society. She is an enormously wealthy young lady, and I know that is what Miss Forbisher intended. I feel it is my duty to guide her. She is so terribly green, you know."

The duke gave his sister one of his rare smiles, thinking that Imogene was not very far from being green herself.

She continued her speech, fortified by the fact that he

was not scowling at her yet. "It will be most difficult to present a governess to the *ton;* I am hoping you will help. Drake, it would mean a great deal to me." Her eyes were anxious as she watched for his reaction.

Rising, the duke went to stand in front of a large window overlooking a small hedge maze in the garden. "It would not be difficult. It would be impossible. A governess would be cut dead if she showed herself in Society," he informed his crestfallen sister.

"But, Drake, we must try," Imy urged. "After all, she is an heiress. Years ago, I wondered if I should be looking around for a young man for Celia. She is so pretty and intelligent. And she is the daughter of a gentleman. With no dowry and her being much too proud to accept a settlement from me, I never really pursued the matter. It is different now; she should be living the life of a lady."

"I agree. Celia is a lady. Under these unexpected circumstances, all should be done to help her in her new life. But if you go about saying she was a governess, you might as well quit before you start," he said, turning from the window to give his sister a pointed look.

Imogene jumped up with a cry of excitement. Running to the window, she threw her arms around her brother and hugged him effusively. "You will help! You are wonderful, and this will be such fun! I thought the ball you are giving for me would be an excellent opportunity to introduce her to the world, so to speak. What do you think?" She pulled back to assess his reaction.

"It will serve. In the two weeks before then we must endeavor to prepare Miss Langston. However, it must not, under any circumstances, be known that she was a governess," her brother said sternly. "I believe the best approach would be to say that Miss Langston has been a friend for many years, which she has, and stayed at Harbrooke because of being orphaned. The less said the better. If we pass Celia off as if it is the most natural thing in the world, this may not be as difficult as you think. After all, she has you and me to give her the proper consequence," he said.

Imogene wondered at the cynical tone in his voice.

"I will explain the situation to Rotham," he continued. "He will add to the credibility of our slight masquerade. Again—and I stress this, Imy—it must not be known that Miss Langston was in service to you." His voice held a note that she could not ignore.

"I never really thought of her as the governess," Imogene said, "not after we became such good friends, anyway. I feel completely at ease now that you are in command, Drake, dear. I must run and tell Celia. Now that you will help, I know she will agree," she said gaily, fairly skipping out of the room. She left her frowning brother to contemplate the changes that, no doubt, were bound to disrupt his well-ordered life.

Celia had spent the first day after hearing the news of Edna's death in her room, crying profusely into the silk coverlet on her bed. She had come down for breakfast the day after, but felt so bereft, she again returned to her room.

Edna's letter, received on the day Celia found out the sad news, had sat unopened on the little desk until the third day. Celia had not felt strong enough to read it until then. She met with Mr. Whitely that morning, who kindly explained in greater detail the circumstances of her inheritance. Upon his departure, he promised to follow her instructions on repairs and other improvements to Harford Abbey. After seeing him out, Celia went back to her room and picked up Edna's letter.

The scrawling handwriting had brought tears to her eyes. Sitting down in the high-backed chair before the fireplace, Celia finally opened the envelope. By the end of the missive she was laughing so that her sides hurt. She read the letter again.

> *Dear Celia,*
>   *I received your letter the day before last and enjoyed it immensely, and so did Matthews. But, my dear, you must endeavor to describe the people in greater detail. I have been to London before and I doubt the terrain has changed much.*

*Haven't you seen any of the fops or dandies
we've heard so much about? I have also heard
that some women (I do not call them ladies)
have actually been seen riding horses astride in
public! Have you seen anything so shocking?
If so, write to me immediately.*

*Perchance you have made the acquaintance of
some worthy young men? I know that in your
position this may be difficult, but do try.*

*You have asked after my health, and I confess
that I have been a bit poorly the last two days,
but nothing to alarm yourself over. I would be
quite upset if you let your stay in London be
marred by any worry over me.*

*All is well here at Harford Abbey. Though I
did have to speak to Jarvis about trying to get
a better price on our groceries. I so dislike to
be overcharged.*

*Write to me soon, Celia, and please endeavor
to enjoy yourself.*

Sincerely,
Edna Forbisher

A better price on the groceries! All this time, Edna had
possessed a huge fortune, and she quibbled about pennies.
How shocked she was to hear about ladies riding astride,
yet she wished to be informed the moment Celia witnessed
such an event. Celia shook her head and reread the letter
yet again. Edna had been such an eccentric old lady and
she would always miss her, yet somehow having this last
letter from her took away some of the pain.

A tap on the door suddenly interrupted her musings.

"May I speak to you, Celia?" Imogene asked upon
entering.

"Of course, Imy. I've just been trying to make sense
of all this," Celia said, gesturing to Edna's letter and the
papers Mr. Whitely had left for her to read.

Imogene sat on the bed and looked at her friend's pale
face. "This is all so amazing, Celia. Do you realize that
you are an heiress?"

Celia shook her head. "No," she said truthfully. "How could Edna have been so rich, yet lived in such penury?"

"I do not know. But obviously she knew what she wanted, and because of that your life has vastly changed," Imogene said seriously.

"Yes, I realize that. I am at a loss as to what to do next," Celia said, gathering the papers together and taking them to the secretary before reseating herself.

"We shall honor Edna's wishes and introduce you to Society," Imy began. "Do not look at me that way. Drake already has it all in hand, so there is nothing to worry about."

Celia jumped up from her chair and stared at her friend with a horrified expression on her face.

"Oh, no, Imy. You did not ask your brother to help!" she cried in alarm. "I do not even feel that I should be here now that all this has happened."

"Do not upset yourself, Celly. Drake has offered to help launch you into Society, which is very kind of him," Imy stated practically. "We shall formally present you at the ball Drake is giving in two weeks. Before then, we shall follow Edna's very express wishes and get you the most glorious wardrobe this side of the channel."

Celia looked at Imy helplessly, seeing that her friend was enjoying all the changes that Celia found so daunting. Sinking back into the chair, Celia said, "This whole situation seems incomprehensible to me, Imy. I don't know how to be rich," she finished plaintively.

"Of course you do. You've been around me all these years, haven't you?" Imy demanded archly, bringing a wry smile to Celia's lips.

"I know you are right about what Edna wanted. We had a conversation shortly before I came to London. She told me I would soon have many choices. Now I understand her words." Sadness colored Celia's voice. "I shall miss her very much."

"I know you will, my dear," Imy replied, going over to lay a supportive hand on her friend's shoulder. "I regret that I never had the honor of meeting her. But from her letter, it is clear that her fondest wish would be for you to jump into your new life. And I think you should begin tomorrow by going shopping with me," Imogene finished hopefully.

Celia hesitated. "Well . . . let's see what tomorrow brings."

Imogene, well pleased with this morning's work, decided not to press her friend. After placing a kiss on Celia's forehead, she went to the door.

"Rest this afternoon; it will help you get over the shock. Remember, Edna is at peace, and she gave you a wonderful opportunity for a new life."

Celia slept the afternoon away. Awakening after the sun had set gave her a strange, disoriented feeling. Turning her head to glance at the clock, she saw that she had only an hour to dress before dinner.

After bathing, she donned the new umber-colored gown that Imy had given her. Celia smiled when it suddenly occurred to her that she could now return the generosity. Coiling her thick hair onto the back of her head, Celia frowned at the reflection of her pale face. After tucking a stray hair away, she gave herself one last look, shrugged, and left the room.

She found the duke alone in the salon, staring into the fire with his hands clasped behind his back. He looked up at her entry and she curtsied.

"I have not had the chance to offer my condolences, Miss Langston," he offered as he turned away from the mantel and approached her. "You have my deepest sympathy at the loss of your friend. She seemed a fascinating person."

Celia looked up at his somber, handsome face and saw that he meant the words. Lowering her eyes, she admitted to herself reluctantly that his kindness touched her heart.

"I thank you, your grace. I confess that I have been overset by the news."

"Most certainly. You must give yourself time to become accustomed to your new situation. Of course, you shall remain here as my guest and follow Miss Forbisher's instructions," he remarked agreeably, as if it were all very natural.

Celia's surprise was so great, she could not bring herself to respond.

The duke did not seem to expect her to say anything and walked over to the liquor cabinet. He offered her a glass of sherry, which she gratefully accepted.

To Celia's relief, Imogene burst into the room in a flurry of deep blue silk, babbling about how late she was for dinner.

Just then Porter opened the double mahogany doors leading to the dining room.

"Dinner is served, your grace," he stated, bowing slowly.

The duke stepped forward and offered both ladies an arm, saying with a slight smile, "Shall we?"

Imogene took her brother's arm and smiled happily at Celia, delighted with her brother's gallantry.

Despite her long-standing friendship with Imogene, Celia did not feel comfortable placing herself as a social equal. Since coming to Severly House she had always followed Imy and the duke into supper. So she hesitated before them now, looking lovely and confused, frowning slightly as she looked from Imy to the duke.

Disengaging his right arm from Imy's, Severly reached over, took Celia's hand, and gently pulled it through his left arm. Celia felt a tingle through her fingers as she gazed down at his warm, long-fingered hand touching hers.

Severly turned to his sister again, offered her his right arm, and said, "Cook will be angry if we let his efforts get cold."

As they all walked arm in arm into the dining room, it suddenly struck Celia how profoundly her life had changed.

The next morning, Imogene would hear none of Celia's protests and bustled her out of the house and into a waiting carriage to go shopping. By the time they had been conveyed to Knightsbridge, some of Imogene's chattering excitement had transferred itself to Celia.

Imogene had informed Celia that Mrs. Triaud of Bolton Street was a very fashionable and creative modiste. They arrived at the elegant little shop, only to be informed that Mrs. Triaud would be much too busy to assist them, for she was in the midst of working on Princess Charlotte's trousseau.

Celia didn't know if she was on her head or heels. How Edna would have loved this! For a moment Celia thought about writing to Edna, until she remembered that Edna was gone. But Celia would never have had the chance to be in this place if Edna were still alive. It was all very sad and ironic, she thought, gazing about the opulent little shop.

Imogene had a brief word with the shop girl. The girl disappeared into the back room, and a moment later a plump woman in a very chic dark gray gown came into the room with outstretched arms.

"Forgive the silly girl, your grace," Mrs. Triaud solicited, sweeping a very deep curtsy to the duchess. "I have, of late, not accepted new clients, as we are so busy with the royal wedding. Besides the wedding dress, there are over a dozen more to complete! But of course I should be delighted and honored to create something for the Duchess of Harbrooke," she fairly gushed in her attempt to placate the duchess. One never knew when the fortunes could turn and some other modiste would take her place as the most exclusive dressmaker to the beau monde. Indeed, she had turned away a few ladies and even the daughter of an earl, but only a fool would turn away the illustrious Duke of Severly's sister.

Imogene inclined her head to the plump woman, not in the least surprised by the woman's consideration.

"Yes, I am in need of one or two ball gowns, but it is my friend, Miss Langston, who is in need of a complete wardrobe."

Mrs. Triaud's eyes bulged from her head as her gaze went to the lovely young woman standing serenely next to the duchess. A complete wardrobe! This was much better. One or two gowns were just an inconvenience, but a complete wardrobe was money in the bank.

Her assessing eyes narrowed as she looked at Celia

from tip to toe. *Good.* She obviously was not making her come-out. Mrs. Triaud disliked dressing young girls, as everything had to be white and missish and not the least bit daring. This young lady, being tall and possessing such a graceful carriage, would show off her creations to perfection. Mrs. Triaud made a rustling bow, and gave a clap of her hands, and the shop girl immediately appeared with bolts of fabric, a measuring tape, and fashion plates for Miss to inspect.

And so it began—the overwhelming task of choosing and being measured and standing for endless fittings. As she decided on more morning gowns, day dresses, tea gowns, afternoon dresses, riding habits, dinner gowns, and ball gowns, Celia's eyes glowed with delight at the appearance of each new ensemble. She had had no idea how wonderful shopping could be, or how wearying.

In the following week, the thrill of being able to purchase anything that took her fancy completely overtook Celia. It was such a new and exciting feeling for her. Imogene had laughingly protested that Celia could not possibly wear all the stockings, gloves, parasols, and shawls that she had bought.

"But they are all so beautiful," Celia had countered laughingly, as a groom followed them to the carriage, struggling with a mountain of boxes.

A week before the Severly ball, the duke, Imy, and Celia breakfasted together in the flower-filled morning room and discussed the plans for the day. They had seen little of the duke of late, as the ladies had been so busy shopping during the days and the duke had been gone most evenings.

Celia felt shy in her new, very fashionable morning dress of periwinkle blue. Secretly, she wondered if the duke noticed that she no longer looked so dowdy. Immediately she squelched the foolish notion. She was still only a governess, no matter what she wore, and thus was beneath his notice. Not that she wished him to notice her, she reminded herself sternly.

"As we are to formally introduce you at our ball next week, Miss Langston, I think it would be wise for you to appear in public once or twice before then. A drive in Hyde Park this afternoon would be a good start. We shall introduce you to our friends so that you may become acquainted with a few more people in London," the duke instructed.

Imogene thought this a capital suggestion and Celia thanked him demurely, finally able to look at him. He really was very handsome, she thought before she could stop herself.

"But we must all be very careful—not a word about this governess business. You are an heiress who has lived with the Duchess of Harbrooke since the tragic deaths of your parents. Perhaps there is some distant family connection that could be brought forth. Do you know anything about your parents' relatives?" he queried, admiring the way Celia tilted her head when she concentrated.

Celia knew full well how important one's family tree was to the *ton*. Her hand cupped her chin as she tried to recall what her mother had told her of the family.

"My father's uncle is Baron Langston. The family settled in Northumberland, I believe. They were of simple means, so they were relieved when my father took up the cloth. My mother was the granddaughter of a French émigré. I know little of my mother's people, save that they did not feel that a second son of a second son was a good match for Mama. It caused hard feelings, so my parents rarely spoke of it. At least, I don't recall much discussion of the family." She strove to suppress the sad tone that always seemed to be in her voice when she spoke of her parents.

She met the duke's astute gaze, and an odd feeling came over her at the look of understanding in his dark-fringed hazel eyes. He seemed to be able to look into her heart and see the pain that her words did not reveal. It must be because he had lost his parents, also. It gave her a slight shock to realize that they actually had something in common.

Imogene clapped her hands together. "Capital! We shall hint that you are the great-granddaughter of a French aristocrat and a relation of a well-respected landowning family in Northumberland. Do you know them, Drake?"

"I am not acquainted with the Langstons of Northumberland. But that shall be our story. Actually, it is the truth, so you needn't feel as if you are deceiving anyone, Miss Langston. We are just leaving out the part about your being a governess, which is of no one's concern."

Celia's head jerked up to look at him. How had he known that she had been feeling a niggling discomfort at the thought of possibly living a lie? He really was the most amazing man, and he had completely alleviated her doubts. He gave her a devilish, yet charming smile and rose from his chair.

"If you will excuse me, I have a few matters to attend to before we meet again . . . at, shall we say, three o'clock?" he asked after consulting his watch fob.

The ladies found this agreeable and the duke took his leave.

"I am so glad that Drake is being helpful. Everything is so much easier now," Imogene said.

"Yes, indeed. He is excessively kind to do this," Celia offered sincerely, busying herself with a piece of fruit.

"I believe you find him more tolerable than you once did." There was a question in Imy's gentle voice.

"Well," Celia began, tracing a pattern with her fingertip in the damask cloth covering the table. "I have gotten a better measure of his temperament since coming to London. He has also been very kind about Edna's death."

"Yes, my brother has a few ~~nice~~ fine qualities that I sometimes think he does not wish to be known," Imy stated archly.

Celia had no answer to this, and the ladies spent the remainder of the morning and early afternoon going over the fine art of deportment. Although Celia had exquisite manners, due no doubt to Imy's fine example for so many years, Celia wanted to be sure she would not make a wrong step. Imogene instructed Celia on how to address various members of the peerage, how to hold a fan properly, how to drape a shawl to the best advantage, and many other essential modes of behavior.

Celia followed Imogene's every move and instruction with firm attention. She felt excited—and a little nervous—about riding in Hyde Park with Imy and the duke, for this was to be her first test on behaving like a lady of quality.

Chapter Eight

An hour before the promised ride, Celia was in her room agonizing over what to wear. Dora, Mrs. Chambers's niece and Celia's newly appointed lady's maid, had been pulling out one ensemble after another for Celia's approval. Celia was in the process of tossing yet another gown onto her already burdened bed when Imogene entered, looking fresh as spring in an apple-green dress with matching bonnet and parasol.

"Celly! You aren't dressed? Drake will be here shortly and he hates to keep his cattle standing," she admonished, staring at the pile of gowns on the bed.

"I know, I know! I can't decide what to wear." Celia felt panicked by her indecision. Never had she had to decide between even two gowns, nonetheless a dozen.

"You goose! Anything you own looks as if it just arrived from Paris. Here, this dark pink gown with the pretty bows on the pelisse is very smart. Dora, please locate the fawn-colored bonnet and gloves I remember arriving with this ensemble, and help Miss Langston dress. We mustn't keep Drake waiting," she said pointedly to Celia.

A little while later Celia calmly descended the stairs in the rose-colored gown and pelisse. As she pulled on the fawn kid gloves she wondered how she could have overlooked this lovely confection.

The duke was waiting for them in the circular drive, controlling a pair of jet-black high-steppers. He handed the reins to a groom and stepped agilely from the vehicle to help his sister alight, and then he turned to Celia.

He noted her hair, swept back into a chignon with tendrils framing her face beneath her smart new bonnet. She bore little resemblance to the badly dressed young woman he had encountered at Harbrooke Hall. She even carried herself differently. Edna Forbisher had been right: clothes did give a woman confidence. Celia appeared a beautiful, poised young lady. He felt an odd pang somewhere near his heart because he knew how deceiving appearances could be. Miss Langston was still the shy, green governess who had never been more than a few miles from sleepy little Harford until a few weeks ago.

Logically, Severly knew it would be ludicrous for her to go on as if nothing had happened to change her life. Few young, unmarried women found themselves the possessor of such fortunes. So there really was only one thing for her to do—enter Society and find a husband who could take proper care of her and keep her away from fortune hunters. This thought brought a cynical quirk to his well-shaped mouth.

He knew the *ton* well enough to know that the sudden appearance of an extremely wealthy and unknown woman would cause a stir. Everyone would be politely trying to find out everything about her. If she would meet personal questions with a lofty stare and a short response, she'd get by, he concluded. From personal experience, he knew that she should have no trouble with giving a short response.

A wave of shyness engulfed Celia as she stood before the duke's direct and disturbing gaze. As he towered over her, she fussed with her reticule nervously.

"May I compliment you on your excellent taste, Miss Langston? I confess that I have been admiring each new ensemble more than the last," he praised in his deep voice.

It was exactly what she needed to hear, and she smiled up at him, though still unable to meet his gaze.

"Thank you, your grace. I confess I've been enjoying

the shops of London prodigiously," she said demurely as he handed her into the phaeton.

The duke's deep laughter set the horses to dancing.

As he tooled the phaeton through the streets of London, Severly contemplated his plan to launch Celia into Society. He had already decided to introduce her to a few of his particular friends. Rotham she already knew, and that would help. He had also decided to take one more friend into his confidence. The duke knew that if he and the Duke of Westlake paid Celia the mildest of attention she would soon be the biggest rage London had seen in years. Westlake, though a rake and deep gambler like Severly, could still be counted on to be a gentleman with a lady. They'd been close friends ever since school days, and Drake trusted him completely. In fact, he was the only person, other than Rotham, whom he trusted with the true circumstances of Celia's situation.

Hyde Park was bright with spring flowers and crowded with everyone who was anyone in the beau monde.

From the moment they entered Rotten Row, Celia became fully aware of the esteem in which the Duke of Severly and the Duchess of Harbrooke were held. More than once, the duke had to use the excuse of his restless horses to move forward several yards, only to be hailed again by another acquaintance hoping for a few words.

"Lady Tayborne, I do not believe you have met my dear friend Miss Langston, visiting us from Harford," called Imogene to a thin matron in brown.

"Sir Mayhew, have you met Miss Langston? She is my dearest friend visiting us from Harford."

To Celia's amused surprise she found herself the recipient of much avid curiosity. She had the odd feeling this was happening to someone else and she was just an observer, enjoying the novelty of all the attention. The word spread quickly that Severly was on the scene escorting his sister and a lovely, exquisitely dressed young lady whom no one seemed to be acquainted with. The crowd around the phaeton grew. Not a few hopeful mamas were brought to near panic at the thought of some unknown chit stealing the elusive duke before they could bring him to heel for their unmarried daughters.

"Who is she?" Everyone seemed to be asking this question.

Celia suppressed a startled laugh when a dandy in a bright green-and-pink-striped waistcoat pulled his conveyance alongside the duke's. In a very deliberate manner, he raised a monocle to his eye, examined her for a moment, and pronounced in a drawling tone, "Charming."

Another fop had shirt collars so high that Celia wondered how he could turn his head without poking his eye out. Glancing to the other side of the conveyance, Celia admired the way Severly's gray-blue coat fit snugly to his shoulders. There was almost a military cut to his clothing, which showed his tall, broad-shouldered, narrow-hipped frame to advantage. She could never imagine *him* sporting such silly and extreme fashions.

The carriage pulled forward, but once again they were hailed, and the duke reined in his horses.

"Oh, dear! Lady Pembrington is coming straight for us!" Imogene whispered quickly to Celia. "She is one of my mama-in-law's cronies. We'll just have to play it off, Celly. I have already written Alice explaining everything, so she'll be up to scratch if questioned."

Celia nodded her understanding quickly and tried to smile confidently as the carriage pulled up next to the duke's.

"My dearest Duchess of Harbrooke! How *vey* delightful to see you!" Lady Pembrington, dressed in scads of orange satin, possessed a booming voice and an open curricle upholstered in deep red leather. Her gargantuan bright orange and beplumed bonnet proved quite the most absurd thing Celia had seen all day.

"I was just saying to dear Richard, my dear son," she went on loudly, "how *vey, vey* delighted I was to see that the Duchess of Harbrooke shall be attending my little ball come Friday. So *vey* delighted." She fairly shouted this last to a politely smiling Imogene before Celia could be presented.

"And here is your dear brother! How *vey* delightful! One never knows where *he* shall pop up. Maybe you, my dear Duchess, can prod him into making an appearance at my little ball. Not that he can be led, I'm sure, dear boy." Her laugh was so loud that a number of fashionables turned to attend the situation.

"Knew he'd be a dasher from the start!" Lady Pembrington said, waving her parasol at the duke, who only gazed at the lady imperiously. She continued, "I wonder if your dearest mother-in-law shall attend? But la! Last I heard from Alice she was *vey* delighted with Brighton."

Celia stared in fascination at Lady Pembrington, amazed that she could say so much without ever drawing a new breath.

Imogene finally wedged a word in and introduced Celia.

Lady Pembrington eyed Celia as if she had suddenly sprung whole from the seat cushions.

"How *vey* delightful! Miss Langston, you say? Langston, Langston . . ." She tapped the side of the curricle with her parasol. "I don't believe I'm acquainted with your family," she stated curiously, making note of the chit's chic clothing and elegant posture.

"The baron, her uncle, is settled in Northumberland. Not fond of town life, you know. I'm sure my mother-in-law must have mentioned Miss Langston. After all, Celia has lived at Harbrooke Hall for the last ten years, since her parents passed away," Imogene rattled on a little nervously, lest Lady Pembrington question her further. But the duke's consequence was such that Lady Pembrington suddenly seemed to recall Miss Langston's being mentioned.

"Miss Langston! Of course! How *vey* delightful to finally make your acquaintance! If I had but known that you would be visiting I would have sent along an invitation to my little ball. How remiss of Alice not to mention it. Any friend of the dear duchess must, of course, be happily welcomed by me! I would be *vey* delighted if you would join us at my little ball on Friday." She took Celia's acceptance as a matter of course and waved her good-byes as she spied another person she wished to speak to and drove away. Celia's and Imogene's eyes met in silent laughter and relief. Celia could not recall ever having so much fun.

After making a little progress, Severly again stopped the carriage. He caught Celia's attention and introduced an elegantly attired gentleman astride a black horse.

"You remember the Duke of Westlake, Miss Langston?" Severly asked with a significant look and a raised brow. "I believe you met some years ago."

Celia was nonplussed at this unexpected address and for a moment couldn't think of a thing to say. Evidently the Duke of Westlake had no such lapse. Even though seated on a horse, he still managed a courtly bow. He was an exceedingly handsome man with very dark hair and green-gray eyes, and Celia thought him almost as dashing as Severly.

"Your servant, Miss Langston. How very pleased I am to meet you again. It has been two, maybe three years since we last met?" He spoke easily and sincerely, and the little crowd that had gravitated around the duke's carriage gaped and murmured. First Severly and now Westlake! The two most sought-after men in London both claimed an acquaintance with the mysterious beauty. Neither of the men was noted for dealing with any female who wasn't married, a widow, or an opera dancer. So the mood of curiosity among the onlookers grew to an almost frenzied pitch. Imogene gave Celia a discreet nudge.

"Er . . . three, I believe, your grace. How lovely to see you again. And may I ask after your family?" Celia said in a rush, throwing the last bit in for good measure.

He grinned wickedly. "Mama is fit as a fiddle, and my sister has just recently been delivered of another baby girl."

"Goodness! And how many does that make now?" she asked, following his lead, smiling into his lazy eyes.

"Three, to Charlie's despair. He's already looking about for husbands for them. How are you enjoying your stay in London, Miss Langston?" he asked in a most

A Hint of Scandal

engaging manner, his eyes sliding to his old friend, who was gazing at Miss Langston with a mixture of pride and concern.

Earlier in the day, Westlake had encountered his old friend at Waiter's, their club. While they were seated comfortably in deep armchairs, sipping brandy, Severly asked him in confidence to acknowledge a friend of his sister's.

"Just a quirk of *your* brow should be enough to set her up for the season, Drake. Why do you need my nod also?" Westlake asked curiously. He had never known his friend to show partial attention to any female, even his mistresses. Drake then explained the highly unusual circumstances in which Miss Langston found herself. There was no need for Drake to request Westlake's silence on the matter.

"She's my sister's closest confidante and a bit lacking in town polish. Imogene insists that I help, and there really is nothing else for it; you know how sisters are. I thought the more arsenal backing her, the better," he drawled, taking another sip of his drink. Of course Westlake had agreed; the whole thing rather amused him. Besides, a gentleman never let down a friend.

Now, looking at the lovely face and figure of Miss Langston, Westlake found himself wondering if it was only at his sister's urging that Drake had roused himself to lend the girl an air of consequence. After exchanging a few more pleasantries with the two ladies, Westlake took himself off, but not before cutting a knowing grin to Severly.

The duke continued to tool the phaeton along Rotten Row, stopping the carriage for a few more notables, before deciding to return to Severly House. Celia was extremely relieved that this first trial was over. She hoped she would remember the names of all the people she had met, in case she should meet them again.

"What a charming man the Duke of Westlake is," Celia said to Imogene as they left the park. The duke snorted derisively.

"Yes, he is. But Drake, I thought that no one was to

know of Celly's situation," Imy questioned her frowning brother.

"Besides Rotham, Alex is the only person I would trust with this. I think with this strategy Miss Langston will find her entry into Society an easier path," he stated firmly.

Celia looked at his carved profile as he expertly guided the horses around a corner. It really was too kind of him and Imy to go to so much bother for her. Her heart swelled with gratitude. She vowed to do nothing that could cause them any embarrassment.

Chapter Nine

*F*riday turned misty by late afternoon. By then Celia
felt almost sick with anticipation for Lady Pembring-
gton's little ball. To distract herself, she sat on her bed
trying to read *The Haunting of Hinchley Manor,* her hair
in rag curls. After staring at the first page for a full quar-
ter of an hour without reading a word, she set the book
aside and rang for Dora to draw her bath. She decided
she would rather start getting ready early than endure
this interminable feeling of expectation.

After her bath, Celia wrapped herself in a luxurious
dressing gown of purple satin and walked to a comfortable chair by the fireplace. Hesitating a moment, she
came to a decision. After she directed Dora to request
her grace's presence, Celia went to the rosewood bureau
and retrieved the red leather jewelry case Mr. Whitely
had given her the day he brought her the sad news
about Edna.

Moments later Imogene entered, a look of curiosity in
her hazel eyes. "Getting ready so soon?"

"Yes"—Celia sighed—"you know how long it takes
me to decide what to wear. Though, I did not ask you
to come here to help me with that decision. Imy, I am
finally going to open Edna's jewel case."

Imogene gasped and sat down quickly in a chair by
the fireplace. "Finally! I don't know how you've resisted
this long," Imy said excitedly, and leaned forward for a
better view.

After a moment's pause, Celia sank into the chair next

to Imy's and slowly lifted the lid, then inhaled sharply.
Imy forgot herself so much that she actually whistled.
The deep, velvet-lined case held a kaleidoscope of jewels.
Ropes of pearls in all lengths, bracelets of varied pre-
cious stones, at least a dozen rings, and a myriad of ear-
bobs, necklaces, and brooches met their wondering gazes.

"It looks like a pirate's treasure," Celia whispered, her
greenish brown eyes wide with astonishment.

"I can't believe my eyes." Imogene gasped.

Lifting out different pieces, Celia marveled at the fiery
glitter of the precious stones, enjoying their weighty cool-
ness in her hands. After passing a few handfuls of jewelry
to Imy, Celia picked out a few more pieces and noticed
something else beneath the jumble.

"Look, Imy, a diadem too! How did Edna ever keep
all this a secret? I would have worn something different
every day if I had been her." She shook her head,
amazed at the sapphires and emeralds in her lap.

"Try on the diadem, Celly," Imy urged, continuing to
sift through the pile of jewels with girlish pleasure.

Celia did, and Imogene helped her on with a diamond
collar also. The young women fell about laughing at the
absurd picture Celia made with her rag curls and wrap.
Half an hour later they were still trying on and admiring
the jewels, like two little girls playing dress-up.

Celia discovered an exquisite set of diamond-and-topaz
earbobs with a matching brooch and bracelet. Instantly,
she decided Imy must have them because they comple-
mented her beautiful eyes so well.

"Oh, no, Celly, do not start giving away your jewels.
Besides, I have enough of my own," Imy protested,
laughing.

"But nothing like this! They match your eyes, Imy.
Please allow me the pleasure of making them a gift. Anyway, you know I could never wear topaz; the color does
not suit me," she cajoled, an impish light in her eyes.

"They *are* lovely and unusual." Imogene hesitated,
then looked to her friend. "Thank you, Celly, I would
love them."

They embraced; then Imy pulled back to look at her

friend. "I'm so happy for you, Celly. I know you grieve for Edna, but I'm so glad that she has given you this new life. I confess that I shall enjoy London so much better now that we can share it."

Celia bit her lip to hold back the emotional tears that pressed against her eyes as Imy moved to the door.

"I must leave you now or I shall never be ready on time. Thank you so much again for the lovely jewels, Celly, dear; I'm quite bowled over," she said on a light note.

Standing in the middle of the beautiful rose and gold room, covered in jewels and with more jewels strewn across the chair and bed, Celia said, "So am I," an ironic smile touching her well-defined lips.

Seated at her vanity table an hour later, Celia watched in the mirror as Dora put the finishing touches on her hair. Celia had been surprised at the jumpy little maid's skill, considering that just a week before she had been a belowstairs maid. It had always been Dora's dream to be a real lady's maid, she had informed her new mistress, and so she had diligently tried to learn all that she could. She had gone so far as to practice hair arranging on the other housemaids.

Celia encouraged the little blonde to talk, and learned that Dora's cousin Sophie, a lady's maid to the fashionable Lady Kendall, had kindly guided her on a few things. But not even Sophie had been elevated to lady's maid this young, Dora told Celia proudly. She was very proud of her new mistress, too. So pretty and kind, and Dora knew Miss Langston would be the perfect subject on which to practice her skills.

Celia felt the gown she had finally decided to wear was breathtaking. It was made of a deep violet silk with silver ribbons threaded through the little puffed sleeves that revealed the tops of her shoulders. Another silver ribbon was threaded underneath her bosom in the very fashionable Empire style. Dora had wound a silver ribbon through her golden brown curls and now stood back to judge her work with critical eyes.

On the night of her first ball, Celia wanted everything to be perfect. She fussed nervously with her new jewelry, changing it at least ten times, still not satisfied.

"If you'll excuse me, miss, but I thought the little diamond earbobs and the plain diamond brooch and bracelet were the most becoming. Simple, like, if you take my meaning, miss." The little maid loved looking at the ladies' magazines that the duchess and Miss Langston left lying about and had developed a good eye for style.

Again, Celia donned the jewels Dora had suggested and, after gazing at herself carefully, felt Dora had hit the right note. "Very good, Dora. You are right. I would just be gilding the lily, so to speak, to add anything else. This dress is lovely enough." She stared at her reflection and knew without vanity that she had never been in better looks. Not too ramshackle for a spinster of nearly six and twenty, she thought with some satisfaction. Her eyes were dark with excited anticipation, and the flush in her cheeks gave her an added glow. Dora then produced a box of very fine French powder and a chamois. Tapping the chamois into the powder, she gently pressed it against Celia's nose, forehead, and chin.

"You don't want to shine, miss," cautioned Dora, circling Celia to judge her handiwork from all angles. She felt more than satisfied with her beautiful mistress.

"No, indeed, Dora. Thank you so very much for making me feel so pretty. You really are a wonder," she said admiringly to the blushing maid.

Dora was saved from trying to respond by the entrance of the duchess, radiant in a pale, glimmering yellow gown accented by the topaz-and-diamond jewels Celia had given her earlier.

"Oh, Imogene, you're so lovely."

"Pish, tosh. This gown is quite old. But you, my dear, are breathtaking. If you don't have a dozen beaux by the end of the evening I shall wonder why," she stated positively.

After Celia collected her silver shawl and reticule, they left the room and went downstairs to the blue salon. The duke was already there, standing by the mantel, gazing into the fireplace.

Celia's breath caught in her throat. Even in evening clothes he still managed to be so handsomely masculine. His black coat hugged his broad shoulders and the color brought out the gold in his hazel eyes. He wore a neck-cloth of such intricately tied folds that she was convinced it must have taken his valet an hour to perfect it. A large emerald nestling in the folds of his cravat was his only adornment.

Imogene had been quite pleased when her brother had informed her that he would escort Celia and her to Lady Pembrington's ball. Imogene had informed Celia earlier that Severly believed this was an excellent opportunity to ease her into Society before their own ball. Again, Celia had been surprised by his thoughtfulness.

"Here you are, and only a few minutes late. But I would have waited the whole evening for such exquisite beauty as this," he said with a slight teasing smile.

His eyes came to rest on Celia and he could hardly comprehend that this beautiful, sophisticated young woman was the same one whom he watched skip stones with his nephews. His eyes met hers briefly as they left the salon.

Imogene chatted excitedly as they rode in the duke's well-sprung town coach, pulled by four matched bloods, with the Severly crest emblazoned on the doors. Celia was grateful for Imogene's incessant prattle, as the feeling of nervous anticipation that had plagued her all day suddenly started diluting into nervous dread. The duke was seated across from Celia, and she gazed at the emerald in his neckcloth as it blinked at her in the lights of the passing lampposts. She wondered what in the world she was doing.

She was a governess, for heaven's sake. Celia knew she was only a country bumpkin trying to pass herself off as a lady of quality. By the end of the evening she was sure she would be considered an antidote by all and sundry. Celia's palms became clammy and she felt the blood pounding in her ears as the carriage moved swiftly through the shadowy streets of London. Surely this was the most cork-brained plan ever to be contemplated—to introduce a spinster governess to the crème de la crème of London Society?

Before Celia could ask the duke to have the carriage turned around, the coach stopped. A footman in green livery opened the coach door and placed wooden steps on the ground; then Severly was helping her from the carriage. They were walking up the steps of a mansion that was brilliantly ablaze and obviously crowded. A crush of people surrounded her in the large foyer, the mass slowly moving forward to ascend the stairs to the ballroom. The plethora of brightly colored gowns and the scent of overblown flowers rendered Celia breathless in the oppressive warmth of the high-ceilinged room.

This was Lady Pembrington's *little* ball? she wondered, gazing about in alarm. There must be three hundred people crowding up the stairs.

Panic seared through her veins as she heard the sonorous tones of the majordomo announcing the guests.

"His grace, the Duke of Roxbury.

"Lord and Lady Hampton."

On and on it went, his voice clearly carrying throughout the assemblage. In a very few moments, Celia would be handing her card to the majordomo and hearing her name almost shouted out.

It was too much! Fear fluttered in her chest as she looked around the densely populated room for a way to escape. Why did she ever think that she wanted to go to a ball? What could she possibly say to all these people? This was horrid!

With her heart pounding fiercely, Celia began to edge away from the crowd, instantly concocting a hazy plan to hide in the cloakroom until the ball was over.

"You may call that particular shade of purple your own, Miss Langston, for no one else could look so well in it as you," Severly's deep voice rumbled just above her right ear. Some of Celia's distress had transmitted itself to the duke and he wondered what to do. The chit

was obviously panic-stricken. Celia turned to look up at
the duke with terrified eyes.

"How kind of you, your grace." She made a heroic
effort to keep the tremor from her voice.

Severly smiled slightly into her troubled eyes. She was
quite lovely, he thought distractedly. The candlelight
from the enormous chandeliers brought a fiery shimmer
to her golden brown hair, which smelled of lilacs, he
noted. Her skin reminded him of the petal of a magnolia,
the most exotic and rare flower in his vast hothouse at
Severly. He felt his hand rise of its own volition to stroke
her velvet cheek.

Shock blazed through his body. What a nine-days'
wonder that would be! The Duke of Severly taking a
liberty with his own guest in public. He must catch hold,
he told himself harshly. Celia Langston was not a light-
skirt, nor even an experienced woman. The only course
for a lady like Celia was marriage, and marriage was
definitely not in the cards for Severly. He enjoyed variety
and freedom too much to ever get caught in the parson's
mousetrap. But if he continued in this senseless manner,
Imy would soon be haranguing him to offer for the girl,
if only to save her reputation.

Yet his eyes still inexplicably held hers.

Celia could not look away from the expression in his
glittering gaze. It seemed almost a physical touch that
reached deep into her being and settled somewhere
around her heart. His presence, the very broadness of
his shoulders, and the glittering gold of his eyes blocked
out the noise, the music, the world, and left only them.

Someone jostled Celia from the side and begged her
pardon. The frozen moment shattered around her and
left her feeling confused and disordered. Dazedly, she
turned her gaze from Severly's and ascended a few more
steps. How close she stood to the majordomo now.

Celia mentally gave herself a shake, and her practical
governess's mind told her not to be a ninny. The duke
was being kind. She had nothing to fear this evening; she
was an independent woman now, not a governess. Hadn't
she always dreamed of wearing beautiful gowns and

dancing at a ball? Imogene would be close at hand, so all would be fine, she told herself sternly, forcing the image of the duke's enigmatic eyes gazing so deeply into hers from her mind.

With a lift of her chin she gracefully ascended the last few steps and handed the majordomo her card.

"Miss Langston."

Chapter Ten

*T*wo hours later, Celia found herself twirling around the crowded ballroom in the arms of Major Rotham. The music of a waltz carried them along on its lilting melody, and Celia felt almost intoxicated by the excitement of the evening. To Celia's mind, all the ladies were beautiful, all the gentlemen dashing, and the room was filled with magic.

Major Rotham swung her near an enormous gilt-framed mirror, where Celia caught a brief glimpse of herself. Her own figure moved amidst a kaleidoscope of twirling dancers and giant bunches of spring flowers that Lady Pembrington had placed everywhere, including the chandeliers. Could that really have been her in the mirror? She smiled in bemusement and hoped the Lady Pembrington's little ball would never end.

Celia thought Major Rotham looked exceptionally dashing in his uniform, and despite his limp he proved an excellent dancer. Or because of it, he explained:

"Never was much of a dancer before the war. But after I came home from France, my physician suggested I take up dancing to speed my recovery and help my agility. Actually, I feel I'm a better dancer now than I ever was, if I don't sound conceited saying so."

"Not at all. You should be proud of yourself. You have recovered remarkably from your injuries. Besides, your very slight limp makes you more romantical. I have heard more than one lady say so," she said artlessly, causing the major to blush.

The waltz ended and he guided her back through the throng of dancers and chattering groups of revelers to where Imogene stood conversing with several people. Immediately Celia found herself surrounded by a small but impressive group of gentlemen.

Major Rotham had been the first gentleman to lead Celia out onto the dance floor earlier in the evening. Celia thought this had been exceptionally nice of him, but she had a suspicion that Imogene had made a gentle request. Afterward, he had introduced several young men to her: Sir Richard Pembrington, son of their hostess, the Earl of Chandley, a quietly handsome man with a military bearing, and Sir John Mayhew, whom she had met in Hyde Park and understood was a much-admired Corinthian.

Each man had requested her hand for a dance, and she had demurely obliged them, her confidence growing. Until the first waltz, that was. Sir John had requested her hand for the waltz. Celia had stood there hesitating, wondering what she should do, for Imy had expressly warned her against waltzing with gentlemen she had just been introduced to.

"You must be very careful of your reputation, Celly. I am still trying to procure your vouchers for Almack's, and all the patronesses are so censorious about unmarried ladies waltzing. Some of them still think it a little fast. Even though you are not making a come-out, you had better only waltz with Drake and David—and Westlake, of course, since you two have such a long acquaintance," she finished with a laugh.

So Celia had hesitated before her new admirer, ready to claim fatigue, when the polished figure of the Duke of Westlake nimbly stepped through the crowd. With a sly grin he said, "Our waltz, I believe, Miss Langston." Celia felt a little self-conscious at the marked attention they were receiving as his arm went around her waist.

"Now, Miss Langston, we are old friends and you must smile at me and tell me of your life since we last met. That will give everyone something to whisper about."

Celia looked at him in surprise and could not suppress

the laugh that bubbled forth. "Indeed, your grace, I believe they will whisper if I smile at you or not, such is your consequence."

"But the whispers shall be much more interesting if you continue to smile at me."

Celia laughed again, unaware that his teasing words were completely true. The easily bored members of Society loved to be distracted, and this mysterious new beauty, who seemed to be intimate with those of the first consequence, was already causing speculation.

Celia continued to banter with the wickedly grinning duke for the remainder of their dance. A reel with Sir Richard followed the waltz, and a quadrille with Chandley came after that. The next dance was again a waltz, and that she danced with Major Rotham.

Now she stood amidst her little band of admirers and felt enough confidence to flip open the silver fan that dangled from her wrist and wave it in the languid fashion that Imy had shown her. She listened to the sincerely offered flowery compliments with much feminine gratitude, but very little belief, for she was of an age and temperament that did not put overmuch stock in flattery.

Imogene had introduced Celia to many people, all with curious eyes. One or two had even suggested that they had been previously acquainted, for Celia looked so familiar. Celia had dealt with this all very gracefully, and many members of the *ton* soon expressed their opinion that Miss Langston possessed an elegant poise.

Before long, the most prolific topic of the evening, second only to the upcoming wedding of Princess Charlotte, was Miss Langston and her wealth. Lady Castlereagh had admired the topaz-and-diamond jewels that Imogene wore, and Imy had casually stated that they had been a gift from dear Miss Langston. "So generous and kind she is. I have rarely met such a thoughtful creature as Miss Langston. Some may say my opinion is a bit prejudiced, since she is my dearest friend," Imy said with a smile.

The story spread in a rapid wave that Miss Langston must be as rich as Midas if she handed about such gifts.

But Imy had an ulterior motive for telling the story to a noted gossip. She wanted the fact of her close friendship with Celia to be established quickly, so that fewer questions would be asked about Celia's background. Being the best friend of a duchess should be enough to shield Celia from most prying questions. Lady Castlereagh had eagerly parlayed this information to many of her friends throughout the assemblage, and by the end of the evening Miss Langston's wealth and generosity had been exaggerated to almost mythical proportions.

As she stood near Imogene, Celia politely listened to her small group of admirers, feeling so enchanted with the evening, she could not recall now why she was so nervous earlier. But in the back of her mind she still saw Severly's disturbing gaze and marveled at the odd, breathless feeling in her chest. She had not seen the duke for some minutes. The ballroom walls fairly bulged with a glittering array of the *haute ton,* and she knew that there were also card rooms and billiard rooms beyond. The duke could be anywhere.

Her gaze continued to travel around the room, and soon, on the opposite side of the ballroom, she found the object of her search, Severly. He stood beneath a chandelier with a group of gentlemen. One seemed to be relating a story using an abundance of expressive hand gestures. After a moment, the duke threw back his head and laughed. Celia caught her breath. Unequivocally, he was the handsomest man in the room. Evidently, she was not the only woman to think so. She watched with an amused smile touching her expressive eyes as a number of ladies tried to attract his attention, and anxious mamas tried to push their daughters into his path.

He had taken the dance floor only three times so far, Celia noted. He had danced first with his beturbaned hostess, who had been effusive in her delight at his appearance at her little ball, then with his sister, and finally with a stunning blond woman in emerald green. Celia had been informed that she was Lady Kendall, the elderly Earl of Kendall's much younger wife. Celia recalled Dora saying that her cousin was in service to Lady Kendall.

Celia wondered if—nay, secretly hoped—the duke would ask her to dance. She was an honest girl and could do nothing but admit to herself that her feelings for the enigmatic duke had undergone a complete change. He was so manly and handsome and kind. His kindness had completely surprised her, for she had always thought him such an ogre, but he had treated her as a welcome guest from the moment she came to London.

How foolish she felt for such thoughts, but she could not help it. Just the sight of his square jaw and even the scar on his cheek sent a frisson of awareness up her spine. One dance would be more than wonderful. Other men had complimented her this evening, she told herself, so maybe he would find her attractive enough to dance with.

As if he heard her thoughts, Severly turned at that moment and met her gaze across the room. The smile faded from his lips, and Celia held his piercing glance for a second before turning away, mortified that he had caught her staring at him like a silly girl. The tempo of her fanning quickened, and Imogene turned from her conversation with Countess Lieven to ask quietly if all was well. Before she could respond, Celia heard a familiar, deep voice requesting her hand.

Several of the young men surrounding her protested that Miss Langston had only just been returned to them, that it was too bad of him to whisk her away in this manner.

"You may trust me to return Miss Langston to you safely," Severly drawled with dry amusement as he drew her to the parquet.

The meter of this waltz was slightly slower than the previous one, and Celia became acutely conscious of how close her body was to the duke's. Again, she noted the many curious eyes upon them and felt a blush rising to her cheeks as she tried to focus on anything but the duke.

"I believe you are enjoying yourself, Miss Langston," his deep voice rumbled above her shyly bent head.

"Yes, your grace. It has all been wonderful," she said with forced composure, trying to hold fast to her new-found confidence.

"Excellent. I confess that I am curious as to how you learned to waltz so gracefully. I know you had few opportunities to enjoy Society at Harbrooke Hall," he said diplomatically.

A dimple appeared at the corner of Celia's mouth. "I could say that your grace instructed me."

"How so?" His tone held surprised curiosity.

Celia took a moment to gather her thoughts. She felt intensely aware of his strong arm around her waist and her hand engulfed by his as he expertly led her through the steps of the waltz. A shameless yearning to feel him pull her closer coursed through her body, and Celia took a deep breath to calm herself.

"On a previous visit to the hall, you taught Imy how to waltz," she began. "She was so enchanted that she purchased sheet music, and I played the piano while she showed Henry the steps. When he became proficient, Imy played while Henry and I danced. So, since you instructed Imy and she instructed Henry, in a roundabout way one could say that you taught me, your grace."

Severly laughed outright at this deduction, and the assembled guests goggled. No one could recall his giving such marked attention to an unmarried woman. Yet here he was, hanging on the lovely Miss Langston's every word. A few dandies wondered if it would be too early to lay a wager.

Severly still had a smile on his lips when he asked how they had persuaded Henry to go along with the scheme.

"He kicked up a fuss at first, but when we explained that you were a very good dancer he agreed to try. The boys try to emulate your grace in every way."

"I shall have to commend Henry on his excellent tutelage," he said in his deep voice as he swung her around the polished floor.

The rest of the waltz passed in a haze for Celia. She couldn't help recalling the look in his eyes as they had stood on the stairs earlier in the evening, and again she felt that odd sensation in her chest. When the lilting strains of the waltz faded away, the duke returned her to his sister instead of her little group of swains. When he bowed over her hand, she felt hers tremble slightly in his strong grasp; then he excused himself. She watched his tall frame disappear into one of the faro rooms.

I have thoroughly misjudged him, she told herself. *He really is a gentleman, and not the rake everyone reputes him to be.* For a reason she refused to examine, her heart felt very light to realize this.

She was pulled from these musings when Imogene took her arm and turned to Major Rotham. "David, would you mind terribly obtaining some champagne for us? I'm positively parched, and I'm sure Celia is too," she requested of him with a sweet smile.

"Happy to, my dear, and it will give you and Miss Langston a chance to have a private coze," he teased with a bow.

Instead of being chagrined at his accurate deduction, Imogene just laughed and said, "How intuitive of you, David," as she pulled Celia to a pair of chairs in a secluded alcove near the dais the dowagers occupied.

"Dear Celia, I'm so proud of you! You are a rousing success! By tomorrow you will be discussed in every drawing room from St. James to Park Lane. Why, even the old tabby dowagers approve of you." She quickly cast a worried glance toward the dais in case she had spoken too loudly.

"I own my dance card is full, but there are dozens of young ladies more popular. Besides, I'm a spinster, not a young miss. This is all quite lovely, but it doesn't really matter if I make a splash or not," Celia explained with a wry smile to her friend.

"You a spinster? Don't be a goose. Not an hour ago Lady Sefton, one of the patronesses, said that not even Miss Corinna Sheffield, this Season's Incomparable, could compare to Miss Langston's beauty, easy charm, and artless wit. I do not want to hear any more talk of spinsters when you have such as the Earl of Chandley and Lord Mayhew dancing attendance," Imy finished firmly, tapping Celia's knee with her ivory fan. Celia made no further arguments, for she was young enough to enjoy the heady feeling of being sought after.

Later in the evening, Celia stood conversing with a few of her new acquaintances, slightly amazed with her own confidence after being so terrified just a few hours earlier. Imogene approached with a very pretty, petite young woman with titian hair.

"Celia, dear, Miss Corinna Sheffield wishes to make your acquaintance. I am sure the two of you shall find much in common," Imogene said, smiling encouragingly to both girls before sweeping off to dance with Lord Beresford.

"Indeed, Miss Langston, I did want to make your acquaintance. I have been admiring you. Your gown is so elegant and you dance so beautifully. My dear mama has been holding you up all evening as the example she wishes me to emulate," Miss Sheffield said in a breathless, almost childlike voice.

Celia was rather taken by surprise by this onslaught of compliments. She almost laughed out loud at the thought of someone wanting to emulate her, but found herself instantly liking Miss Sheffield's unguarded pale blue eyes.

"How obliging you are, Miss Sheffield!" Celia began. "And I am very happy to meet you. Shall we take a turn about the room and visit?"

With that, the two young women curtsied to the gentlemen Celia had been conversing with and set out to get to know one another.

"Miss Langston, I must admit that I am quite envious of you," Miss Sheffield stated baldly, but there was a smile in her voice.

"How so? Obviously you have no reason to envy anyone."

"But I do!" she said in earnest as they strolled through the crowded room. "I am one and twenty. This is my first Season because I have been in mourning for a number of years due to the deaths of my grandfather and uncle. Yet now that I am finally here, my mother still insists that I dress as the other girls do, in these boring white gowns that do not flatter me. She does not seem to understand that I am no longer seventeen."

Celia felt a brief pang of guilt at the mention of

mourning, because she was not properly mourning Edna. Instantly she dismissed the feeling because she knew Edna would have preferred her to attend a ball, instead of mourn her.

Tilting her head to the side, Celia paused to examine the petite girl from head to toe. She thought her very pretty, but had to agree that the white gown with its ruching and bows did look rather juvenile.

"I think you look delightful," Celia said diplomatically.

Miss Sheffield stopped beneath a chandelier. "You are too kind, Miss Langston, but I know I look silly. Seeing you in your lovely violet gown has given me hope. Mama so approves of you, and how could she not, as a number of the most eligible gentlemen in London have partnered you this evening? Maybe she will bend a little and let me wear something with color."

Though Celia blushed a little at the younger girl's frank manner, she found it refreshing and saw no harm in supporting Miss Sheffield in her desire. Resuming their walk, they continued to discuss clothes and dancing and other feminine things. They parted a little later after agreeing to call upon each other during the week. Celia was delighted to meet such an unaffected creature as Miss Sheffield.

Returning to Imogene and Major Rotham, Celia thanked them both for making her first ball such a wonderful experience.

"You did most of that on your own, my dear," Imy said. "You have taken London by storm. Dozens of people have asked me about you."

"I can't believe I am as popular as all that," Celia demurred.

"You shall see; by the end of the week you will have so many invitations, your head will spin," Imy vowed, and Major Rotham seconded her opinion. *agreed*

Celia did not encounter the duke again for the remainder of the evening, though her eyes did scan the room occasionally. She told herself not to be silly and resolutely turned her attention to her little circle of beaux, who did their best to keep her attention on them.

Sometime after two in the morning, Severly emerged from the billiards room and requested the carriage, even though the ball showed no signs of slowing down. Celia did not mind a bit, because she was much too happy and, in truth, she was beginning to stifle a yawn or two.

As the footman handed her into the duke's town coach, Celia could not help but recall how, just a few hours ago, she had been terrified. Imy and the duke entered and settled back into the soft leather squabs as the coach moved forward.

"So, Miss Langston, did your first ball meet your expectations?" the duke questioned with an enigmatic smile.

Sighing with remembered pleasure, Celia looked directly at the duke. "Exceeded them, your grace."

The morning after her first ball, Celia lingered in the cozy warmth of her pretty chamber long after Dora had opened the curtains to let in the spring sunshine. Stretching her arms over her head, she thought over last evening and savored the afterglow of the enchantment. Her first ball! She had actually attended a ball and danced with handsome gentlemen, and maybe even made a new friend in Corinna Sheffield. It was all rather wonderful, she thought, as she finally got out of bed.

After dallying over her toilette, she went downstairs for breakfast. At the bottom of the stairs, she gasped in astonishment at the veritable hothouse of floral arrangements that met her wondering gaze. The entire foyer was filled with bouquets, nosegays, and baskets of fruit and flowers of every description.

Almost hesitantly she stepped forward to touch an immense arrangement of roses and snapdragons. The envelope nestled among the green leaves bore her name. She read the brief missive and was enormously flattered that the sender was the Earl of Chandley. She checked other bouquets and discovered that many of the senders were gentlemen with whom she had not even danced. Celia marveled at the abundance of the blossoms and delighted in their beauty and sweet scent, touched beyond reason that they were for her.

Severly came downstairs at that moment, dressed for riding and looking even more handsome than he had last evening. Celia's cheeks grew pink at being caught standing in the midst of all the flowers with her nose buried in a bunch of violets.

The duke took in the scene with a lazy eye and raised a brow. "It would seem, Miss Langston, that every buck who saw you last evening has sent you his garden."

Surprised, Celia could not help laughing. "It does look as if someone has brought in the greenhouse." Her shining eyes met his, until she remembered the moment on the staircase just before she had entered the ballroom.

Dropping her gaze, she self-consciously placed the violets on the entry table. "I hope we aren't so late that Imy must breakfast alone," she said shyly. As she stepped past him, Celia quietly asked Porter if he would be so kind as to have the flowers removed to her room.

When they entered the sunny breakfast room they found Imogene full of last evening's merriment and plans for the day. "We must pay a call to Lady Pembrington; then we must call on Lady Cowper. I'm positive that she will give you your voucher to Almack's." This was extremely exciting news, Imy informed Celia, since it would be impossible to be considered a true success if one did not have a voucher to attend the assembly at the much-vaunted Almack's.

The duke said very little over breakfast, but Celia often felt his eyes upon her. She refused to take notice, feeling too confused about her changed opinion of him to know how to behave.

Soon she was released from his nerve-racking presence as Imy bustled her from the room almost before she had completed her breakfast, admonishing her not to linger over dressing, as they did not have all day. Celia did glance back at the duke and wondered at the deep frown creasing his brow as he gazed down at his paper.

Chapter Eleven

*T*he lovely spring days that remained before the Severly ball passed swiftly while Imogene and Celia threw themselves into London town life. They shopped, went to museums and the theater, and paid numerous visits and received countless visitors. Imy was enjoying herself prodigiously over Celia's come-out, and felt sure the coveted vouchers to Almack's would soon be arriving.

The floral tributes continued to flow, and, to Imy's delight, Celia received dozens of invitations from the grandest hostesses in London. Celia had even gone for a carriage ride with the Earl of Chandley, whose company she found she enjoyed very much—though, at first, Imogene had been very concerned about this outing.

"Celia, you must not say anything about taking care of the boys." Imogene stared intently at Celia as she was buttoning her pelisse. "One slip about your past would be a complete disaster."

"I understand, Imy; I shall be very careful." Celia gave Imogene the most reassuring smile she could muster before leaving Severly House.

At first, sitting next to the earl in his high-perch phaeton had made Celia nervous to the point of muteness. Soon the task of making conversation was eased when Corinna Sheffield and her mother pulled their carriage alongside the earl's and hailed a greeting.

"I say, Miss Langston, are we to see you at Lady Sefton's musicale this eve?" Miss Sheffield asked.

Celia said that she would.

"I do hope the prince regent decides to attend. But one never knows with his royal highness," Corinna stated with some asperity.

"No, indeed," put in the earl. "He promised 'pon his honor only a week ago to attend my rout. But we did not see hide nor hair of him."

The honorable Mrs. Sheffield nodded her understanding. "How vexing of him. He promised to attend our ball, but sent his regrets at the last moment."

"I was terribly disappointed," Corinna piped in. "I so wish to be presented to the regent. Don't you, Miss Langston?"

"Oh, but I have met his royal highness," Celia responded before thinking.

After a moment of surprised silence the earl laughed and said to the other two ladies, "Will the mystery of Miss Langston never cease?"

"Do tell how you've stolen a march on me and met the regent, Miss Langston," Corinna said in mock demand.

Celia paused a moment, very aware of the expectant faces before her. She knew she needed to be careful, lest she give too much away about her past in the telling.

With a self-deprecating gesture she said, "My encounter with the regent is not so very exciting. We were both guests at the Duke and Duchess of Harbrooke's wedding. I told him he was handsome; I recall thinking his green waistcoat was divine. He kissed my cheek and told me I was a very good girl. I was a mere child."

"What a lovely story," Mrs. Sheffield said.

"Be careful, Miss Langston; it may get around town that the regent is smitten by your charms. You know how gossip can be distorted," the earl teased.

This caused laughter all around, and after a few more pleasantries the Sheffield ladies bade Celia and the earl adieu. Celia waved her farewell, promising to see Corinna later at Lady Sefton's.

Celia was grateful for her growing friendship with Miss Sheffield and was pleased to discover that they did, indeed, have much in common. Both girls enjoyed reading

and loved gardening, and to her delight, Celia felt they
were fast becoming good friends. They had shopped together several times, and Celia fond it quite impressive
that Corinna could tell the owner of a carriage just by
glancing at the crest on the door. Corinna seemed to be
acquainted with everyone in the *ton,* and Celia's confidence grew as she gained some much-needed town polish
from her new friend.

"Miss Corinna Sheffield is a most delightful creature,"
Celia pronounced.

"She is indeed," the earl agreed.

As they rode along, Celia smiled to herself, for she
was very pleased with her outing with the earl.

After the earl returned her to Severly House, Celia
went to her room to rest before the evening's festivities
and wondered if the duke would join them at Lady Sefton's musicale. Celia saw little of him of late. She knew
the duke was often in his private library or gone much
of the day. She did not know if she felt relieved or not.
As much as she tried, she could not banish the image of
his intense gaze and broad-shouldered presence from her
mind. She found herself reliving, over and over, the moment on the stairs at Pembrington House when his look
had been almost a physical touch. Sometimes she would
lie awake at night and wonder if the slight noises she
heard were those of the duke returning home.

Why had he not married? She pondered this question
the next morning while helping Sims, the gardener, cut
flowers. She knew the duke to be near two and thirty.
Surely it was not because of a lack of candidates, she
thought as she snipped a few larkspur and placed them
in her basket. She had witnessed for herself how practically every unattached female in London pursued him.
Maybe he had found no one to whom he could truly
give his heart. She shrugged this thought off because she
couldn't imagine the duke giving his heart to anyone. To
her, he seemed completely self-sufficient.

The day before the Severly ball, Corrina and her
mother invited Celia to take a carriage ride in Hyde

Park, as it was such a fine day. Celia and Corrina stifled a few giggles at the attention they received from a number of young bucks who were doing their best to show off.

The honorable Mrs. Sheffield, an older, less talkative version of her daughter, had finally agreed that Corrina could wear colors, but nothing bright. Nevertheless, Corinna was happy with the concession, and excitedly informed Celia she would be wearing palest lavender to the Duke of Severly's ball.

"I am so glad Mother relented," Corinna confided, glancing back to make sure Mrs. Sheffield was still conversing with Mrs. Drummond-Burrell on the other side of the carriage. "For it would have been too lowering to wear such a missish white gown to what I'm sure will be the most exciting ball of the Season."

"Fustian! You are lovely no matter how you are clothed," Celia assured her.

"Well, I shall be much happier in my lavender gown. What shall you be wearing, Miss Langston?"

"A gown of white silk, Miss Sheffield," Celia said with a mischievous twinkle in her eye.

Corrina looked aghast. "No! You must be hoaxing me," the younger girl said.

"Not a bit of it." Celia laughed. "Mrs. Triaud vows this gown is a masterpiece. And I assure you, it is the farthest thing from missish."

"I wish I had your confidence," Corrina lamented.

"What in the world do you mean?" Celia turned a surprised face to her friend, for she would never use the word *confident* to describe herself.

"You are all the rage. All the *ton* discusses your attire and jewelry. You are setting a fashion with the angle at which you wear your chapeau. All the patronesses praise your manners and you sail along, unperturbed by any of it," Corrina explained.

"Now you are hoaxing me." Celia felt her cheeks growing pink. She scarcely knew what to say.

Miss Sheffield continued, "And the most toplofty bucks in London attend to you. The Earl of Chandley,

Sir John Mayhew. Even the Duke of Westlake, whom everyone knows finds the polite world a dead bore, danced with you twice at the Pembrington ball. And of course, the Duke of Severly." Corinna clutched her hands to her heart expressively. "Severly is so imperious and intimidating. To be in his set is to be all the crack. And you behave as if it is all a ride in the park."

Miss Sheffield was rewarded for this speech by the look of incredulity that came upon Miss Langston's face.

"I can scarce find a word to say to you, Miss Sheffield," she began at last. "I believe you are being exceedingly kind, so before my head turns from your flummery, we shall change the subject."

As the carriage moved along, Corinna's laughter rang out merrily. "Poor Miss Langston, your modesty will only add to your popularity."

When the day of the Duke of Severly's ball finally arrived, Celia felt as ill-prepared for this ball as she had for Lady Pembrington's little ball and set about getting ready in a state of anticipation and dread.

The silk gown she finally decided upon was the shade of white found on the inside of oyster shells. The little puff sleeves were intricately tucked into hundreds of tiny folds and dotted with seed pearls. Celia again marveled at Mrs. Triaud's cleverness.

As she stood before her mirror with Dora buttoning the dozens of little pearl buttons down her back, Celia noticed the gown showed more décolletage than she was comfortable revealing. Even though she knew her low-cut gown was the height of fashion, she pinned a large emerald brooch at her cleavage to make it less daring, unwittingly drawing more attention to the creamy expanse of her bosom.

Edna's jewel case had rendered a half dozen hairpins with large emeralds on their ends. Dora had, with painstaking care, arranged them becomingly in Celia's upswept hair. Celia draped her oyster shell–white shawl to her elbows and donned her long satin gloves while trying to examine her appearance from all angles. Dora had already stated herself satisfied with her mistress, but Celia still stared at herself with critical eyes. Even as she told herself it did not matter, she wondered if the duke would admire her.

During their many discussions about the ball, Celia had learned from Imogene that the receiving line would form on the landing above the wide marble steps that descended into the ballroom on the ground floor.

Years ago, the fourth Duke of Severly had decided the ladies looked particularly charming descending a staircase. The only problem was that the architect he had commissioned had made the staircase so enormously wide that it could be intimidating to walk down the middle unaided. Celia and Imy decided it would be too gauche to descend clinging to the side of the balustrade.

The numerous steps caused Celia to chew her bottom lip in worry over tripping in front of four hundred people. "I shall probably stare at my feet and walk so slowly that I will appear an oaf," she predicted to Imogene. Imy expressed the same concern, and so they decided to meet in the ballroom to practice their descents before any of the guests arrived.

Leaving her room with Dora's good wishes for the evening, Celia walked swiftly to the west wing of the house, fearing she might be a little late. Reaching the wide-open double doors, Celia stood at the top of the steps, her breath catching at the glowing beauty of the huge ballroom below her.

Several footmen were engaged in lighting the innumerable candles in the three massive crystal chandeliers that hung from the gloriously painted ceiling. There were a large number of gilt-covered chairs, and huge bunches of tuberoses, gladioli, lilies, and irises stood in Grecian-style urns on tall marble columns. Floor-to-ceiling French doors opened to the gardens, where the trees and shrubbery sparkled with a multitude of fairy lights.

Celia sighed with pleasure at the opulent, glowing splendor, and a quiver of excitement touched her at the thought of dancing with the duke in such an enchanted setting.

Imogene wasn't to be seen, so Celia decided to practice by herself. Lifting her chin, she flipped open her fan and carefully attempted to walk down the middle of the massive marble staircase, with some elegance, she hoped. She turned her head this way and that, as if the guests were already assembled, reminding herself not to look at her feet. When she reached the bottom she curtsied deeply to an invisible prince regent. Dissatisfied, she decided to go back up and try again, but stopped short at the sound of clapping reverberating through the room.

"Very graceful, Miss Langston. I especially enjoyed the languid fan movement."

Celia looked up to see the duke dressed in evening clothes, standing at the top of the stairs. He was gazing down at her with a slight but devilish grin on his face.

Celia didn't know where to look and felt ready to burst into flames from embarrassment. How lowering to be caught behaving in such an unsophisticated manner when she wanted him to think her elegant and poised. But something about his handsome, amused face turned her chagrin to anger. He had probably never been embarrassed in his life, she thought resentfully.

"I would not be so condescending, your grace, as *you* do not have to worry about tripping over your skirts when you go down the stairs," she said archly, meeting his glittering gaze with a cool look. He descended the stairs as she spoke and halted a step above her. To her surprise he reached for her reluctant hand.

"You are too harsh with me, my dear," he said in a deep yet gentle voice. "I only teased you a little. You must forgive my clumsy attempt at friendliness. I have noticed that you and my sister are great ones for teasing each other. It was but a poor bid on my part to join in."

The heat from a fierce blush stained her cheeks, and Celia could not take her eyes from the duke's solemn gaze. "It is quite all right. Please forgive me for being so waspish," Celia said faintly, greatly touched by his words.

"Not a bit of it, my dear. You have every right to take me to task, less harshly next time, perhaps? I often joke when I wish to be serious. It is a fault I am well aware of."

He still held her hand in his strong grasp and seemed to have gotten closer to her without even moving.

"What did you wish to be serious about?" she couldn't resist asking, noticing how the candlelight gleamed on his dark hair.

"I wished to be serious in complimenting your poise and grace, which you are already aware of from the multitude of floral tributes you have received. But I noticed it long before anyone else did. I noticed how elegantly you hold yourself even while skipping stones on a pond."

Something strange was happening to Celia. Her heart pounded wildly at his words, even though they made little sense to her. Suddenly she wanted to touch him, to put her arms around his neck or lay her head against his broad chest.

Shakily, she took a deep breath and parted her lips to speak, but no words came. Her wide eyes locked with his. She lifted her hand, whether to push him away or draw him near she did not know, but he took it in his and held it tight.

"Celia," came a rough whisper, and his head lowered to hers.

"Celia? Are you there? I'm sorry I've taken forever; we must hurry if we are to practice before everyone arrives." Imogene's lilting voice cut through the magical moment just as the duke's warm lips brushed Celia's. With an unintelligible curse, he lifted his head and turned to look at the top of the stairs.

"We are here, Imy."

"Oh, good." She skipped down the stairs in a girlish fashion. "Drake, be a lamb and critique us. We want to cut a dash, but we're afraid of tumbling down the stairs." She looked past her brother's broad shoulders to stare curiously at Celia's flushed face.

"You'll have to pardon me, Imy, but I must speak to Porter before our guests arrive." He bowed slightly to both ladies, then turned and ascended the stairs two at a time.

Imy looked at her friend. "Is all well, Celly?" she queried gently.

Celia chewed her lip at the duke's treating back. "Of course, I just came here early and practiced by myself," she lied with a bright smile to her friend.

"Well, let's have a go, shall we?" Imy said, deciding not to press Celia further.

"Yes," Celia agreed, but more than anything she wanted to run back to her room and think about what had just happened.

It was almost time to go in to supper and Celia had not decided who would be her escort. Her current partner was Sir Richard Pembrington. Though he had been solicitude and attentiveness itself and had called on her several times in the last few weeks, Celia could not like him overmuch. There was something weak about his hand on her waist, and she noticed that he rather liked malicious gossip.

The Earl of Chandley, with whom she felt more comfortable and who was becoming one of her particular beaux, had already asked her. But she had playfully avoided answering him. After the quadrille with Sir Richard ended, her last little hope that the duke would ask was dashed. To her disappointment, when the doors to the dining room opened, she saw Severly's tall frame escorting his sister. *not done*

She felt foolish for hoping, for she should have known he would not seek her out, since he had danced with her only once this evening. They had made up the numbers in a country reel, which had afforded little opportunity for conversation.

She left Sir Richard then, almost abruptly, lest he renew his offer to escort her. She moved to stand by a marble column entwined with orchids and ivy, trying to force her thoughts to some order. It was no use; every other moment she recalled the two of them on the marble steps, his smoldering expression reaching into the depths of her being and touching something that she had not known existed. She couldn't forget the image of his head as it lowered to hers, the length of his lashes before she closed her eyes and felt the briefest touch of his lips on hers. She reached up and touched her lips, wondering that they didn't feel different to her fingers when they felt so different to her heart.

She looked up to see Chandley making his way through the crowd toward her, a hopeful smile on his lean face, and she was glad that she had not completely discouraged him with her earlier evasiveness.

"There you are, my lord. I had begun to think that I had been abandoned," she said brightly, taking the arm he offered.

Chandley proved an engaging partner for supper, which was a buffet of titanic proportions. The tables looked about to buckle from the amount of pheasant, lamb, roast beef, and turkey savories. The guests had their choice of every kind of summer fruit imaginable and luscious French pastries.

Celia encouraged the earl to talk, as she did not feel as if she had anything to say, and thus added to her growing reputation as a good conversationalist. A number of people she had met at the Pembrington ball joined Celia and the earl. Soon, she was somewhat able to distract herself with the lively conversation.

In particular, she enjoyed the company of Sir John Mayhew, and was pleased when he strolled over, bowed with a flourish, and asked if she would permit him to be seated.

"Pray be seated, Sir John. We have enough room for you to join the fun," she replied, smiling her encouragement.

Sir John was a rarefied dandy whose sartorial elegance could be quite blinding. Celia did give him credit, though: Only one of Mr. Mayhew's lithe frame and blithe confidence could carry off such high collar points without looking too silly.

"Miss Langston, I am not able to express to you how utterly charming you look this evening. I believe I shall have to write a poem to do you justice," he effused as he held up his champagne glass for a passing footman to refill.

"You flatter me greatly, Mr. Mayhew." Celia laughed.

"I am sure you can find a worthier subject for your poetic talent."

The other gentlemen at the table disagreed vigorously with her opinion and were soon arguing about who could write an ode, paint her likeness, or even compose a song that would do justice to one so a charming as Miss Langston.

Celia found this conversation more amusing than flattering and soon found her attention wandering. The noise and laughter in the grand dining room, glowing with candlelight, easily caught her attention. Corinna Sheffield waved at her from across the room, and Celia smiled to see that her friend was surrounded by a number of charming young men, and indeed looked lovely in her lavender gown.

Celia continued to scan the room. It did not take her long to spy Severly's tall frame. He was speaking to the lovely Lady Kendall.

Celia remembered her from the Pembrington ball and wondered what her husband was like. She had heard that the London air did not agree with him. The countess was very young, probably not yet four and twenty, Celia surmised, feeling every one of her six and twenty years. Celia admired and even envied slightly the way the petite countess could meet the duke's gaze so easily and converse with so much confidence.

"Miss Langston shall have to be the judge of that," Chandley said, calling her focus back to the gentlemen around her. Celia felt rude for letting her mind wander from the conversation at hand.

With a determined smile, Celia talked with Chandley and with whomever else approached them until the music from the ballroom began again. She resolutely pushed her confused thoughts about the duke aside and concentrated on being as engaging as she could.

It was well after one o'clock in the morning, and the Duke of Severly's grand ball was in full swing. To the surprise and delight of his guests, the duke had arranged for a number of magicians and jugglers to entertain throughout the room. He was pleased that he had been able to keep his plan a secret; not even Imogene had known. The enjoyment on his sister's face as she watched a juggler balancing on his back, keeping three balls in the air with his feet, caused him a rare smile.

Standing near the orchestra, the duke let his eyes seek out Celia, and found her holding court in the midst of several admiring bucks. Her cheeks were flushed, her eyes sparkled, and her gown was incredibly alluring.

He gave Celia credit: For a green girl she handled herself with an engaging combination of dignity and wry humor. No giggling or simpering from Miss Langston. It was obvious that she had stolen more than one dandy's heart with a glance from those bewitching brownish green eyes, he thought with a cynical twist to his lips.

He watched her look of surprise as a magician made her fan disappear. When the magician pretended to abscond with the trinket, Celia grabbed Westlake's arm and laughingly beseeched him to retrieve her fan. The magician made a mock sad-face and produced the fan from behind her ear. Celia's eyes went wide and she accepted the ornament with a pert little curtsy.

Without a doubt, Celia was a rousing success. The young bucks in the faro room had already toasted her as a diamond of the first water. And no wonder—the *ton* was always willing to welcome a beautiful heiress, Drake's cynicism continued. The sight of Miss Langston surrounded by so many attentive males vying for her attention set his teeth on edge. Even Westlake, who had arrived late, had gone to her side immediately after greeting Imogene, Drake remembered with disgust.

Turning away, Drake made his way through the throng of revelers, and entered the relatively peaceful atmosphere of his billiard room.

As he declined a brandy from one of the vermilion-and-gold-liveried footmen, he greeted a number of older gentlemen who preferred the less strenuous sport of billiards to dancing. It also enabled them to take a pinch of snuff, which, of course, could not be done in front of the ladies. Severly's mind turned again to the strange scene earlier on the staircase. Her artlessness had touched and amused him, he admitted to himself. How exquisite she looked in a gown that made her skin glow like a pearl, the candlelight sparking off the jewels in her hair like emerald fire that mirrored the green in her eyes.

He had actually kissed her, albeit very briefly, he thought, with something close to astonishment.

A guest in his own home, an innocent young woman without the least experience with seducers like himself. Severly felt an uncomfortable and unfamiliar feeling of self-disgust. He had been raised a gentleman and he'd always prided himself on his self-control and sense of honor and decency. The thoughts that he had been having of late for the enchanting Miss Langston were neither honorable nor decent. A gentleman would never consider seducing an innocent lady, especially one living under his protection, and his sister's closest friend.

With his eyes on the painted ivory balls being scattered across the billiard table, Severly told himself that having Celia so close at hand was the trouble. She was a beautiful and charming woman. In his world, when one felt desire for a woman, it was worked out discreetly, with both parties knowing exactly where they stood. That was why married women had always been so attractive; they never confused love with passion.

It was no wonder why he felt this unprecedented frustration where Celia was concerned, he rationalized, running long fingers through his hair. She did not know the rules, and there was no way he could explain them to her. If he followed his desire, she would soon expect a marriage proposal. Marriage was not in Severly's plans for many years to come. His grandfather, whose portrait Celia had stifled a giggle over, had not married until he had been a decade older than Severly was now. The duke planned to follow in his footsteps. It was his opinion that wives were inconvenient, and a mistress was better suited to his life.

Now that he had that settled he was determined to rid himself of this bad humor.

The sound of clinking glass pulled him from his musings. Across the green baize–covered table, Sir Richard Pembrington was raising his brandy snifter in a toast.

"To Miss Celia Langston, the incomparable of incomparables!" he said in a drawling, slightly affected tone. A chorus of "Hear, hear" and "Quite so" came from the other gentlemen in the room as they raised their glasses in tribute. With a thunderous frown on his dark brow, Severly turned on his heel and returned to the ballroom.

The orchestra was at the end of a minuet as Severly walked to the edge of the parquet. A passing footman offered him a glass of champagne and he accepted it gladly, finishing it in two gulps as his golden-hazel eyes scanned the room.

"I've been wondering where you had disappeared to," came a soft, feminine voice at his elbow. Looking down, he saw Leticia Kendall gazing up at him with limpid blue eyes the exact shade of the daringly cut gown she wore.

"I've just been playing at being a good host," he informed her.

"And you play so well," she practically purred.

"Have I told you how lovely you look this evening, Letty?" the duke said, meeting her bold gaze with some amusement.

Lady Kendall tried to gauge from his enigmatic eyes his sincerity. The Duke of Severly was not the first lover she had taken during her five years of marriage, but he was certainly her favorite. It was not just the cachet of having the elusive duke as her lover that held such appeal; it was that she had never been with someone so completely masculine, yet so fascinating. The frustrating part of their relationship was that, of late, she had become the pursuer instead of the pursued. With shrewd insight, the countess realized the tenuous hold she had on him was slipping. In her insecurity, she had grown quite jealous of him and, therefore, threatened to destroy the one thing that had attracted him in the first place; her undemanding passion and good humor.

Of late, Letty had grown almost desperate in her demands upon Drake, because she sensed he was growing bored. That was something the petite blonde could not tolerate. He had not visited her in over a fortnight. He had explained to her that he needed to be on hand to squire his sister and Miss Langston around town. At first, his regrets had mollified her.

Now, she wondered if duty was the only reason the duke had curtailed his affair with her. For the life of her, she could not understand why the *ton* was all agog over Miss Langston. She was so tall, she observed with scorn. And a spinster, too.

Glancing up, she watched with narrowed eyes as Severly tracked the Langston chit making her figures in a quadrille. The countess pulled her gaze from the duke's chiseled profile to see Miss Langston leaving the floor on the arm of the Duke of Westlake. Miss Langston made a pretty display of casually waving her fan as she stood conversing with Westlake and a number of other notables.

The situation was more desperate than she at first thought, Letty realized with a touch of fear. Forcing a serene smile to her lips, Leticia laid a gentle hand on Drake's arm. "Would you think me terribly bold, your grace, if I asked you for a waltz? But I forget you have ofttimes told me you like me when I am bold," she finished on an intimate whisper, hoping to remind him of the passion they had so mutually enjoyed. Her desire was satisfied when he turned to her with a smoldering glance.

"Indeed, I do, Letty." He gave her a slight hard smile and swung her onto the floor to the opening strains of a waltz.

Celia was anxiously trying to recall the name of the gentleman with whom she was dancing. He was a fair young man with a florid complexion and little to contribute by way of conversation. After two useless attempts at dialogue, Celia gave up and contented herself with thinking about the duke. Her heart fluttered as she recalled his deep voice telling her he thought her graceful even while watching her skip stones on a pond. What could he have meant by that? Had he happened upon her and the boys during one of their outings? That really was the only explanation for his comment, she decided. Could it be possible that he had admired her when she had looked so plain and dowdy? A shiver brought the gooseflesh to her skin, and her partner roused himself enough to ask if she was chilled.

Before she could answer, they made a half turn to avoid another couple, and the sight of the duke dancing with the beautiful Lady Kendall caught Celia's attention. Severly's dark head was bent close to the petite blonde's and he held her closer than was correct. They whirled closer and Celia observed them gazing into each other's eyes, the countess with her head tilted back, lips parted, and lids alluringly lowered.

A disbelieving sense of shock almost caused Celia to stumble. There was no mistaking the blatant passion exhibited on their faces. Looking away in confusion, Celia stared at her partner's snowy white neckcloth. Could the countess and the duke be lovers? The thought came like a thunderbolt to her mortified thoughts. What else could explain the emotions she had so plainly seen? Surely, she must be wrong. She cast about desperately for another explanation. No woman of breeding would ever degrade herself or her husband in such a way. And the duke? Indeed, she had known of his reputation. All the world called him a rake, but an affair with the wife of a peer? It was beneath him as a gentleman.

Finally, the music ended and her nameless partner returned her to Imogene, departing with a bow. Celia, fanning her flushed cheeks, searched the mass of people for the duke, wanting to convince herself that her eyes had deceived her.

Easily locating his dark head above the others, Celia craned her neck to see him better. He was with the countess, her arm through his, and she was still gazing at him with that blazingly intimate expression. They stepped through the open French doors and disappeared into the garden.

Chapter Twelve

*O*pening her eyes as little as possible, Celia squinted down at the dappled light pattern playing across her bed, caused by the sun beaming in from the windows on the other side of the room. Groaning, she realized that it must be well after noon and she rolled over, burrowing deeper into the silky bedclothes, trying to recapture the slumberous feeling that was fast slipping away. Soon aware that sleep was futile, she kicked off the covers and pulled herself out of bed. Dora must have been listening right outside of the door, for immediately there was a light tap and the little maid slipped in, offering to draw Miss her bath.

"Yes, thank you, Dora," Celia said dully, causing Dora to frown in concern.

After the bath, Celia dressed in an exquisite silver-blue tea gown. Her temples throbbed, and she noticed there were shadows under her eyes as she stared at her reflection while Dora arranged her hair.

"You should see the flowers that have come for you and you grace, miss. I'd wager every flower seller in London is blessing the day you arrived," Dora predicted, putting the finishing touches on Celia's hair.

A faint smile touched Celia's lips, but she was in no mood to think about flowers.

"Thank you, Dora; I believe I shall read until tea," she said as the maid straightened the bottles on the vanity table.

With another concerned look at her mistress's face, Dora bobbed a curtsy and left Celia to her thoughts.

Pushing away from the vanity, Celia came to the realization that she could no longer put off thinking about last night. She walked over and sat down in one of the chairs by the cold grate. Staring down at the fingers clenched in her lap, Celia felt as if the proverbial scales had been lifted from her eyes.

A wave of shame swept over her, leaving her racked with anger and self-disgust. What a fool she had been, she rebuked herself, wincing as she recalled the moment on the staircase before the ball and how she had not even pulled back as his lips brushed hers.

What a ninny I was to believe he could grow partial to me, she thought with piercing embarrassment. How easily she had succumbed to his practiced charm. She continued to berate herself as she rose from the chair and moved to the window, pushing aside the curtains to stare out at the duke's magnificent gardens. She had actually believed, she marveled, that there had been something inexplicable growing between them, when in truth he had just found her gullibility amusing. He was an arrogant, jaded rake, and she hated him for so effortlessly snaring her heart.

Last evening, the remainder of the ball had passed in an odd dreamlike manner. She had stood in the midst of the opulent beauty looking at her surroundings with new eyes.

Lady Cowper, the lovely, respected patroness of Almack's, looked so different to Celia now. Obviously, she was Lord Palmerston's mistress and took every opportunity to make her husband the butt of one of her witty little jokes. How could she have missed this before? Celia wondered with a bemused shake of her head. Look at the Duke and Duchess of Falton; they arrived in separate carriages and had never acknowledged the other's presence the entire evening.

She had spent the rest of the ball, which had gone on until the sun was breaking over the horizon, pretending that she was enjoying herself. And whenever the duke got within ten feet of her she moved to the other side of the room.

Before last night it had all seemed so beautiful and amusing. But now, she saw the gossip and infidelity and felt like an idiot for being so deceived. All the clever little stories she had heard took on a new, cynical meaning. A hard, pretty shell masked an empty, frivolous world. Was this what was expected of her. To marry the best title her money could buy and find love and passion where she could?

She could not live that way, Celia thought stubbornly, turning away from the window.

How dared the duke tell her he admired her, Celia thought, her eyes flashing in anger as a dull little ache settled around her heart. How dared he look deeply into her eyes, hold her hand, and kiss her when it all meant less than nothing to him. It had just been social patter to be repeated to other women, she decided with new-found cynicism.

Her very first impression of him, when she had been only sixteen, had been correct. She had just been naive to put any import on his attention toward her. Celia realized she had been too unsophisticated to know this, and vowed to herself that she would not be so foolish in the future.

With new resolution, Celia determined not to let this ruin everything. She was a woman of means now, and her life would go on much better than it had before. Somehow this thought was little comfort to her bruised emotions.

Late in the afternoon, unable to stand her own thoughts a moment longer, Celia decided to leave the sanctuary of her room to wander in the gardens and clear her head. After walking through the formal gardens for a bit, Celia circled back toward the house and came upon Imogene lounging in a chaise on the veranda.

"Hello. I've been wondering where you've been," Imogene called. "Come have tea with me." She gestured to the tea cart next to her.

Determined to be cheerful, Celia seated herself on a little chair near Imogene and accepted a cup of tea.

"I have told Porter that we are not at home. I am just

no, must receive "thank you" visits

too fatigued to receive any callers today," Imogene said gaily, pouring milk into her cup. "Wasn't the ball too lovely? Why, Lord Allyn told me he hadn't a nicer time in years."

Celia managed to muster the proper responses, and felt relieved that Imogene did not seem to notice anything amiss. Soon they were both quietly enjoying the beauty of the garden, and the sight of the iridescent hummingbirds flitting from flower to flower helped to soothe her ragged emotions.

"Here you are. I thought the two of you were going to lie abed till dinner."

Jolted from her reverie, Celia looked up to see the duke coming toward them, dressed in buff-colored breeches, a white shirt, a bottle green coat, and black top boots. His dark hair gleamed in the afternoon light, and the odd ache in Celia's heart intensified. Stiffening her spine, she rebuked her heart for quickening and told herself to behave calmly.

"Drake, dear, we didn't think to see you until the Marmans' soiree this evening," Imogene called. Her brother seated himself on a wicker settee next to his sister and sat back in his characteristically languid pose.

Celia continued to watch the hummingbirds with determination.

"Our ball was the highlight of the Season, Drake," Imy continued. "Porter has been run frazzled from answering the door every other minute."

"Indeed, I see my foyer again looks like a hothouse." He flashed an amused glance to Celia, but she seemed to be finding her tea of great interest.

"And Celia! Being toasted from here to St. James!" Imogene said proudly. "What a wonderful idea to bring us to London, Drake. We are having the loveliest time, aren't we, Celly?"

Lifting her chin, Celia said with newfound sophistication, "Yes, indeed, I am finding London vastly diverting."

She met the duke's gaze squarely and coolly to prove to herself that she could. Even so, she was the first to lower her gaze.

"Are we to see you tonight, Drake?" his sister asked.

"I may put in an appearance. But you shall be well looked after with Rotham as your escort."

"Yes, he is very kind," Imogene said airily, a blush rising to her cheeks.

"Kind? I certainly would not describe Rotham's behavior as kind." There was a teasing note in Severly's voice.

"Don't be silly. David and I are old friends," Imogene rebuked, and fussed with her handkerchief.

"Is that so?" Drake's glance went to Celia, and his conspiratorial grin invited her to join in his teasing.

Setting her cup down, Celia stood up and said, "If you will both excuse me, I have some correspondence to attend to." She was proud that her tone betrayed no emotion.

Severly rose at her curtsy and stood, watching her slim, retreating figure with narrowed, speculative eyes.

Later that afternoon, the Duke of Severly stood before the Earl of Kendall's fashionable town house on upper Brook Street. Using his silver-handled walking stick, he rapped lightly on the front door. Letty's ancient and discreet butler answered the door and greeted the duke solemnly. Drake was long used to running tame in Letty's house, so after handing over his hat and cane, Drake strode past the butler and went to the staircase. He was halfway up, headed for the withdrawing room, before it occurred to him that he had no desire to be in his mistress's home.

For reasons he refused to examine, he felt irritated and restive and thought it would be wise to avoid his own house as much as possible. After Letty had approached him last evening, he realized that he had been neglecting her in the last few weeks, and was here now out of a sense of duty more than desire. He had always found Letty's boldness and wit amusing and hoped this afternoon would prove diverting. But now that he was here, standing on her staircase, he wanted nothing more than to go back down and out the front door.

With a dismissive shrug, he continued on. Entering the elegantly appointed room, he was not surprised to find it occupied by a few choice members of society.

There was the Marquis of Dale, an old friend of the duke's; Lady Baldridge, a frowzy woman whom Letty tolerated because when she stood next to her she showed to such advantage. Then came Viscountess Callon, wearing a vulgar amount of diamonds, sitting next to Lady Baldridge on the settee. Letty's fourth guest was Harry Smithe-Downe, a fop who prided himself on his garishly embroidered waistcoats.

Letty didn't hide her surprise and pleasure at seeing Severly. She leaped up, leaving her conversation with the Marquis of Dale, to cross the room and clutch the duke's arms and whisper in his ear.

"You grace, how divine to see you." Her voice was almost a purr.

Drake took her hand from his arm, kissed her fingers lightly, and turned to the assemblage.

The other guests greeted Severly as he accepted a cup of tea from Letty. After numerous compliments regarding his ball, the general conversation resumed, but with very little contribution from the duke, who had gone to stand by the fireplace. Even so, his presence dominated the room.

"What a fierce scowl you wear, your grace," Letty teased as she poured tea for her guests. "What could cause such a thing?" She tilted her head to the side and gazed at him with wide china-blue eyes.

Drake pulled himself from his private musings to attend Letty. His thoughts had been on Celia and how beautiful and regal she had looked last night descending the marble staircase, her alluring figure showing to advantage as she walked down the center of the staircase unescorted. It probably wouldn't be wise to relate this to Letty, he thought, with self-deprecating humor. With a charming smile he made an effort to be more attentive to his mistress.

Mr. Smithe-Downe, who also prided himself on having the best gossip in town, turned to the duke.

"I say Severly, I believe I heard yesterday that Miss Langston is going to buy herself a racehorse."

This startling bit of news caught everyone's attention and all turned to Drake for confirmation of this *on dit*. Before Severly could respond, Letty's childlike voice interjected, "Well, good for her. The poor dear needs some amusement."

Her tone was sweet, and she flashed a quick yet significant glance to her friend, Lady Baldridge.

"Er . . . what do you mean, Letty?" The rotund lady took the prompt happily, always ready to help her friend annihilate someone else.

The duke's eyes narrowed slightly as he watched Letty sigh in dramatic sympathy.

"At her age, one needs to take up interests. I'm sure it would be very comforting," she explained in a kindly tone.

"Heavens, she's not an ape leader yet," the marquis said, laughing at the notion.

"No? Well, I just can't imagine how . . . discouraged I would be if I weren't wed by the age of six and twenty," she said, casting innocent eyes around the room.

Lady Baldridge and the birdlike Viscountess Callon exchanged knowing looks. This was rich gossip indeed! The Countess of Kendall had virtually called London's latest rage a spinster. Each woman decided that Miss Langston must somehow hear of this. It would make the next assembly so much more interesting.

The scowl creasing the duke's brow deepened, but Letty wasn't finished yet.

"Miss Langston is such an interesting, mysterious woman. I am curious to know what she was doing in the country all the years before she came to London."

The duke's cup and saucer met the mantel sharply. Bluntly surprised at Letty's attack on a guest in his home, Severly gazed down at Letty coldly.

"Miss Langston was the ward of my sister and spent many years living quietly in the country since the deaths of her parents. A subject I'm sure Miss Langston would rather not discuss with strangers" the duke said in an implacable tone.

Realizing her mistake with some alarm, Letty beat a hasty retreat.

"There!" She smiled brightly. "I knew it could be explained easily. Another cup, Severly?"

The duke declined and took his leave a short time later, leaving Letty feeling more threatened than ever.

A large clock struck half past midnight as the duke, stretched out in a leather chair with his ankles crossed, stared down at a pair of deuces. He wasn't very intent on the game and had come to his club only to avoid going home. Earlier in the evening, he had sat in the common room drinking brandy and conversing with a few friends, but to the duke's mounting annoyance, they all seemed to turn the conversation to his charming houseguest.

So when Westlake entered, Severly immediately excused himself and invited his old friend to play cards. They exchanged the usual pleasantries, and Drake appreciated that his friend had not mentioned Celia once.

"Where is Rotham this eve?" the handsome Duke of Westlake asked, trying for the tenth time of the evening to engage his friend in conversation.

"Dancing attendance upon my sister, I'm sure."

"Looks as if those two will make a match," Westlake observed.

"Possibly."

Raising an amused brow, Westlake gave up and concentrated on winning the hand. He lost.

"You wagered your matched grays on a pair of deuces?" Westlake said in amazement, impressed that his friend would take such a chance with so cool a demeanor. Both men were so wealthy they usually wagered something they valued more than money, just to make it interesting.

"What if I had called your bluff, Severly?"

"You didn't," Drake said, giving his friend a grim smile.

At that moment several young bucks entered the elegant wood-paneled room. Severly glanced up from his cards at the noise the rowdy, dissolute bunch made. Sir

Richard Pembrington was in their midst. Even though Pembrington was from a fine old family and their parents had been close, Severly had no time for him. Severly viewed Pembrington as a man who couldn't hold his liquor, gambled beyond his means, and sat a horse poorly.

So the duke was mildly surprised when Pembrington and his crony, Viscount Treman, approached the table and asked if it was a closed game. After a glance at Severly's careless face, Westlake directed a footman to bring two more chairs.

After seeing himself comfortable, Pembrington asked the limits. When Westlake told him how deep the play was, the color drained from the younger man's face.

As Westlake shuffled and dealt the cards, Sir Richard cleared his throat a number of times in a nervous fashion.

"It is the consensus, Severly, that you have the two most beautiful women in London residing under your roof," Pembrington began jovially.

"I'm sure my sister and Miss Langston would find this information gratifying," Severly said dryly, not lifting his eyes from the cards in his hands. With weary annoyance, he wondered what Pembrington was playing at. In the past, they spoke to each other only when it was socially unavoidable, and this situation was certainly avoidable.

"I was introduced to Miss Langston in Hyde Park the other day," offered the viscount, a drawling exquisite who thought himself a ladies' man. "Utterly charming. Her beauty is surpassed only by her good humor."

Severly made no comment.

The play continued for a while, with the stakes going higher after each hand. As the stakes grew, the two younger men took longer and longer to place their bids.

"I say, Severly . . ." Pembrington cleared his throat. "Are you . . . That is, I wondered . . . is Miss Langston free to decide . . . or does one need your permission?" Pembrington finished this disjointed sentence lamely.

So that was the way of it, Severly thought, turning his unblinking eyes to Sir Richard's pale face. Pembrington wanted to know if he needed to get through him before asking for Celia's hand. Pembrington was an ass. No gentleman would bring up such a subject in a gambling club, Severly thought, continuing to gaze at the younger man derisively. Sir Richard swallowed hard.

Taking his time, Severely threw a number of chips into the middle of the table. "Miss Langston is a family friend of many years and a guest in my home. I naturally feel a certain responsibility for her, but I am not her guardian." Something in the tone of his voice made the fact that he was not her guardian inconsequential.

As it was Pembrington's turn to bid he was saved from responding to the duke, which was a good thing, since he had nothing to say.

Severly lost his taste for the game. His jaw muscles worked reflexively and he found it difficult not to insult the atrocity that Pembrington called a neckcloth just so he could call him out. Damn it, he thought, it was hard enough to ignore Celia without her being mentioned everywhere he went.

He certainly hoped Celia had enough good sense not to become involved with Pembrington. She could not be that green, he hoped. Pembrington would throw her fortune away on gambling and opera dancers, leaving her to rot in his moldering estate in Hampshire. Severly refused to examine why these thoughts made him so angry.

Westlake had to inform him twice that it was his turn to bid.

Chapter Thirteen

Bees hummed happily around the hydrangea hedges, and an orchestra played Mozart near the enormous yew-hedge maze at the Earl of Chandley's glorious estate situated one hour outside London.

It was obvious to all that the young earl had gone to great expense to entertain the easily bored beau monde. So far, it was proving a rousing success.

Rowboats bobbed on the man-made pond for the Corinthians to show off their athletic prowess. Even the dandies tried their hand at the archery ranges set up on the velvet green lawn, and the ladies especially enjoyed the swings and the gypsy fortune teller.

Servants dressed in old-fashioned country garb circulated amongst the guests, serving an impressive alfresco luncheon. There were even braziers set up for those who might find it a novelty to cook their own food.

Earlier that morning, as they were setting out for Chandley in the duke's open, shiny black landau, Celia was determined to ignore the duke. Now that she knew him to be an unrepentant libertine, she could not possibly find him attractive, Celia decided, tugging on her kid gloves with more force than necessary. Even so, she was annoyed that her thoughts so frequently dwelled on him. After Imy was settled across from her, Celia waited impatiently for the duke to join them, ready to display her new disregard for his presence.

To her chagrin, the duke rode up next to the landau astride his horse.

"Blackwind has become restive with these tame trots in Rotten Row. I shall meet you at Chandley," he informed the ladies, tipping his beaver hat. After a brief glance to Celia, he spurred the horse with a flick of his heel and was off at a fast trot. Celia watched his broad back until he disappeared around a bend, leaving her more confused than ever.

"What a lovely day for a ride to the countryside," Imogene opined as the coachman guided the team from the drive to the main road.

"Indeed, the earl could not have picked a better day," Celia agreed a little absentmindedly.

The landau rolled along at an impressive speed. Imogene kept glancing at Celia, who seemed to be lost in her own thoughts.

"A letter from the boys came in the post yesterday. Peter thanks you for your letters and hopes you'll keep writing, even though he hasn't written back."

Celia laughed. "How like Peter. I hope they are enjoying their visit with their grandmother." Celia adjusted the angle of her parasol to keep the sun from her face.

"They are. No doubt Alice is spoiling them terribly. But no matter; it is only for a couple of months."

The two young women fell silent for a time as the landau left the outskirts of London and entered a country lane.

"Celia," Imogene began suddenly, "are you enjoying your stay in London?"

Noting the tone of concern in Imy's voice, Celia pulled her thoughts from her musings and looked across to her old friend.

"Enormously," she stated earnestly. "Sometimes, I still cannot believe that this has happened. If not for your care and guidance, where would I be?"

Waving away Celia's gratitude, Imogene said, "I am pleased you are enjoying yourself. I, for one, am having a bang-up time watching you lead your beaux such a merry chase. And isn't it fun to be toasted the most fashionable young lady in London?"

Celia made a self-deprecating face. "That is only because I gave Mrs. Triaud her head. I certainly had no idea what is considered the mode in London."

"Maybe so, but if you weren't so poised and pretty it wouldn't matter what you wore."

"Thank you very much, Imy. And what of you? It has not escaped my notice that Major Rotham is often at your side."

Celia watched Imogene's cheeks grow pink. "I confess that I do enjoy his company," she said, suddenly finding the surrounding terrain of great interest.

Once they reached the estate, Celia's new friends surrounded her and she threw herself into the gaiety full force. The number of gentlemen who paid court to her, including their host, soothed and gratified her pride. And it pleased her that she had given the enigmatic duke very little thought, at least for a while.

The day was lovely, if a bit warm, but Sir Richard Pembrington proved to be very obliging by continually bringing Celia cups of the tart and refreshing punch. She smiled at him sweetly, wondering if her opinion of him could be mistaken.

Soon Celia began to feel as if she hadn't a care in the world, and led her band of admirers a merry chase across the Earl of Chandley's perfectly manicured lawn.

Viscount Delford approached Celia and playfully challenged her to a game of horseshoes. Celia obliged him with an impish grin.

"Pray lead the way, my lord," Celia said, taking the arm he offered. They moved to the horseshoe pit, a flat, grassy area a little away from the rest of the activities.

A footman raised his eyebrows in surprise as he handed the lady her first horseshoe. Evidently, the notion of a lady playing at horseshoes was novel enough to draw a crowd around the two participants. Viscount Delford bowed to Celia, saying, "Ladies first."

Celia took her time before throwing, touching her hankie to her brow for a moment. For some reason she felt a bit light-headed. Swinging the shoe back and forth a few times, Celia squinted at the distant stake, trying to measure the distance. The crowd was extremely quiet.

She tossed the shoe underhand and watched it fly across the lawn. The distance was good, but the throw was too far left of the stake for Celia to be satisfied with her first attempt.

Delford did not fare much better, but then, he seemed more intent on flirting with Celia than making a good throw. That was until her aim improved with each try. She beat him by barely an inch and he insisted on the best of two out of three.

Celia thought him a very good sport when she bested him again. The little crowd cheered, and, with a smile, she dropped a curtsy to the bowing viscount.

Pleading fatigue, Celia walked back to the other guests and sat on a swing fashioned like a swan. A few swains jockeyed for the privilege to push her, but Celia became dizzy and begged them to stop.

Despite her resolution to put the duke out of her mind, Celia found it impossible to ignore him completely. She noticed him everywhere—winning the trophy at archery, holding a crowd of society's notables engrossed with one of his entertaining stories, and just looking breathtakingly handsome.

She turned away when she saw Lady Kendall, dressed in an exquisite confection of pink gauze, move to his side and stay there. Sir Richard brought Celia another cup of punch and soon she felt better.

For his part, the duke was also finding it an effort to keep his eyes from constantly straying to Celia. He thought she looked utterly charming in her chic, spring-green dress with its sprigged pelisse and her bonnet tilted at a fetching angle. He smiled sardonically at how artlessly she handled her entourage. In fact, he found it dashed annoying that Celia seemed to be enjoying all the attention, even flirting in return.

He also couldn't help noticing how often that pup Pembrington was at her elbow. He turned from his conversation with Leticia to look across the lawn to his sister, standing with Rotham and Lady Sefton by a sundial. Severly noted that Imy kept glancing at Celia with concern as she became bolder and more flirtatious. Not that

Celia's admirers seemed to take exception to her comportment, he thought cynically.

He continued to socialize, but kept an eye on Celia.

A little while later, the duke moved to lean against a large oak tree. From here, he had a very good view of Celia. Soon, to his annoyance, Letty approached arm in arm with Lord Petersham.

"Severly, you must see milord's latest trinket," Letty called to the duke.

"I would be delighted," the duke said drolly. He usually found Lord Petersham a diverting sapskull.

Lord Petersham was showing off his newest bejeweled snuffbox when Severly caught sight of Celia making her way to the pond in a mode that was suspiciously like a prance. This put the duke very much on alert. When she started skipping stones, Drake adroitly disengaged himself from Lord Petersham and Letty. With feigned casualness he strolled across the lawn to join Imy and Major Rotham.

"Oh, Drake, what shall we do?" Imogene whispered to her brother anxiously, twisting her beribboned parasol around and around. "David has just informed me that one of the punch bowls has been contaminated with spirits! That scoundrel Pembrington, who I'm sure is the culprit, has constantly been at her elbow with a full cup. Celly is obviously unaware of what she's been drinking." Glancing back at her friend, the duchess continued, "If Celia continues to act the hoyden, she will never get her vouchers for Almack's. Countess Lieven has not taken her eyes from Celia in the last five minutes."

Drake did not answer his sister immediately, as he continued to assess the situation with an enigmatic expression across his handsome face.

"Celia is unused to spirits," Imy said in a hiss, using Major Rotham as a screen from the other guests. "No wonder she is behaving in this uninhibited way. How can we intervene without calling more attention?" Imogene looked up at her brother anxiously.

Coming to a decision, Severly turned to his sister with a grim smile. "We shall join in the fun. It is a fine spring day and there is no harm in kicking up our heels a bit," Drake reasoned, watching Celia clapping excitedly as Chandley's stone skipped several times.

A moment later, Celia was scrambling around the water's edge, encouraging her admirers to help her find a suitable stone. Drake gritted his teeth as he saw a number of other guests turn their full attention to Miss Langston's antics.

Westlake joined them at that moment, saying with a wicked grin, "Our Miss Langston certainly has a good arm."

"Yes, and we've decided to find it charming," Drake told his friend pointedly. "Rotham, let's join in. After a bit, Imy, you come and persuade Celia to go to the gypsy's tent with you," he directed, starting toward the crowd by the pond.

"I'll go with you," Westlake offered helpfully, falling into step with his old friend. "I hear she's taking wagers that no one can outskip her stones."

"Good lord," Drake said through clenched teeth.

Celia was extremely surprised, a moment later, when the duke suddenly appeared at her side. Peering up at him, Celia wondered why there seemed to be two of him. Following several deliberate blinks, he settled into one, and Celia smiled beatifically.

"Would you care to try your arm, my lord Duke? I have just found the loveliest stone and will let you have it, if you think you can beat six skips." She held out the rock just a little too far to the right of him.

Severly took the stone, relieved to see that she was at least steady on her feet.

"Thank you, Miss Langston. It is indeed a fine stone," he said, hefting the rock and taking a couple of steps closer to the pond. With a powerful yet graceful flick of his wrist, the duke sent the stone sailing across the surface of the pond.

"Good show!" said Rotham.

"Was that nine or ten skips?" someone in the group questioned.

Celia looked up at the duke with admiration. "What

hidden talents you have, your grace. I would never have guessed." She was almost flirting with him, she realized, but found she didn't care.

"There is much about me you don't know, Miss Langston," Severly said. Celia wondered at the stern note in his voice.

Because the Duke of Severly had sanctioned the rock skipping, soon a number of gentlemen were trying their hand, laying wagers and having a rousing good time.

"Celly, you must have your fortune told. Come with me now," Imy urged, pulling Celia by her elbow away from the fun.

Celia resisted her at first, but Imy continued to drag her across the lawn to the brightly colored tent.

Pushing aside the canvas that covered the tent door, Celia entered cautiously, blinking several times against the low lighting. She saw in the corner of the tent a small, wrinkled old woman sitting on an ornate red velvet chair. Looking around, she saw that the walls were draped in dark velvet. Celia also noticed a sweet, musky smell hanging in the dimly lit tent and closed her eyes as a curious, dizzy feeling came upon her again.

"Come in, come in." The old woman's voice was a raspy whisper. "I've been waiting for you."

"You have?" Imogene said in an awed tone.

Celia only snorted inelegantly, and then placed a hasty hand over her mouth, surprised by her own uncharacteristic behavior.

The crone, wrapped in a black shawl, fixed her beady gaze upon Celia.

"So, you do not believe that Maria can tell the future?"

"Well, I beg your pardon, but no, I don't," Celia said a little breathlessly. She found the tent oppressive and wanted to remove her bonnet.

Never taking her eyes from Celia, the old woman gestured for her to come closer. After glancing at Imy, Celia took a few steps nearer the wizened old woman.

"Let me see your palm," the crone demanded.

Wishing she didn't feel so muffle-headed, Celia hesitantly held out her hand, palm up.

Imogene drew closer as the old woman squinted a moment over Celia's palm.

"Mmm . . . I see two paths before you. You must chose wisely. Long life, great wealth, and happiness, or despair and solitude," the old gypsy muttered as she continued to peer at Celia's palm.

Considering the vagueness of these statements and how easy it would be to guess that she was wealthy, Celia was not impressed and pulled her hand away, disappointed.

"Will she find love?" Imogene asked quickly.

Celia paused, frowning at Imy before looking back to the strange gypsy woman.

Pulling her shawl closer, the old woman cackled hoarsely. "She already has it, but her stubbornness may cause it to die."

"Oh, Celia," Imy exclaimed, looking at the old woman with awestruck eyes.

"Imy, you can't possibly believe any of this!" Celia cried. "Even I could make better predictions. And I don't even claim to be clairvoyant."

"You will see that Maria is right," the crone interjected, pointing a gnarled brown finger at Celia. "You may lose what is most precious to you through your own stubbornness."

Suddenly, Celia wanted nothing more than to be away from this stifling tent and strange old woman.

"Will you read my palm?" Imy requested eagerly.

"Sit, sit," the gypsy directed, indicating a chair next to hers.

Seeing that Imy was caught up in having her palm read, Celia slipped from the tent. A wave of dizziness came over her again, leaving her feeling unsteady. Looking around for a place to sit, she saw that the great house was close by and decided to go in and rest for a while instead of joining the other guests.

A maid spied her and curtsied as Celia entered a spacious drawing room from the garden.

"Is there a place I may rest, please? I am feeling a little overcome by the heat," Celia explained.

"Yes, miss. Please come this way."

The maid led her to a charming anteroom and offered to bring her some refreshment.

Celia thanked the maid as she removed her bonnet and pelisse before seating herself on a comfortable little settee.

How long she sat there, she did not know, and found she did not care. It was much cooler inside, and if she did not move too quickly her head did not swim so dreadfully. It was actually a relief to be away from everyone.

"There you are. I was just about to become worried that you had wandered off to challenge someone at darts or had gotten lost in the maze."

Celia looked up swiftly and saw the duke standing in the doorway with an amused smile on his lips. She jumped up in surprise and immediately wished she hadn't. The room spun in a dizzying fashion. She hoped she was not becoming ill.

Severly moved swiftly to her side, catching her elbow as she swayed slightly. He watched her closely, recognizing all the signs of being slightly disguised. His grin widened.

"Are you well? Pray, Miss Langston, be seated." He helped her to the settee.

His unexpected presence so unsettled her that she could not look at him, and consequently occupied herself with carefully arranging her skirt and fanning herself. A definite flush stained her cheeks.

"Thank you, your grace, I am quiet well. But I admit I feel it is a bit warm in here, don't you?"

Severly sat down next to Celia. "No, but I expect you do. How many cups of punch have you had?"

Celia continued to fan herself and look around the room vaguely. "Two or three, I believe. Everyone has been fetching me cups." She turned to the duke and gazed at him quite boldly, very aware of how handsome and strong he looked. In fact, there seemed to be something different about him. A hazy glow seemed to surround the duke. The blood pounded in her wrists and temples, and Celia wondered why she felt so muzzy.

"More like four or five," the duke said archly.

"Four or five what?" Celia asked, her eyes fixed on the scar on his cheek, and she thought that it was most attractive.

"Cups of punch, Miss Langston," he explained patiently.

"Oh, yes, cups." Celia had no idea what he was talking about and continued to gaze at his face, admiring his strong jaw and angled cheekbones.

Setting her fan in her lap, Celia reached out a gentle hand and lightly touched the scar on his cheek. The duke was suddenly very still.

"How did this happen?" she asked, looking at him with soft brownish green eyes. It seemed perfectly natural to Celia, wrapped in her warm golden glow, to be sitting quite alone with the duke, touching his cheek.

Severly captured her hand and silently cursed Pembrington. He brought her hand up and lightly brushed her fingertips over his lips. "In Spain." His voice was almost stilted. "I don't recall exactly how, there was so much happening. A gash on the cheek went unnoticed at the time."

"It's really rather nice," she complimented him as she met his intense gaze.

Celia's heart thudded wildly as he leaned closer to her, still holding her hand.

"I feel very strange," she said faintly, unable to look away.

"You are utterly entrancing." The duke's voice was a husky rumble.

"I am?" Celia questioned, feeling a thrill go through her entire being at his words.

"Yes, you are. And if you continue to look at me in that fashion I shall have to beg your pardon."

"My pardon? For what?" She gazed at him in confusion, acutely aware of her hand clasped in his and how she desired to feel his lips on hers. Ever since the day she had rebuffed Squire Marchman's fumbling attempt to kiss her after church, she had often wondered how it would feel to kiss someone she wanted to kiss.

Severly saw the open invitation in her glorious eyes
and found her irresistible. Telling himself there was no
harm in one chaste kiss, he leaned the few inches that
separated them and gently took her lips with his.

As the warmth of his mouth held hers, the world
stopped for Celia. Everything became part of this moment; the sunlight filtering in from the widow behind
them, the scent of tuberoses and lilies, all became part
of this, her first kiss.

Tilting his head slightly, Severly slipped an arm around
her and drew her closer, deepening the kiss.

In her wildest dreams Celia would not have believed
that a kiss could cause her to feel such intense new sensations. Of its own volition, her hand moved to his chest.
She marveled at the strong beat of his heart beneath the
heavy muscles her fingers caressed.

His lips continued to hold hers, full of tenderness and
barely veiled passion. Celia did not want him to stop.
Ever. When he felt her tremble, he pulled back reluctantly to look into her dark, passion-filled eyes. He put
his long fingers against her cheek.

"Celia, I . . ." he began purposefully, then shook his
head in frustration. "Why did you have to drink that
damned punch?"

"What does punch have to do—" Celia began on a
shaky note when the door opened and Imogene entered.

The duchess gasped upon seeing her brother and Celia
seated so closely together with Drake's hand on Celia's
cheek!

"What is going on here, Drake?" Imy demanded,
twirling around to shut the door lest anyone should happen by.

Celia looked at Imogene and thought that her voice
seemed to be coming from a great distance. Everything
seemed slightly distorted, and she was terribly disappointed when the duke's hand left her cheek. Had he
just kissed her? Had he really told her she was entrancing? The world must be upside down, she thought, putting a hand to her head.

"Drake, I demand to know what is happening." Imogene was so incensed and shocked she even stamped her foot on the Aubussen carpet.

"Imogene, please do not make yourself ridiculous," the duke said sharply, rising from the settee. "What has transpired between Miss Langston and myself is private," he said in a tone of voice that would brook no further questioning.

After one intense, searching glance at her brother, Imogene rushed to Celia and knelt at her side. "My dear, are you all right?" she cried, reaching for her friend's hand and looking at Celia's flushed face with concerned hazel eyes.

Celia did not know if she was all right or not. Looking past Imy to where the duke stood watching her, she wondered what had just transpired between them.

"I feel a little muzzy, that's all, Imogene," she said, beginning to feel confused and embarrassed.

Imogene brushed her hand across Celia's brow. "Oh, Celly, I should have told you about the punch! It was too bad of that beast Pembrington to ply you with it," she said angrily.

Celia was becoming annoyed with this odd obsession everyone seemed to have with punch.

"Drake, go have the landau brought around," Imy ordered her brother. "We shall say that I have the headache. You will have to make our excuses. Go, go." She waved him away.

The duke stood where he was for a moment, watching with a thunderous frown on his face as Imy fussed over Celia. He was a man used to strong drink on occasion, and knew from experience that one did things when foxed that would never be considered in a sober state. The duke had the sudden feeling that that was the case here.

With a last look at Celia's distressed face, he turned and left the room, still feeling her gentle fingers on his scarred cheek.

Chapter Fourteen

*C*elia sat in the breakfast room staring dismally across the room at a mural depicting a cheerful medieval garden party. John, the footman attending her, frowned as she pushed the food around on her plate, her cheeks unusually pale.

Below stairs, the servants had discussed how much they enjoyed having Miss Langston as a houseguest. She was so cheerful and kind, but today there was obviously something distressing her. John poured more hot water in the teapot, hoping she wasn't sickening for something.

Sighing with relief that no one had joined her for breakfast, Celia wondered how she could possibly face the duke after what had transpired between them yesterday. Resisting the urge to massage her temples, Celia squinted slightly as a dozen little men with very sharp picks mined in her brain. She knew she could not face anyone just yet and was glad to have time to herself to decide how to tell Imogene of her plans.

Looking down at the beautifully prepared food in front of her, Celia gave up trying to force herself to eat and signaled to John that she was finished. She rose, deciding she must go back to her room and start making plans. There was so much to do. She didn't quite know where to begin.

She left the breakfast room and was halfway across the entry hall when she saw the duke step from his library and stop a few feet in front of her.

With her heart thudding wildly in her chest, Celia froze

midstep. She stared at him with surprised embarrassment as he stood before her, so straight and tall, looking at her in a way he had never looked at her before.

Celia pulled her gaze from his and continued toward the staircase, feeling a mortified blush scorch its way to her cheeks. So desperately did she desire to be out of his presence, she had no care that she was being terribly rude in not acknowledging him.

"I desire a word with you, Miss Langston," he requested. His voice was unfamiliar to her with its tone of gentleness and intimacy.

His words halted her on the first step, and slowly she shook her head. She shook her head because at that moment it would be impossible to trust her voice. His sudden appearance jolted her tenuously set emotions. She had purposely avoided thinking about what had happened yesterday at Chandley, for her confusion was such that she didn't know if she would cry or throw something at him.

Anger came to rescue her pride. Celia had no desire to hear him explain away the kiss that had transpired between them yesterday. With an effort, she turned toward him and lifted her chin. "I would prefer not to, your grace."

Taking a step toward her, his solemn eyes fixed upon her, he said quietly, "You do not feel it necessary to settle things between us?"

Continuing to keep a tight rein on her roiling emotions, Celia said in a surprisingly calm voice, "What is there to settle? If you are worried that I misinterpreted the situation yesterday, put your mind at ease. I am not a naive child."

A frown creased his dark brow. "Just what do you perceive the situation to be?"

Taking a few cautious steps up the staircase, Celia tried for a haughty tone. "Isn't it obvious? I was disguised and you displayed your true nature—nothing more needs to be said on the matter." She hoped fervently he would allow this embarrassing subject to be closed. She jumped at his sardonic bark of laughter and was a little alarmed at the anger suddenly flashing in his hazel-gold eyes.

"My dear Celia, if I had displayed my 'true nature,' as you put it, you certainly would have experienced more than a chaste kiss."

Chaste! Celia could hardly believe her ears as she stared askance at his amused face. Her high-strung nerves could take no more, and the slim hold she had on her temper snapped.

"Chaste?" she said in outraged scorn, looking up at the mural on the ceiling in vexation. "I don't know why you are arguing with me, your grace. Considering how forgiving I am being over your rakish behavior, I should think that you would be relieved."

The duke stared at Celia with his square jaw tightly set, but made no immediate response to her intemperate statement. When he first approached Miss Langston a few moments ago, he had expected embarrassment, shyness, and even confusion. But this lofty self-possession was surprising. Beneath his frustration he found himself admiring her poise under such awkward circumstances. Even so, he was beginning to find her stubbornness extremely provoking.

Taking a deep breath to calm himself, Severly lifted his massive shoulders in a self-deprecating manner and said as gently as he could, "Believe me, I am not unaware of my seemingly improper behavior, but we are off the subject. Celia, if you will allow me—"

"Seemingly?" Celia's voice rose with outrage and she pounded her fist once on the balustrade. "Your arrogance has no boundaries, *your grace*. My first impression of you was correct—you are unfeeling. You practically flaunt your mistress, the wife of a peer, in front of all the *ton* and then kiss me when I was . . . my judgment was impaired," she continued, her voice rising with each word.

She stood looking down at him from the third step of the staircase, as he sauntered forward until they were standing almost face-to-face. She refused to look away from his arrogantly amused countenance.

Though his lips were quirked in cynical amusement, Severly's gaze was assessing. He was a little surprised that she knew about Letty, but that was of no consequence compared to her opinion of him. Perhaps, at last, he would discover the reason she had been avoiding him in the past. His eyes continued to scan her face, taking in how regal she looked in her anger.

"What about your first impression of me convinced you that I was unfeeling?" His tone was deceptively mild as his eyes kept her riveted to where she stood. Celia could no longer force herself to meet his piercing scrutiny and allowed her eyes to drop to the gold chain of his fob. He was the most vexing man! She had an overwhelming urge to take him down a peg. Maybe then he would not dally with the hearts of unsuspecting females, she thought, bolstering her anger.

After a brief hesitation she spoke quickly. "When I first went to Harbrooke Hall you told Imogene I shouldn't take care of the boys. You thought I should be sent away." As soon as the words left her mouth, Celia wished them unsaid. How foolish she felt for bringing up something that had happened over ten years ago. He would think her a child to attack him in this way. The last bit of amusement left his eyes. For a moment, the duke's expression was completely blank, until the full implication of her words became clear.

"What the hell are you talking about?"

Celia began to tremble at the anger in his voice, but it was too late to stop now.

"In the first few days of my stay at Harbrooke, I overheard you tell Imogene that I was not suited to look after Peter and Henry. You felt I was too young to take charge of the boys and told Imy to send me away."

"What the hell are you talking about?" he said again, fairly shouting.

"I just told—"

"I know what you said. I can't believe you believe what you are saying," he claimed in a biting tone. "I may have expressed my concern about your tender years, but I had no care about Imy having you in her home. Why should I?"

Frowning, Celia tried to recall his exact words those many years ago as he continued in a bitterly angry voice.

"So this is your opinion of me. So many things become clear. I now understand your peculiar avoidance of me during my stays at the hall. And why you gave me the cut direct that day in the village." He paused to stare at her in cold anger. "Allow me to assure you, Miss Langston, albeit ten years too late, though I may be a bit beyond the pale, I haven't quite stooped to throwing orphans into the streets." His tone was so harshly scornful Celia felt almost seared by it.

Turning her head from him, Celia whispered hoarsely, "I will not discuss this further. This situation has become untenable, your grace. I thank you for your hospitality but I shall be leaving London tomorrow," she finished, hazarding a quick glance at his face.

The unconcealed rage on his countenance sent her up another step.

"No, Miss Langston, there is no need for you to leave London. I understand from my sister that you have received your voucher for Almack's. Your leaving would upset her greatly. Are you so willing to disappoint her over this absurd misunderstanding?"

Celia bit her bottom lip as she took in his closed expression. The truth of his words defeated her. Of course she would do nothing to disappoint Imy. Her tear-clogged throat prevented her from speaking.

"Somehow I find this ironically amusing, Miss Langston. But to reduce your distress over my presence, *I* shall do my best to avoid *you*: Rather the opposite of the situation at Harbrooke Hall, wouldn't you say?" he queried with mild sarcasm.

With a half-suppressed sob Celia turned and fled. She ran blindly up the stairs past Imy's room to the sanctuary of her own. Very gently she closed the door behind her before throwing herself on the bed, burying her face in the coverlet to muffle her heart-rending sobs.

Down the hall, Imogene was in the midst of dusting

off a note to David Rotham, postponing their outing. After sending her maid off with the missive, Imogene paced her room for a few moments, deep in thought, before going in search of her brother. She was determined to speak to him about what has transpired between him and Celia. To her annoyance his valet informed her that his grace would be away from home the rest of the day. Frowning, Imogene went to the library and made herself comfortable in one of the deep armchairs. Instructing a footman to see to it that she was undisturbed, except to be told of the duke's return, the duchess leaned back in the chair to think things over.

Some time later, at the sound of a light tap at her door, Celia sat up and wiped her tear-wet face with the back of her hand. Dora stepped in, looking very concerned. "Begging your pardon, miss, but Miss Sheffield is downstairs. She says you were to go to Kensington Gardens with her."

"Oh! I had completely forgotten," Celia cried, putting her hands to her face. "Dora, please tell Miss Sheffield I shall be with her in fifteen minutes."

Jumping from the bed, she splashed her face with cold water from the porcelain basin, admonishing herself for allowing the duke to so upset her. Patting her face dry with a flannel, Celia forced her turbulent emotions to some order and went to her dressing room to choose a promenade ensemble.

How nonsensical this situation is, she thought as she stepped into an exquisite dress in sophisticated shades of peach and gray. It was so unlike her to behave in such an overemotional manner. She felt as if she no longer knew herself.

Dora returned to button Celia's gown, informing her that Miss Sheffield was in the salon being entertained by the duchess.

Relieved that Corinna was not cooling her heels in the foyer, Celia took a few extra moments to rearrange her hair and place a dashing little bonnet at the perfect angle.

Though she did not want to cry off her outing with

Corinna, Celia recoiled at the thought of spending the afternoon being falsely cheerful. But she owned that taking a walk in the gardens was certainly preferable to reliving, over and over, the scene between herself and the duke. Could it be possible that she had misunderstood what he meant all those years ago? Shaking her head, she forced the disturbing thoughts from her mind.

Gathering her gloves, reticule, and lace parasol, Celia moved to the door. Before reaching for the knob, she turned to Dora.

"Is his grace at home, Dora?" she queried in a tone she strove to make casual.

"No, miss, he left more than an hour ago and is not expected back until late," Dora said as she straightened the bed coverlet.

Celia expelled her breath in a rush of relief and bade Dora good-bye.

Within half an hour Celia and Corinna were strolling among the well-ordered and lushly blooming flower beds of Kensington Gardens, with Corinna's lady's maid a few paces behind them.

"Are you well, Celia? You are very quiet today," Corinna asked her friend after a few moments. She could not help but notice that the taller girl was unusually pale.

"I am sorry to be so dull today, Corinna." Celia smiled an apology to the younger woman. "This whirlwind of parties has caught up with me. But come; we shall continue to walk in the sun, and the fog will clear from my head."

Forcing thoughts of the duke from her mind, Celia strolled through the grounds with Corinna chattering excitedly about Princess Charlotte's wedding, which was now only a few days away.

"Look, Lady Baldridge, 'tis Miss Sheffield and Miss Langston!"

Celia and Corinna turned at hearing their names to see the Countess of Kendall and the rotund Lady Baldridge fast approaching.

Celia knew there was nothing for it but to stop and let the other two ladies catch up. *This is all today needed,*

Celia thought, groaning inwardly. The last thing she wanted right now was to be forced to speak to Severly's mistress.

"What a delightful picture the two of you make," Lady Kendall said in her high, sweet voice. "I was just saying so to Lady Baldridge, wasn't I?" She turned to her companion for confirmation, and the heavier woman nodded vigorously in agreement.

Before Celia or Corinna could respond to this unorthodox greeting, Lady Kendall looked straight at Celia and said, "May I please have a word with you, Miss Langston? Lady Baldridge, Miss Sheffield, you will pardon us for a few moments, won't you?"

"Of course we will, Lady Kendall," Lady Baldridge said forcefully, drawing her arm through Corinna's and steering the young lady away. Corinna looked over her shoulder at Celia with a very surprised expression. Celia could do nothing but smile politely and wait for Lady Kendall to speak. She owned that she was very curious as to why Lady Kendall would seek her out so pointedly.

"Let us go over to that pretty little arbor and have a nice coze. We really must make an effort to know one another. After all, it's almost as if we were family."

"Oh? How can that be?" Celia raised a brow and followed her into the arbor, seating herself next to the countess on a little stone bench. It was clear that she would not be able to get away until the countess had her say. "I am not related to the duke or his sister. Are you?"

"La, no." Letty giggled. "What I mean to say is that you are so close to the duchess and I am so close to Severly. . . . Well, naturally, we should be friends. I do feel as if I know you because Drake has told me all about you," she lied blatantly, irritated by Celia's cool, self-assured demeanor.

Celia stared at the pretty little blonde, and found herself speechless. For a split second Celia wished she were ill-mannered enough to get up and walk away. She had a very strong feeling that she did not want to hear anything else Lady Kendall had to say.

Lady Kendall continued.

"Anything that concerns Severly is very much a concern of mine. He has told you of how . . . special our relationship is?" she inquired, raising both brows in question.

"No, he has not." Celia was surprised at her own calm reply.

"How like Drake." Letty's laughter lasted a little too long to be natural. Sobering, she turned long-suffering blue eyes to Celia. "It is rather unconventional, I own, but can true love ever be denied? Should it be? Drake has loved me for years. Tragically, my parents forced me to marry a very old man. Drake was away because of the war, or he would have eloped with me." She sighed poignantly, setting the artfully arranged golden ringlets of hair dancing beneath her bonnet. "He's the only reason I can bear to go on."

The region around Celia's heart seemed to freeze. In her heart of hearts, she had hoped that his relationship with Lady Kendall was just a dalliance based on nothing more than mutual desire. But Lady Kendall's words changed all that. Drake was in love with his mistress, a woman he couldn't have. This explained why he hadn't married and why he made no effort to be discreet about their relationship. It explained the blatant look of passion she had seen on the duke's face when he danced with Lady Kendall.

Celia could not recall ever feeling so much pain in her heart. What a fool she had been not to accept what she had seen so plainly. She suddenly felt quite naive.

"If this is so, I see no reason why you would share this information with me." Celia tried to keep all evidence of distress from her voice.

"Well . . ." Letty shifted on the stone bench and looked at Celia with a frown creasing her brow. "Drake is quite concerned about your growing feelings toward him. I thought it might help if I explained our unfortunate circumstances to you. Drake does not wish you to be embarrassed. You take my meaning, I'm sure."

Celia could not believe her ears. Obviously, the duke

had told Lady Kendall that he believed Celia was in danger of making a cake of herself over him. Why else would the countess waylay her in this manner? How dared he, she fumed silently, feeling almost relieved at the surge of anger replacing the pain in her chest.

Letty watched the emotions play across Celia's face, and felt a sense of satisfaction at the angry, embarrassed flush that rose to her cheeks. So she had not been wrong to be suspicious yesterday at Chandley when Drake and the spinster had disappeared.

The countess had been in a panic ever since returning home from Chandley. In a frantic gamble, Letty had sent her lady's maid, Sophie, over to Severly House to see what she could learn. She had done this in the past, because Sophie's cousin was a belowstairs maid in the Severly household. Sophie had often come back with useful information, usually about the duke's plans and such. But never before had Letty needed to know what was going on at Severly House as badly as she needed to now.

Impatiently, she had waited all morning for Sophie to return. When Lady Baldridge had arrived at two o'clock, Letty had decided not to vex herself further by waiting. And so they had set out for Kensington Gardens. Letty thought it was the greatest good luck to spot Miss Langston, deciding almost instantly to have a private word with the older girl. Woman

Now she felt she had played it perfectly. For certainly, if the spinster had been harboring any romantical ideas about Severly, she would now be too ashamed to make them known, Letty thought, continuing to watch closely the play of emotions across her rival's face.

Gathering the shreds of her torn feelings as best she could, Celia took a deep breath.

"I have no desire to be privy to such intimacies, Lady Kendall. I bid you good day."

Without another word, Celia rose and walked out of the arbor. With difficulty she forced herself not to run through the beds as she spotted Corinna nearby.

Corinna came to her friend's side immediately, for she

did not have a good feeling about this meeting. Seeing Celia's composed, yet very pale face caused her further concern. She was too polite to ask what had transpired, but everyone knew that Letty Kendall was the Duke of Severly's paramour, and that he had been neglecting her of late. Corinna put her arm through her friend's, noted that it was trembling, and suggested that they return home.

Celia agreed at once.

Chapter Fifteen

*P*orter opened the front doors to a weary-looking Celia. She wanted nothing more than to lie down and nurse her head. It was aching even worse than it had been this morning. She winced, putting a hand to her throbbing temple.

"Lord Pembrington is in the blue salon, miss. He insisted on waiting for your return."

The butler's usually noncommittal voice seemed to hold a faint tone of disapproval, Celia noted as she looked up at him in surprise. What was Lord Pembrington doing here?

"Good lord, what next?" Celia said half under her breath as she untied the ribbons to her bonnet.

"I beg your pardon, miss?" Porter said as they walked toward the blue salon.

"Nothing, Porter." Celia sighed. "May I give you my bonnet?"

"Of course, miss," he said, before opening the salon door for her. "May I bring you a cup of tea?"

She smiled wearily at the butler. "Thank you, Porter. A cup of tea would be lovely," she said before stepping into the blue salon.

Celia found Lord Pembrington pacing the floor and speaking. Curiously, Celia looked around the room to see if Imogene was waiting, too. Seeing no one else, Celia cleared her throat.

"Good afternoon, Lord Pembrington. You wished to see me?"

Pembrington stopped pacing at the sound of her voice, and blushed to the roots of his red hair at having been caught muttering to himself.

"Miss Langston! How good of you to come. I mean, that is, I see you have returned."

A short silence fell as Celia tried to determine whether Lord Pembrington was foxed. Stepping farther into the room, she said, "Yes, I have returned. Porter said you wished to speak to me?" she repeated.

Moving to stand before her, Lord Pembrington nodded his head vigorously. "Quite so. But you see, when you first came in, I was not really talking to myself. I mean, of course I was speaking You heard me . . . just practicing. But that is of no import. I came here to talk to you about something else."

"I gathered that." Celia was becoming convinced that he truly was in his cups. He had probably wandered into the wrong house and did not know how to extricate himself, she surmised.

"Yes, very important You see, Miss Langston, ever since you came to town, you've been all the kick. That is to say . . ." He began pacing again.

Celia was beginning to feel slightly alarmed.

"What I mean to say . . ." He tried again. "You are beautiful. Chandley says you are the incomparable of incomparables. Since he feels that way, I thought I should toddle over here first, just in case."

Celia's mouth was agape as Pembrington continued.

"And since one doesn't need to have Severly's permission . . . well, you take my meaning." He stopped pacing the floor long enough to grin at her in a very self-satisfied way.

"I have no idea what you are prattling about, Lord Pembrington. And I am not sure I wish to know," Celia took a few steps toward the door.

"I see that I have not made myself clear, Miss Langston. I feel . . . that is, I discussed it with my mother and she agrees that I should bestow . . . that is, ask for . . ." He quit speaking and suddenly lunged forward, grabbing her hands in his. "I want you for my wife, Miss Langston."

Gasping with surprised indignation, Celia struggled to pull her hands free. If this was not the outside of enough! First the horrible scene with the duke this morning, then being forced to attend to Lady Kendall, and now this! She could hardly comprehend that Richard Pembrington was making a complete booby of himself in the middle of the duke's salon! She gritted her teeth and tugged harder.

"Miss Langston, say you will let me honor you—that is, please honor me with your hand."

"Let go!" Celia was quivering with anger now. Mustering all her strength, she gave one last pull before resorting to kicking his shins. Her hands were suddenly free, and Pembrington stumbled forward, landing flat on his face on the Oriental carpet. Celia could only stare down at his prone figure in stunned silence.

" 'Pon rep, Pembrington, I had no notion you were so interested in my rugs."

Whirling around on her heel, Celia saw Severly and the Earl of Chandley standing in the doorway.

Frozen wide-eyed with mortification, Celia could only guess their thoughts by the expressions on their faces. Chandley's countenance was easily read, for he was staring down at Pembrington with angry disgust. The duke, leaning casually against the doorjamb, was not so easy to gauge. His expression, except for the slightest twist of a smile, was closed.

Of their own volition, Celia's hands flew to her flushed cheeks. Her eyes went from Pembrington, who had not moved from his place on the floor, to the two gentlemen sauntering into the room.

What in the world were they doing here? she wondered desperately. And how was this odd scene to be explained?

Pembrington slowly pushed himself up to his knees. He was scowling intensely, and Celia saw that his cheek was red from where his face had hit the floor.

"Zounds! Did you plant him a facer, Miss Langston?" asked Chandley with admiration, for he had also noted the red cheek.

Celia had the most overwhelming urge to laugh hysterically. She could only shake her head, her hands still on her cheeks.

By now, Pembrington was on his feet. Glowering at Chandley, he said, "No, she did not hit me. I merely slipped and fell." He straightened his jacket and began brushing off his knees.

Celia could feel the duke's eyes upon her. Desperately, she cast around for something to say, and could think of nothing. This ridiculous encounter had occurred so quickly, she wasn't even sure what exactly had happened.

Severly's languid gaze went to Pembrington. With a raised brow he waited for the young wastrel to give an account of himself.

Feeling like a butterfly pinned to a board, Pembrington cleared his throat several times before attempting to speak. "I was just asking . . . er . . . I wished to speak to Miss—"

At that moment, Porter entered the room carrying the tea service.

With relief flooding her heart, Celia finally found her voice. "Here is the tea! Porter, you may serve the gentlemen. I am sure they have much to say to each other, and as I am feeling rather fatigued I shall leave them in peace."

Porter nodded his understanding to Miss Langston and wondered why she was saying all this to him.

With a shallow curtsy, Celia quickly left the room, not caring what any of them thought of her. She was halfway up the staircase when she heard Imogene call to her.

"Celia, what in the world is going on?" Imy called, walking up the stairs toward her friend.

"Oh, Imogene, I cannot begin to tell you how odious this day has been," Celia began, as they continued to ascend the stairs.

Meanwhile, in the blue salon, Severly and Chandley were still eyeing Lord Pembrington. After throwing a harried glance to the butler, Pembrington gave up. With a churlish look to the other men he muttered, "I have nothing to say and will take my leave."

Without another word he left Severly House before Porter could get the door.

"Well," Chandley said, "that was devilish queer."

"Indeed," responded the duke coolly. "I wonder if the offense of being a ninny is enough cause to call him out."

"In Pembrington's case, it is more than enough," Chandley responded. Porter offered the gentlemen tea.

"May I offer you something stronger than tea, Chandley?" The duke gestured to his liquor cabinet.

"Yes, I believe I am in need," Chandley replied.

Porter instantly procured a bottle of whiskey. The two gentlemen raised their glasses in a silent toast.

Severly had to own that young Chandley had certainly gone up in his estimation this afternoon. Earlier, while the duke was taking Blackwind for a bruising run through Regent's Park, he had scarcely noticed another rider bearing down upon him. It wasn't until the other horse was abreast of his that the duke slowed to a trot. Severly had been in no mood to talk, but his innate good manners made him rein in his horse and greet the Earl of Chandley.

"I say, Severely," the younger man began a little breathlessly, "I hope I'm not overstepping, but I have need to speak to you."

Severly had gritted his teeth in an effort to control his tongue. If this were another buck hinting at offering for Celia, he would be hard-put not to be rude.

After the duke nodded for the younger man to proceed, Chandley said, "Was just at my club and encountered Pembrington. Not to tell tales, but he was already a bit over the boughs."

This statement had caught the duke's attention.

"Well, he was prattling on about making Miss Langston an offer. Said you weren't her guardian and he was going right over to Severly House. Heard him give his coachman your direction." He paused a moment. "It would not at all be the thing for Miss Langston to be embarrassed. And with Pembrington being halfway foxed . . ." His voice trailed away.

"I take your meaning," the duke had said, swinging his mount around. "Would you care to accompany me, Chandley?" He made this offer out of sheer politeness.

"If you'll permit, your grace," the earl had replied.

The last thing Severly had contemplated happening, as he and Chandley rode posthaste back to Severly House, was to find Pembrington laid out on the rug, Severly recalled with a grim smile.

Now, standing in the middle of his salon having a drink with Chandley, the duke pondered the disturbing question of Miss Langston.

The assembly rooms at Almack's were prodigiously warm. Celia fanned her flushed cheeks vigorously as she stood with Imogene and Major Rotham at the edge of the parquet floor.

So this was the much-vaunted Almack's, she thought as she gazed around the rather plain room. Granted, those assembled were the crème de la crème of the beau monde. Everywhere she looked she saw beautiful ladies with bare shoulders and gentlemen in black satin knee britches.

As they made their way around the room, Celia smiled at those who greeted her, unable to be heard well enough to converse through the waves of laughing chatter around her.

Almack's was not at all what Celia had been anticipating.

"I do not believe that Miss Langston is properly awed by Almack's," Major Rotham said to Imy with a grin.

"No, indeed, David. Celia, don't you think this is the most beautiful place in London?" she asked with a mischievous smile to her friend.

"I will admit that for a place I've heard described as the zenith of society and the seventh heaven, this is not what I expected," Celia admitted with chagrin.

"If you are not impressed with the decor, you will be even less so with the refreshments," Major Rotham said with a laugh.

Celia looked upon her friend's smiling face and couldn't help wondering when they would marry. It was obvious to her that Imy was in love with the major. And looking at the major's handsome face smiling down at

Imy, he had probably never been out of love with the beautiful duchess.

Knowing how much it meant to Imogene for Celia to have received her voucher made Celia determined to behave in a manner above reproach. During the coach ride over, Imogene had cautioned Celia about the patronesses who ruled Almack's with iron fists.

"No one, despite rank or wealth is permitted to enter Almack's a minute after eleven o'clock," Imy informed. "Even the Duke of Wellington was turned away when he begged entrance after eleven."

Celia also knew that the patronesses could be terribly censorious. They were not beneath using their influence to blackball from the hallowed halls of the most exclusive club in London anyone who displeased them.

At that moment, Sir John Mayhew approached her and claimed his dance, expressing in his drawling tones that she had never been in better looks.

Smiling at the very slim gentleman, Celia beseeched, "Oh, Sir John, I find I am quite fatigued by the last reel. Would you mind attending me while I catch my breath?"

"At your service, Miss Langston. I would gladly bask in your stimulating presence, dancing or no," he said with a flourishing bow.

Within moments, Celia saw the Earl of Chandley making his way through the crowd toward her. Trying to steel her emotions, Celia gave Imy a look of panic.

"Do not fret, Celia; just remember what I said yesterday," Imy whispered her encouragement.

Yesterday. Celia would rather not be forced to think of that horrid day. After she had told Imy of the whole sorry incident with Lord Pembrington, Celia had asked in distress, "How can I ever face Chandley again? How am I to explain?"

When Imogene had finished laughing, she brushed a tear away and said, "There is no need to explain, Celly, dear. The earl shall never mention the incident; nor shall Drake. Needless to say, Lord Pembrington has no desire to bring it up. So in public, behave as if the whole silly thing never occurred," she explained. "But in private I shall endeavor to mention your first proposal as often as possible," she teased, setting off into gales of laughter all over again.

Continuing to keep the polite smile on her lips, Celia met the earl's smiling blue eyes with some trepidation.

"Miss Langston, your servant." He made an elegant leg before her. Celia instantly relaxed and greeted him as naturally as she could.

Celia stood trying to converse with the gentlemen as she allowed her eyes to scan the room for a certain dark head and broad shoulders. There was no sign of Severly.

The strain of trying to keep up this polite chatter so set her nerves on edge that Celia considered feigning illness. Just as quickly, she dismissed the notion, knowing Imy would insist on returning home with her. Celia could not bear to cut short the evening for her friend. Imy was so proud of her. She could hardly hide her triumph over Celly's rapidly filling dance card.

But Celia could find no satisfaction in the number of her admirers this evening. The duke had made good on his promise to avoid her, for she had not encountered him since she had escaped the blue salon yesterday afternoon.

Of their own volition, her eyes again scanned the crowded room, and her gaze clashed with a pair of china-blue eyes. Lady Kendall, standing nearby, was staring at Celia with narrowed eyes and excited, flushed cheeks.

Celia immediately looked away. Celia had no desire to risk a repetition of the embarrassingly personal conversation they had had at Kensington Gardens. If she hadn't been so distracted, Celia might have wondered over Lady Kendall's curious behavior. But she was much too occupied with her own disturbing thoughts and trying to attend to the many attentive gentlemen hovering around to take real note of anyone else.

Forcing her gaze to the earl's face, Celia pushed thoughts of the duke from her mind for the tenth time of the evening.

At that moment, the noisy chatter in the assembly room reduced by half and all heads turned to the doors.

The Duke of Severly, with a grim expression on his face, made his entrance.

Celia's heart leaped at the sight of him. Fanning herself vigorously, she came to a difficult decision: She was going to apologize to him as soon as he asked her to dance. After much reflection, she had come to realize that she had deeply insulted him with her accusations of his heartlessness toward her when she had been younger. Now, reflecting upon the past with the eyes of an adult, she could see that she had been mistaken about him. He had not intended for Imy to put her out, and she had been childish to harbor such grievances all these years.

She still refused to examine the kiss that had transpired between them at Chandley, but she was determined to do what she could to put their friendship back on the former easy footing they had established since coming to London. Celia watched him make his way through the crowded room.

He looked in her direction and she gave him a tentative smile. His gaze passed over her coldly. Celia barely suppressed a gasp. He had snubbed her. He must hate her for what she had said to him, she realized with a numbing pain in her heart. A welcome wave of shock rolled over the pain that gripped her chest. She blindly turned to Sir Belford as he claimed her hand for a country reel.

Lady Kendall had also noticed Drake's arrival.

Handing her glass to a passing footman, she approached a small group of her intimates with an unflattering set to her jaw. Calling a gay greeting, she said, "Lady Baldridge! Lady Pembrington! I have the most shocking news. You must swear not to breathe a word." The ladies immediately ceased their own conversations and gathered around the countess in excited anticipation.

"We have all been duped!" Letty made her eyes go very wide. "I have it on the most reliable authority that our delightful Miss Langston is not what she appears to be."

"She's not an heiress?" Lady Pembrington asked urgently, the green plumes in her turban dancing. She had not spoken with her son since he had informed her of his intention to ask Miss Langston for her hand. "It would be *vey* distressing if she were not an heiress."

"No, she is an heiress." Lady Kendall paused dramatically. "But before she received her inheritance, she was the Duchess of Harbrooke's *paid companion.*"

After a moment of complete silence, the small group gasped and tittered at this most delicious gossip.

"No, you must be mistaken!"

"Are you *very* sure, Lady Kendall?"

"Of course I'm sure," she said haughtily, "I have it firsthand. She has only recently come into her inheritance." Lady Kendall was not quite as confident as she sounded. Her information regarding Miss Langston's past was sketchy at best. When Sophie, her maid, had come home from Severly House with this tale, and the news that Miss Langston would be at Almack's, Letty knew she could not possibly pass up such a perfect opportunity to expose the chit.

Letty felt incredible pleasure at the avid expressions surrounding her. She had been so pleased with her maid; she had even given the young woman a few of her old gowns. What a stroke of luck that Sophie's cousin had become Miss Langston's lady's maid.

By the knowing looks her friends were exchanging, Letty was confident that the information would be heard by all the *ton* within half an hour. And soon, Miss Langston would be held in such contempt no one would deign to speak to her, Lady Kendall's thoughts continued gleefully.

A short time later, as she stood conversing with Lady Jersey and Imogene, Celia suddenly noticed some odd looks cast her way. A few ladies even seemed to be whispering and giggling in her direction. The Countess of Milfordhaven approached them, apologizing profusely, but insisting she must speak with Lady Jersey. The two women went off with their heads close together.

Imogene turned questioning eyes to her friend, wondering if Celia had an idea as to why they suddenly seemed to be the object of speculation. Celia gave a helpless shrug to Imy's unspoken question.

A moment later, they were set upon by Lady Cowper and a few of her acid-tongued cronies.

"La, the Duchess of Harbrooke and Miss Langston, what a delightful sight the two of you make. So *companionable!*" The ladies tripped off with gales of laughter. Celia and Imy looked after them in surprised confusion.

The orchestra opened a quadrille, and Celia unexpectedly found herself partnerless. She gazed around the assemblage trying to hide her growing confusion and embarrassment. She avoided the knowing looks as best she could. What could explain this odd turn of events? Could they be following the duke's example? She knew he was a leader of Society—where he went others did also. It seemed the only explanation to this mystery.

She wanted to leave. Being stared at and whispered about was unnerving in the extreme.

She turned to Imy, ready to express her desire, when Lady Kendall approached. By now, a large number of people were paying close attention to Miss Langston.

Watching her mischief at work, Letty had grown triumphant in the last half hour. She was delighted that Severly had not gone near Miss Langston since his arrival. Half of those assembled seemed to be watching in curious anticipation as Lady Kendall greeted the duchess and Miss Langston. After a few stilted pleasantries, Letty turned sweet eyes to the duchess.

"I've been hoping to ask your advice, ma'am."

"Certainly," Imy said graciously, trying to hide her suspicion.

"You seem to have such luck in finding good help." She looked pointedly to Celia. "How would you advise I go about finding a good lady's companion?" Those nearest them gasped and goggled. Letty was a bold one indeed.

The murmuring grew.

Westlake, who was standing near enough to hear this exchange, turned away angrily to seek out Severly.

He found him playing cards in an antechamber. After catching Severly's eye, Westlake gave him a significant look and tilted his head toward the door. Momentarily, Severly excused himself from the game.

"Severly," Westlake began as soon as they were private, "I've grown to admire your Miss Langston. Her poise is to be commended."

"She is not my Miss Langston," Drake responded in a tight voice, wondering what his friend was about.

"Be that as it may, she is a guest in your home. You have not danced with your guest this evening, and that curious fact has added credence to the rumor that is now circulating the assembly rooms."

"What are you speaking of?" the duke said irritably, running impatient fingers through his thick hair. He wondered why he had stirred himself to attend this evening. He had always found Almack's a dead bore.

"Miss Langston is now the object of vicious gossip. It is rumored that she has been trying to pass herself off as a lady. Everyone is giving her the cut direct and whispering. Lady Kendall had just asked your sister her advice on finding a good lady's companion. Your sudden inattention toward Miss Langston seems to confirm these rumors." Westlake spoke casually, as if he were discussing the latest play.

Severly stared at his friend in growing comprehension. "Devil take it," he said in a growl, striding out of the room. Once he reached the ballroom it took only a moment to take in the situation. There was an odd hush over the guests, and his sister's face was frozen in a polite, dignified mask. Letty's chin was thrust up in a haughty tilt, and even at this distance he could see the gleam of malicious triumph in her blue eyes.

Celia was speaking to the young Earl of Chandley. Severly was grimly pleased to see she had not been completely abandoned.

The duke watched as Chandley led Celia out to the opening strains of a reel. Severly moved to his sister's side, trying to force the scowl from his face.

"Severly!" Letty twittered when she saw him. "Shame

on you! There are not enough gentlemen who dance well, and you go off to play cards. Why, poor Miss Langston has only had one dance in the last five." Her laugh was delighted.

At that moment Severly could not comprehend why he'd ever found Leticia Kendall attractive. He liked gold-brown hair not blond. He wanted to look into brownish green eyes that tilted up, not childishly wide blue ones.

"There must indeed be a shortage of gentlemen, for I would dance with Miss Langston every dance if she would consent." He turned to his sister and offered his arm, ignoring the shocked gasps of those near enough to have heard his comment.

Leading his sister to a pair of empty chairs, Severly quietly asked, "How bad is it?"

Imogene sighed dejectedly. "Rather bad. None of the patronesses has actually snubbed her yet, but everyone is talking and staring. Drake, this is awful. Celia shall be so hurt if all the friends she had begun to make now turn," she whispered, hoping she did not look as upset as she felt.

"Don't worry, Imy. The situation can be salvaged."

"How?" she asked doubtfully.

"Leave it to me and keep your chin up. And do not leave for at least an hour," he ordered.

The beau monde was treated to an evening of many surprises. Speculation grew to enormous proportions at the sight of the elusive Duke of Severly watching Miss Langston with a frankly admiring gaze. He could barely pull his eyes from her when someone spoke to him.

The room was abuzz when the very fickle Duke of Westlake danced with her twice and seemed to hang on her every word. It could barely be believed when Westlake asked her for an unprecedented third dance, which Miss Langston demurely declined.

The Earl of Chandley also asked Celia for a second dance, and still, Severly stayed on the side, casually leaning against a wall, with his eyes never leaving Miss Langston's graceful form.

Lady Jersey, one of the most redoubtable patronesses

of Almack's, had been watching this scandal brewing and could not stand another moment of ignorance. Having been on good terms with Severly for years, she took matters into her own hands.

Marching across the assembly room, with most of the eyes of the *ton* upon her, Lady Jersey called a greeting to the duke.

After dispensing with the necessary social patter as quickly as possible, Lady Jersey got to the point. "Now, Severly, there seems to be something havey-cavey afoot. Why have we not seen Miss Langston in town before?"

Severly pulled his eyes from Miss Langston to give Lady Jersey a very out-of-character sheepish look.

"Naturally, I've been protective of Miss Langston. Having watched her grow from a sweet girl to a beautiful young woman, I was not eager to see her pursued by every buck in town, so I have always discouraged the idea of a London Season."

Turning his eyes back to Celia, the duke continued with this unprecedented speech. "But Celia . . . er . . . Miss Langston, like most young ladies, would not hear of settling down until she had her trip to London. I am sure you understand this desire," he finished, giving Lady Jersey one of his rare and charming smiles.

Nonplussed at these unexpected revelations, Lady Jersey, for once, was speechless. The high and mighty Duke of Severly had practically declared his intentions toward the mysterious Miss Langston, and it appeared, at least according to the duke, that Miss Langston was not in any hurry to bring him to scratch.

Before the avidly curious Lady Jersey could ask another question, Severly begged her pardon, gave the lady a courtly bow, and sauntered across the hall to gain a closer vantage point of Miss Langston.

Within half an hour, Severly felt the tide turning. Many of the people who had been watching Celia began to turn speculative eyes toward Lady Kendall.

Everyone knew the countess and Severly had been having an affair. Could Letty, in a jealous fit, have started the rumors to discredit Miss Langston? A new speculation grew.

During the orchestra's intermission, Severly approached Celia, who was standing near the refreshments table with Imy. It did not matter if she accepted or declined his request for a dance; either way, it fit into his plan to discredit the rumor circulating the room. Celia's guarded eyes met his in a question.

"May I have the honor of the next waltz, Miss Langston?" His tone was deeply gentle.

For an instant, Celia found herself about to say yes. "I'm sorry, your grace, I am quite fatigued," Celia said with dignity, moving to his sister's side.

It spread like wildfire through the assemblage that Miss Langston had actually declined to dance with the Duke of Severly.

No one could recall that ever happening.

"A mere lady's companion could not be so confident," opined Lady Jersey to Princess Esterhazy, after recounting her conversation with the duke. "Lady Kendall must know that she is losing her thrall over the duke."

Lady Cowper nodded her agreement. "Out of jealousy she obviously spread this vicious gossip. Why, Westlake has known Miss Langston for years. He would not dance attendance on a mere servant."

Desperately wondering how her plan had gone wrong, Letty cast about for a way to save her dignity. Placing herself in the duke's path proved futile. He never asked her to dance. Soon, she became so discomfited with the attention she was receiving, she angrily called for her carriage.

In her distress, Celia was unaware of the changes in the demeanor of the other guests. She had no idea how she was going to get through the remainder of the evening. To her mortification, she had somehow been found out, and she just wanted to leave. The minutes creaked along with agonizing slowness. With each passing moment her distress grew.

Even people Celia had never met were approaching, just to give her the cut direct.

Unbeknownst to her, Celia's inner anxiety showed outwardly as icy calm, impressing a number of the *ton*, even as they savored the delicious gossip.

When Chandley returned her to Imogene after dancing a minuet, Celia turned to her friend and said in a tightly controlled voice, "If it's convenient, Imy, I would like to leave."

"Of course, we may go now." Imy frowned in concern over Celia's pale face.

The ride home was silent, for Imogene truly did not know what to say to her friend.

Upon arriving at Severly House, Celia quickly ascended the staircase and gained her room. Dismissing Dora as soon as she helped her disrobe, Celia sat at her dressing table, feeling strangely emotionless. The tears that had been threatening to fall for the last two hours had somehow dried up, and she was left with the crystal-clear knowledge that she was in love with the duke.

She also knew that she could not stand another day in London.

Chapter Sixteen

*T*he road had gotten quite rough over the last few miles. Celia had been bounced from one side of her new coach to the other until she felt sore to her bones.

Looking out the small window, Celia frowned at the heavy, dark day. It had rained, off and on, since the carriage had taken her from Severly House early that morning. At least the countryside was now looking more familiar. She should be at Harford Abbey, her new home, in an hour or so. She wondered why this information gave her no satisfaction. Feeling the tears well up once again, she searched for her crumpled hankie.

"You must stop this silliness," she admonished herself after wiping her watery eyes.

Feeling sorry for herself was useless. She must face the facts as they were, and go on.

Taking a deep breath, Celia knew the time had come to be honest. She loved the duke. There. She had faced it and she had not dissolved. So she had made a fool of herself at Chandley's picnic and later in the foyer. Wishing differently could not change what had transpired. With a great sigh, she stared out the window at the waterlogged countryside, forcing her thoughts to more painful subjects.

Everyone in the *ton* knew she was not a lady. Everyone in the *ton* knew she had tried to pass herself off as something she wasn't. This could not be changed either. "So far, so good," she told herself, straightening her shoulders against the soft leather squabs. She was facing the facts. They would not destroy her. She forced her weary heart to look at the most difficult fact of all.

Severly loved Lady Kendall.

Celia's shoulders sagged. She buried her face in her hands. No matter how hard she tried to face this, it pierced her heart sharply. She loved him so much it was inconceivable that he did not love her in return.

But he did not, and she was not a child who would die from a broken heart.

Celia recalled the events of earlier in the day. Her leavetaking had been awkward, and she had almost weakened at Imy's pleadings.

"Celia, you can't." Imogene had been horrified when Celia had informed her that she would be departing immediately after breakfast. "Everyone is coming around now. There's no need for you to leave. No one believes— well, no one of any import to us—that you were in my employ. Wait and let us discuss this with Drake. Do not be hasty," Imogene urged with concerned hazel eyes.

"No, Imy, I must leave. I have no desire to be in London any longer. Besides, if I stay I shall probably make a bigger fool of myself than I already have." She tried to smile at her frowning friend.

"Don't be silly. You just can't leave. Tomorrow is Princess Charlotte's wedding."

"I know. Please, Imy, I can't stay. I cannot." Celia's tone told of her distress as she stood before Imogene in her wine-and-gray traveling costume.

Though Imogene still frowned, she did not continue to harangue Celia. However, she told Porter to inform her the moment his grace returned from his morning ride.

Following a brief repast, Celia had gone upstairs to see how Dora was coming along with the packing.

"Almost done, Dora?" she asked the little maid.

"Yes, miss, and I've packed me own belongings, too." Dora's little chin hardened.

"What?" Celia was startled.

"I'm your lady's maid, miss," Dora said simply.

Touched by the maid's loyalty, Celia stepped forward and put her hand on Dora's shoulder.

"I know you'll like Harford, Dora. 'Tis a pretty place. Mr. Whitley tells me the repairs on my home are well under way."

"I'm sure I'll like it, miss. I've never been to the country afore."

Within an hour Celia said good-bye to Imogene, assuring her that she would see her friend again soon.

Imogene stood on the steps, wringing her hands anxiously. Pleading her case one last time, she said, "Oh, Celia, I know things have taken a turn, but won't you please stay and let Drake help us straighten everything out? Besides, I will miss you."

As the footman opened the carriage door, Celia gave her friend a beseeching look.

"Please, Imy, don't press me further. I have my reasons for leaving. You will return to Harbrooke Hall soon, so there will be no time to miss me." Celia embraced the duchess tightly before stepping into the coach.

Dora rode up top with the coachman, for she tended to become ill in an enclosed carriage. This left Celia alone in the coach to torture herself, mile after mile, by living the last few days over and over again.

Because they had set out bright and early with fresh horses, the coachman assured her they would reach Harford Abbey before nightfall.

In an effort to resist her depressed emotions, Celia forced her thoughts to the state of affairs at her new home. During one of her meetings with Mr. Whitley, Celia had asked him if he would arrange to have the abbey renovated. He had been delighted to carry out her instructions, for he believed the house could be comfortable if properly attended to.

The sun was beginning its descent when the coach turned onto the newly smoothed surface of the abbey road.

As the coach got closer to the house, Celia raised the shade and looked out the window. When Harford Abbey came into view, she was quite taken by all the changes so immediately apparent, despite feeling exhausted from her emotions and the rough journey. The overgrowth of ivy and shrubs had been reduced, the roof reshingled, and new doors and window frames gave the manor a fresh face.

Jarvis was on the steps as the coachman leaped down to open the coach door and help Celia alight.

"Miss Celia, we wasn't expecting you till after the Season was well done and gone. Matthews will be happy to see you, miss. Hasn't been herself since the old miss passed on."

Celia forced a cheerful greeting to the wizened butler. The old miss. How many years would it be before she was referred to in such a way?

"I'm so glad to be home. How wonderful everything looks," she said as she started to tug off her gloves. "I'm very tired, Jarvis, and I'm sure Dora is also. She shall be part of our household from now on. Are there any rooms suitable to rest in?" she asked as they entered the much-altered foyer.

Celia wanted to be alone. She couldn't face any questions right then. It was too poignant to be in Harford Abbey with memories of Edna so close.

Matthews hurried in from the kitchen with cries of greeting and delight that the young miss had returned home.

"The young miss is looking for a place to lay her head, Matthews. She's that weary from her travels," Jarvis informed the matronly housekeeper.

"I've had a room ready this past week. You follow me, miss. Will you be needing a bite to eat?"

"No, thank you, Matthews. Just a bed." Celia noticed Dora hanging back in the front hall, and gestured for the girl to come closer. "Dora, you must meet Matthews. She knows everything about Harford Abbey." Celia knew Matthews would draw the petite girl under her wing.

They followed the housekeeper up the stairs. Matthews chattered nonstop about the renovations that were being made and how good it was to have the young miss home.

Matthews showed her to a room sparsely furnished,

but very clean, with a southern exposure. Celia was relieved that she hadn't been shown to Edna's old room.

Dismissing both women when they offered to help, Celia leaned against the door after closing it behind them.

What was the duke doing at this moment? Enjoying himself at his club or a soiree, more than likely. He had probably been very relieved when he found she'd left.

Before her departure she had given Porter a note to give to the duke. She had written a polite little missive thanking him for his hospitality and explaining that she felt she needed to check on the work being done at Harford Abbey.

She hoped he inferred from her dignified letter that she had no intention of continuing to embarrass him with her presence.

A pang of sadness touched her heart. Now that she knew she loved him, she understood him so much better. No wonder the duke had been austere and somewhat cold. The woman he truly loved belonged to another.

A flush of shame stained her cheeks at how harshly she had judged him. Could she blame him for having an affair with Lady Kendall? She had heard that the earl was quite decrepit. It was so sad. The duke and the countess made such a handsome couple. She continued to torture herself, biting her tender lip at the memory of them dancing so close. Severly was so tall and dark, the countess so fair and petite. Celia felt tall and clumsy next to such a pretty butterfly.

Wearily, Celia removed her clothing and lay on the bed in her chemise. As hard as she tried, she could not prevent the silent tears from slipping past her closed lids.

Earlier that day, after watching Celia's coach turn down the drive, Imy went back into the house to find Severly's butler.

"Porter we are not at home today. And please inform me the moment his grace returns."

"Very good, your grace." The stately butler inclined his head as the duchess returned to the drawing room.

After wondering listlessly for a short while what she should do next, Imy searched the room for quill and paper.

Taking a moment to think, she finally dusted off a note and directed one of the footmen to deliver it to Major Rotham. She went to sit in a leather-seated chair by the window, deciding the only thing she could do was wait as patiently as she could.

From the other side of the house, Imy became aware of the continual knocking at the front door.

No doubt the whole of the polite world planned to call, Imy thought with sheer annoyance. She had no intention of accepting visitors, knowing full well that the gossip and questions would start all over if it were known that Miss Langston had departed London.

It was no wonder that Celia wanted to leave. Last night's assembly had been a near disaster. But, to his credit, Drake had somehow turned the tide of scandal. Celia's poised behavior had also done much to salvage her own reputation, Imogene mused futilely. She wished again that Celia had not insisted upon leaving Severly House.

At that moment the drawing room door opened and Porter announced Major Rotham.

Imy jumped up and held out her hands. "David!" she exclaimed, pleased that he had come.

The major swiftly crossed the room and took her hands in his. "I came as soon as I received your note."

Pulling him to a chair near hers, Imy looked at him with bewildered eyes.

"Thank you so much for attending me. I'm at sixes and sevens. Celia has packed up and left. My brother cannot be located, and the knocker has been banging incessantly." Listening to herself now, Imy suddenly felt silly for calling him to her side.

The major dismissed her sudden shyness. "And you have summoned me to help you defend Severly House against an onslaught of gossip seekers," he said with a pleased smile.

Imy laughed, relieved that he so quickly grasped the situation.

"Yes, if I have to be holed up with the curtains drawn, I would prefer to have you here with me." She dimpled, feeling much better.

The major's smile faded as his eyes locked with hers. "I hope you always feel that way, Imogene," he said seriously.

Imy felt her heart skip as her eyes met his. "Of course I will, David," she said simply.

Suddenly they were standing, and Imy was in his arms. Pressed against his warmth, Imy felt like a girl again.

"There is much to say. Much I wish to ask you," he began, as she allowed herself to relax against him.

"Is there?" she queried, waiting for his kiss.

"Yes, but words can wait."

His head lowered and their lips met in a kiss as sweet as it had been long awaited.

Moments later the double doors to the drawing room opened and Severly charged in with a scowl on his face.

"God's teeth, Imy! I can't even traverse my own drive. There are too many damned conveyances clogging the way."

Upon seeing his sister in Rotham's arms, Severly stopped dead in the middle of the room. A look of pleased surprise spread over his face.

"Beg pardon. Didn't you know you had company, Imy," he said to his sister with a slow smile.

Parting from Imogene reluctantly, Rotham turned to his old friend. "I know I should have spoken to you first, Severly—"

"Not a bit of it, my friend," the duke interjected. "You two have been smelling of orange blossoms since your visit to Harbrooke Hall. You have my blessing."

The gentlemen shook hands while Imogene looked on, a serene smile gracing her pretty face.

At the sound, once again, of the distant knocker, Imy suddenly came back to the problem at hand.

"Oh, Drake, everything is amiss. Your drive is so crowded because the entire beau monde has decided to pay us a visit. Everyone is still agog at last evening's entertainment," she said archly. "But that is not all. Celia has departed. She has gone off to live at Harford Abbey."

"Bloody hell you say." The duke lost his characteristic composure. "Doesn't she know the gossipmongers will start all over again?" He slapped his gloves impatiently against his thigh, a frown returning to his brow.

"I don't believe she cares, Drake," Imy pointed out gently.

Severly began to pace the room with long strides. Imy turned to the major with a helpless look. He shrugged in response, having nothing to offer to the conversation.

All of a sudden, a loud commotion was heard outside the drawing room doors. The room's occupants turned with startled curiosity as the doors flew open.

The Countess of Kendall dashed in, her face flushed and her bonnet askew.

"I beg your pardon, your grace. I did inform the countess you were not at home. But she insisted." Porter stood behind the lady, a pained expression on his usually placid countenance.

"That's quite all right, Porter," Severly said icily, turning to the unexpected guest.

Nodding, the butler stepped out of the room and closed the door. The four people remained in awkward silence.

Ignoring the duchess and Major Rotham, Letty approached the Duke with a pout. "Severly, I would have a word with you."

With cold anger the duke realized this scene could not be avoided. It was his own fault, he told himself grimly.

"Imy, Rotham? If you would pardon us for a moment?"

"No. I will not pardon Lady Kendall," Imy said angrily, her chin held high as she looked at Letty accusingly.

Cutting the duchess a nasty look, Letty pulled a hankie from her reticule and made a show of dabbing her eyes.

"Please, Severly," Letty whimpered, gazing up at him with beseeching eyes. Severly gave his sister a firm glance, and Rotham took Imy's elbow and drew her to the doors.

"I will leave the room, but I *shall not* pardon Lady Kendall," Imogene bristled before exiting with the major.

After watching the doors close, Letty turned tear-filled eyes toward the duke.

"Why is your sister so mean to me?" she asked innocently, moving to the chair the duchess had recently vacated.

"She has little reason to be kind," the duke responded calmly.

For the first time, Letty wondered if coming to Severly House had been such a wise idea. Her plan had been to brazen the whole thing out, and throw herself into Severly's arms. But judging by his unyielding expression, her desire might not be so easily achieved.

"Why have you come here, Letty?"

Disregarding the duke's cold countenance, Letty plunged ahead. "Drake, darling, say you are not angry at me about last evening. If you are, you must forgive me, for I was terribly jealous," she sulked. In her vast experience, gentlemen loved a woman to be jealous. It flattered their vanity.

The duke gazed down at his former mistress for a moment, his face unreadable.

"Letty, your behavior at Almack's was beyond the pale. It is one thing to goad me, but to denigrate someone who is completely innocent is inexcusable." His tone was so even and calm that, at first, Letty mistook his meaning. But as the words sank in, her face grew scarlet.

"But, Drake, I was jealous. You were neglecting me for that spinster." Her tone was petulant.

"Then you will continue to be jealous, Letty, for our time together is over."

Lady Kendall's jaw dropped. "You are throwing me over? Drake, you can't mean it. I thought you loved me," she accused shrilly.

"Now, Letty, why would you think that? Love was never part of our game." His tone was deceptively gentle.

Letty sputtered in her outrage. "But you can't throw me over. Not me." She practically stamped her foot.

"Then you may throw me over. I care not," he said dismissively.

The statement threw Letty into a fit of crying hysterics. "I cannot accept that you prefer that wretched ape leader to me," she cried as Severly went to the bellpull.

"Lady Kendall, you will never refer to Miss Langston again. Have I made myself clear?"

Letty stopped crying. There was something in the duke's harsh voice that made her very afraid. She realized that if she defied the duke in this she would surely be committing social suicide. With a hiccup, she knew that his influence might cause the patronesses to blackball her from the assemblies at Almack's. This thought sent her into another fit of noisy crying.

At the duke's summons, Porter reentered the drawing room. "Yes, your grace." The butler kept his eyes averted from the countess.

"Have Lady Kendall's carriage brought around."

"Very good, your grace."

When the door closed behind the butler, Severly turned to Letty. "You may make use of this room as long as you like. I bid you adieu and thank you for the pleasure you have given me in the past," he drawled with exquisite politeness, and strode from the room.

Chapter Seventeen

Celia had set out quite early for Harbrooke Hall three mornings after arriving at Harford Abbey. Despite the beautiful summer day, the long walk had been bittersweet.

Taking a different route to her former home, Celia walked to the burial ground by the little stone church she had attended since childhood. After stepping through the iron gate, Celia spotted a place, a short distance away, where the grass had not yet grown to cover the recently turned earth. Edna's resting place had not been difficult to locate.

Walking amongst the headstones, Celia came to kneel at the simple marker bearing Edna's name. Tears gently escaped her eyes and rolled down her cheeks. Memories were all around her. She now realized Edna must have been planning for many years to leave the fortune she had painstakingly built to Celia. Edna had been an ill and troubled woman, but Celia was grateful that she had come to know her kind heart.

"Thank you, Edna," she whispered aloud.

After kneeling in silence for some time, Celia finally left the churchyard knowing she would return again soon.

Crossing a field, she joined the road that led to Harbrooke Hall. Presently, she was pulled from her musings when she noticed an old-fashioned rig coming toward her, down the lane. As it neared, the vehicle slowed, and Celia saw that it was Squire Marchman at the reins.

At the sight of her, he lumbered down from his seat, doffing his hat. His heavy face registered great surprise.

"Miss Langston! I heard that you had returned to Harford," he said, gawking at her quite openly. His small eyes traveled up and down her form.

Celia, though not in the mood for company, greeted him kindly, asking after his health.

"I am hale and hearty," the squire proclaimed in his rather blustery voice. "I have never seen you looking so well, Miss Langston. You look as if you are about to attend a ball." He was still staring at her walking dress.

Laughing, Celia looked down at her lilac-colored dress with its pale green buttons and bows. Even her walking shoes were the palest green. Undoubtedly, in London, she would be commended for her modish sense of style, she thought wryly. She determined to remind herself to have some new, simpler gowns made up. Her current wardrobe was far too sophisticated for her new life, here in the country.

"All the old tabbies in the village have been talking of the changes taking place at Harford Abbey," he said, moving the conversation to a more interesting topic.

"I daresay they have been," she stated roundly, knowing how the village thrived on gossip. She was certain that the news of Edna's hidden wealth had been more than a nine-days' wonder.

"You are no longer living at Harbrooke Hall?" he questioned curiously.

"No I am now living at Harford Abbey." That fact might as well be established as quickly as possible, she thought.

"And will you be residing at the abbey alone?"

Celia looked up at his jowly face, beginning to be uncomfortable with his many questions.

"Yes," she said shortly.

A speculative light entered his small eyes. Shifting from one foot to the other, the squire hemmed and hawed for a moment.

"See here, Miss Langston. May I call upon you soon?"

Closing her eyes for a moment, Celia took a deep breath.

"I am sorry, Squire. Harford Abbey is still undergoing

a number of repairs, and is not fit to receive company." Her tone was very polite. "You mustn't let me keep you. I see that your horses are becoming restless."

Sketching a quick curtsy, Celia left the squire standing in the lane, looking after her with a befuddled expression.

Upon arriving at the hall, Celia was greeted by Grimes and Mrs. Potts. It quickly became apparent by the butler's formal demeanor that the servants of Harbrooke Hall would no longer treat her in the easy manner of old.

Obviously, they had heard of her unexpected inheritance, Celia thought as she removed her bonnet and pelisse.

"I've come to see my old room," she said breezily moving toward the sweeping staircase. "I shall be packing my belonging and taking them back with me to the abbey."

Grimes bowed deeply at her words. Celia raised her brows at this uncharacteristic gesture.

Determined to ignore his formality, she smiled and continued to her former room.

She worked steadily for some hours, relieved to have a purpose to occupy her mind.

After some time, there was a knock on her bedroom door. Not looking up from her task, she said, "Enter."

The butler opened the door and asked if he could be of help.

"Yes, Grimes, you can have a footman deliver these trunks to Harford Abbey," Celia instructed Imy's butler.

"Very good, miss. May I have a tray with a light repast brought up to you?" the dignified butler questioned.

Seated at her old desk, in her old room at Harbrooke Hall, Celia smiled wanly up at Grimes. "No, thank you, I am perfectly comfortable."

"Very good, miss," he said again, leaving her to her task.

Smoothing back a loose tendril of hair, Celia sighed and resumed going through a large cedar chest containing old clothing and a few precious things left to her by her parents.

Now, as she lifted green silk from the chest, Celia realized it was her mother's old gown that she had altered and last worn at the dinner with Imy, Major Rotham, and the duke. It had been decided that night that they would go to London for the Season.

Could it have been only a little more than six weeks ago? she wondered with a bemused shake of her head. A world of change had occurred since then. Recalling that evening now, she realized that it was that night her opinion of the duke had begun to change. She held the gown tightly against her bosom.

"I will never get rid of this dress," she whispered to herself aloud, unwilling to examine her reasoning.

In truth, every memory she had of the duke seemed like a dream. Had she imagined it all? she mused, smiling sadly as she refolded the gown. Had she also imagined that look in his eyes, that day at Chandley, which even now made her heart beat faster? No matter how she scolded herself to be sensible, she could not forget what had transpired between them.

Soon, she forced herself to become absorbed with packing all the items she had accumulated during her years at Harbrooke Hall.

While sorting through a pile of papers, she paused and told herself, almost desperately, that things had worked out wonderfully. She was sure Imy and Major Rotham would soon wed, and it was better for her not to be underfoot. It was also wonderful that Harford Abbey was close so that she could still see the boys.

But if everything had worked out so wonderfully, she mused miserably, why did she feel so awful? She chided herself again, as the duke's handsome face immediately came to mind. Would she have had preferred not to discover that she loved the duke? In her heart of hearts she knew, as shameless as it was, she would always savor the memories of dancing with the duke, of being in his arms with his lips on hers. No. She sighed. She would never regret her feelings for Severly.

The duke was in the past, she told herself firmly. After wiping her hands on the oversize apron she wore to protect her dress, Celia opened another drawer and was in the midst of removing old letters and other memorabilia, when one of the upstairs maids entered the room bearing a paper-wrapped bundle.

"Hello, Mary," Celia said as she rose from the stool, glad to be distracted from her depressing thoughts. "What have you there?"

"Beggin' your pardon, miss, but Mrs. Potts thought you might want to take your pretty cloth with you to Harford Abbey." The maid offered the package to Celia, who accepted it with a puzzled frown.

"Cloth? I don't believe I have any new cloth," she said as she untied the heavy twine wrapped around the brown paper holding the package together.

As the paper fell away, Celia gasped in confused disbelief as a bolt of violet-blue velvet appeared. After some moments of incomprehension, she realized the fabric was the same velvet she had admired the last time she had visited Finchley's in the village. It had been much too dear for her then. That was the day the duke had walked her back to Harbrooke Hall, she recalled instantly.

She stroked the soft material with shaking fingers, trying to understand how it had come to be here.

"Where did this come from?" she whispered to the maid, not taking her eyes from the fabric.

"His grace's man said it was for you."

Celia's hand froze on the velvet. Mary must have meant "her grace" and said "his" by mistake. It would be just like Imy to be so thoughtful and make a gift of the exquisite cloth. But how would she have known that Celia had desired the material?

"His grace?"

Mary looked at Celia quizzically. "Well, the Duke of Severly, of course, miss."

"When . . ." Celia cleared her throat and began again. "When did his grace's man say this was for me?"

"In March. Before they left for London. Johnny, his grace's tiger, gave the parcel to Mrs. Potts, saying that his grace had sent him into the shop to purchase the fabric you had been looking at right afore he came in.

but Johnny didn't know what to do with it, so he gave it to Mrs. Potts. She forgot to give it to you before you left for London. 'Tis very pretty cloth, miss."

Something began to well up deep inside of Celia. The beginnings of a radiant smile started at the corners of Celia's mouth as she picked up the folded fabric. "Yes, Mary, it is very pretty cloth. Thank you very much for telling me this, and for bringing me the fabric," Celia said sincerely to the maid.

"You're welcome, miss," Mary said as she bobbed a slight curtsy.

"I must return to Harford Abbey immediately. Would you be so kind as to have a carriage brought around?"

"Very good, miss," Mary said, and left the room.

Celia's head was spinning with a multitude of conflicting thoughts. The duke must have seen her through the window at Finchley's as the proprietor had shown her the material. That was the only explanation, she thought as she pulled off the apron, quickly forgetting about the contents of the cedar chest. Why had the duke purchased the fabric? Should she write to him? No, her fevered brain protested. She must speak to him.

It seemed to take an interminable time to reach Harford Abbey. When they finally rounded the drive, Celia did not wait for the coachman to help her from the carriage. Dashing into the foyer, she began calling for Matthews and Dora as she ran up the stairs toward her rooms.

"Heavens, miss, what is wrong?" Matthews called out in alarm as she lumbered after Celia.

"Nothing is wrong," Celia called behind her as she almost ran into Dora on the landing. "Oh, there you are, Dora. Come, you must help me pack. We must leave for London before first light."

"We must?" Dora squeaked, following her mistress into her room. "Is something wrong, miss?"

"No, Dora, everything is fine. At least, I think it is!" Celia put her hands to her head and laughed out loud. "No, I don't know if everything is fine or not, but I'm going to find out."

                        *   *   *

Later that afternoon, seated at her desk in the newly refurbished library, Celia impatiently dashed off notes to the vicar and her solicitor in preparation for her journey back to London.

She steadfastly refused to examine her emotions, or why she had this overwhelming desire to question the duke about the velvet. She would not even allow herself to think about what she would say to him once she returned to London. All she knew was that it was vitally important to discover why the duke had purchased the fabric.

At that moment, Jarvis opened the grand double doors. Celia laid her quill down and turned to her butler curiously. She was immediately struck by his flushed and nervous countenance.

"His grace, the Duke of Severly," he announced, much too loudly for the quiet room.

This statement had the effect of a cannon's discharge upon Celia. After one shocked, frozen second, she jumped up and ran to the other side of her desk, just as the duke's tall frame strode past her butler to stand in the middle of the room.

A squeak of trepidation escaped Celia as she saw his thunderous expression. She stared at him in shock. He was devastatingly masculine in his fitted buckskin riding britches and dusty black Hessian boots. His chiseled features looked harsh and his long hair a little windblown. Celia's reeling mind could not accept that he was standing in the middle of her library. Her heart fluttered like hummingbird wings. She didn't know where to look.

"What the hell are you doing here?" His tone was abrupt. His piercing hazel eyes impaled her where she stood.

Casting him a quick, startled glance, Celia could only stand mutely. Considering that he was the one who had unexpectedly appeared in her home, Celia thought this question odd. After a false try, Celia gathered her courage.

"I live here, your grace." She hoped her tone was cool.

"Devil take it, Celia. You know what I am speaking of. Why did you leave London? Your abrupt departure has only caused more speculation," he charged, yanking off his gloves and tossing them onto a nearby table.

Celia could not look at him. His presence was so overwhelming, so unexpected, it left her trembling. She tried to take herself in hand. A moment ago she wanted nothing more than to be in his presence and ask him about the violet bolt of fabric. Instead, "I have found I do not care for London, your grace," was all that she could manage.

"Really," he said archly, taking a few steps closer. "I was under the distinct impression that you enjoyed dancing, shopping, and going to the theater. Was I mistaken?"

Wishing he would not bark at her in such a harsh manner, Celia felt indignation overtaking her shock at his unexpected appearance.

Clenching her hands together, she said, "I did enjoy those things for a while." She glanced at him out of the corner of her eye, unable to think of anything else to say.

"Celia, if you run off like this, everyone will think you have a reason to be ashamed. You should have stayed and stared them all out of countenance." His tone had gentled slightly.

Celia shook her head. "I care nothing for what is being said. After all, it is not far from the truth."

His hazel eyes surveyed her pale face for a moment. The room was very quiet. "If you do not care, why did you leave?"

Celia turned away from him completely, too ashamed of her weakness to face him. She shook her head mutely again, unable to answer his question.

"Was it because of me?" he prodded harshly.

He knew! Mortification spread through Celia's body. If only the Oriental rug would open up and swallow her. What a fool he must think her. Had her love for him been so obvious?

"Yes," she whispered honestly.

"So it meant nothing? That moment upon the stairs?

That day at Chandley's? You were just playing with me?" His tone was so icy she shivered.

Casting a look over her shoulder, Celia stared at him with confused eyes. What on God's earth was he speaking of? His words made no sense to her.

As she turned to face him, her befuddled senses finally noticed that something was different about the duke. Her eyes searched his face. He had always been so supremely confident, and on occasion even a little arrogant. The expression on his face now seemed out of character.

Did she detect a hint of vulnerability beneath his angry words? She could not account for it. Playing with him? He loved the countess, she acknowledged painfully. All the *ton* knew he had been her lover for years.

"I do not understand. I would never play—" She spread her hands in confusion.

"Do not be coy, Miss Langston," he cut in sharply. "I was quite in your thrall. You should be pleased with the feather in your cap. It is plain. The moment you captured my attention you grew bored and ran off," he said brusquely.

"Are you daft?" Celia gasped, looking up to gaze at the duke as if he had taken leave of his senses. "You completely ignored me at Almack's. You are in love with the Countess of Kendall," she informed him, as if he did not know this common fact. "You are the only reason she can tolerate her deplorable life with her old husband."

Severly's well-muscled body stood tensed. "I beg your pardon?" he questioned with a raised brow.

"Lady Kendall was forced to marry the old earl while you were away at war. She is the only woman you have ever loved," she stated quickly and impatiently.

"Who the hell told you that?" he questioned, watching her beautiful, confused face closely.

Celia shrugged slightly. "Lady Kendall. Also, I saw the way you looked at her when you danced together at Severly House."

Severly suddenly felt ashamed of himself. With a bitter twist to his lips, he recalled how he had flaunted his mistress. He was the Duke of Severly. He didn't follow fashions—he set them. If Society had certain conventions, he was above them. How arrogant he had been, he thought now with regret. How could he explain the truth to this beautiful, naive country girl? He walked forward until he was within inches of her.

"I do not love Lady Kendall. I never have. I did not know her well before the war. Her husband is not so very old." He shrugged. "And from everything I have heard, she pursued him avidly. I will not lie to you, Celia. Lady Kendall and I had an understanding. I wish it were not so. But I assure you, my heart has never been involved with any woman."

The deep timbre of his voice seemed to vibrate through her. Not knowing what to think of his admissions, Celia turned her back and moved away from him again. Trying to organize her chaotic emotions, she was hardly willing to comprehend what he was saying to her. Celia lowered her head, exposing the graceful curve of her nape to him.

"I do not understand you, your grace," she whispered, and meant it. There had been a time when she had hoped he might care for her. But then she had seen him with the countess and had realized his intentions were not to be trusted. Could she allow herself to trust him? He came from such a different world than she, Celia thought sadly. His world took vows lightly. Commitment lasted only until the next amusement.

Severly watched her unyielding back and lowered head. It took a great effort not to press his lips to her pale nape. The silence stretched between them for some moments.

"I believe you do understand me, Miss Langston. You have made it plain that my intentions are disagreeable to you. I will beg your pardon and take my leave," he said quietly and formally.

Celia heard him walking away from her. Suddenly galvanized by an inexpressible and overwhelming emotion, she whirled around, only to see his retreating back.

"Wait, please, your grace. I must ask you about a certain bolt of fabric I received from the housekeeper at Harbrooke Hall. I was told it was meant for me," she questioned breathlessly, suddenly recalling the violet material.

The duke stopped and slowly turned upon his heel. "A bolt of fabric? What significance does a bolt of fabric have to this conversation?"

Celia hesitated, not quite knowing how to continue but certain she could not allow him to leave before he explained. "Well, I admired it several months ago while shopping in the village. It had been much too dear for a governess to afford. Do you know how I have come to possess it?"

It was the duke's turn to appear uncomfortable. "I had taken note of your admiration of the material and thought the color might suit you," he stated after a moment. "I had my tiger make the purchase, but had not the chance to give it to you before we left for London."

The fear and confusion that had settled around Celia's heart dissolved. It was a revelation to know that before she had received her inheritance, while she was still dressed so plainly, the duke had thought well enough of her to want to give her something so lovely. A wave of joy swelled deep within her heart.

The duke made an impatient and dismissive gesture with a sweep of his hand. "The material is of no import."

"But it is very important to me, your grace. Please explain to me why you purchased something so intimate for a dowdy governess," she asked, her eyes shining, revealing plainly what was in her heart.

The duke's face was unreadable as he hesitated before her. "You were never dowdy. I thought you the loveliest and most interesting woman I have ever encountered. When I had chanced upon you and my nephews skipping stones on the pond, at that moment you stole my heart," he said quietly. His deep voice was measured and sincere.

The room suddenly seemed to spin around. Celia knew that her heart had been waiting all her life for this moment. Still, she could hardly allow herself to believe what she saw in his eyes.

"You really admired me when I was a spinster?"

Standing before her, motionless, Severly knew by her shy expression that she had placed her trust in him.

The duke reached her in three strides, pulling her fiercely to his chest. As his hungry lips pressed against her pulsing neck, Celia was exquisitely aware of his muscular arms around her. Breathlessly, she marveled at the quick beat of his heart, matching hers.

Pulling back, he looked deep into her eyes. His large hands came up to cup her beautiful face gently. Someday he would write an ode to the splendor of her eyes. Soon, he would compose a sonnet declaring the depth of his love.

All that would come later. For now, he could only say, "Yes."

That one word, so huskily spoken, filled Celia with the deepest sense of wonder and joy she had ever known.

As she leaned into his embrace, his lips took hers in a kiss that began gently, but soon held the promise of their passion.

His arms tightened around her slim body, pulling her closer against him. *This is not a dream,* Celia thought to herself in a haze of growing desire. Severly was truly here, at Harford Abbey, and he had declared his love for her.

Their kiss deepened, and with newfound confidence Celia's hands stroked Severly's chest before stealing up to his neck. She savored the new sensations coursing through her veins. Standing on her tiptoes, she pressed herself even closer against him, wanting to show him how much she loved him.

After some time, Severly reluctantly pulled back, fearing for the first time since he'd been a lad that he would not be able to control the passion flaming through him.

Standing in the middle of her library, still loosely encircled in his arms, Celia felt her face glow with a new inner light as she gazed up in wonder at the expression on Severly's face. Never had she thought to see such tenderness and passion so plainly evident. All for her, she thought with humble amazement.

"You have come all the way from London," she marveled out loud.

"To the ends of the earth, if need be, my darling torment," he said with the slightest touch of a wicked grin. Her heart seemed to catch and stop for a moment. "Imy sends her love," he continued. "She hopes you will send her and David your good wishes."

For a moment, Celia was too enthralled by his presence to fully take his meaning.

"Drake!" she said in a dawning surprise at his words. "Are Imy and David betrothed?" This news would only make her happiness complete, Celia thought with delight.

Severly, greatly pleased with Celia for saying his name so naturally, pulled her back into his arms. "Yes," he murmured against her temple. "They shall be wed at Harbrooke Hall next month."

Celia snuggled her cheek against Severly's shoulder. "Next month? So soon?" she said, wishing he would kiss her again.

With a deep chuckle, Severly's warm lips traveled down her cheek.

"Soon, my love? It is my deepest desire to precede my sister to the altar."

As the revelation of his love coursed through her body, Celia raised her radiant face to his.

"What a lovely idea, your grace," she said as his lips captured hers once more.

Epilogue

*S*everly Park, the duke's family home in Kent, was ablaze with lights as the numerous liveried footmen, maids, and kitchen staff scurried about in preparation for what promised to be the county's most glittering social event in years.

Despite the gloom of the late-fall weather every one of the ninety-odd guests to receive an invitation from the duke and the new duchess had accepted eagerly.

A number of them, who were not actually staying at Severly Park, were now arriving at exactly seven o'clock.

"How unfashionably prompt," the duke remarked drolly to his new brother-in-law, David Rotham, as they strode through the wide hallway to the main salon. A footman opened the impressively wide double doors and the two men passed through them into a huge room with large mullioned windows that opened into the rose garden.

"What do you expect?" David asked his friend. "Everyone is eager to meet your new bride."

More than two dozen guests immediately surrounded the duke, most from neighboring estates, who had not yet had the pleasure of meeting the new Duchess of Severly.

Soon everyone was enjoying themselves, helped in part by the bounty produced from the duke's excellent cellars.

As guests continued to arrive, it became apparent that one very important ingredient seemed to be missing from the festivities—the Duchess of Severly.

The duke continued to circulate among the colorful

and increasingly curious revelers. He greeted old friends and distant relatives, all with one topic on their lips—his wife.

As he directed a footman to bring Lord Graston another glass of champagne, Severly had to own that he found it amusing to know that the most recent rumor being spread about was that he and Celia had been secretly engaged for years before their marriage.

He was looking forward to sharing this latest *on dit* with Celia. That was, if she ever came downstairs, he thought with wry tenderness toward his beloved's tardiness.

As more guests arrived, Severly caught sight of Alex, the Duke of Westlake, threading his way toward him through the crowd.

"Westlake!" he greeted his old friend with pleasure. "Celia and I are well pleased that you will be staying this week. It has been too long since we have had your company."

Accepting a glass from a passing footman, Westlake gave his friend a knowing grin.

"Sink me, Severly, if you hadn't taken such a shockingly long honeymoon, you would have had my company long before this."

Severly laughed at his friend's comment. He had been receiving much the same roasting from a number of his guests, and accepted the teasing good-naturedly. After all, he and Celia had not been home to anyone save Imy and David for more than four months.

"My dear Severly," Lady Ardale loudly interrupted the two gentlemen, "never tell me the duchess has taken ill?"

Severly smiled fondly down at the petite Lady Ardale. Her family and his had been neighbors for generations, and she had been one of his mama's dearest friends. Having no sons of her own, she had always taken a keen interest in the duke's affairs.

"Fear not, Lady Ardale; I have no doubt my wife shall be along presently. My bride has but one fault: She takes a prodigious time over her toilette," he said with a slightly conspiratorial smile that set the old lady's heart aflutter.

"Oh, you," she twittered, hiding her face behind her fan.

The guests continued to stream in and yet there was still no sign of the duchess.

Excusing herself from a group of old friends, Imogene made her way across the crowded room to her brother. Severly thought his sister looked magnificent in an evening dress of bishop's blue.

"Drake, I am going to see what's keeping Celly," she said with a mischievous smile. "You must stop purchasing her so many gowns. You know what a difficult time she has deciding what to wear."

Severly nodded his agreement, glad of his sister's offer, before turning his attention to Lord and Lady Darnham. He wanted Celia next to him, for he was eager to show her off.

It took Imy some minutes to make her way out of the salon and up the massive oak staircase of her childhood home.

Upon reaching Celia and Drake's suite, she lightly tapped on the door. A moment later, the door opened a fraction and Imy saw Dora's blue eye peering at her.

"Oh, it's you, your grace," the little maid said with a deep sigh of relief before stepping back and opening the door wide.

"What on earth?" Imy said, wondering what could cause such odd behavior. Curiously, she looked around the beautiful room. It was decorated in shades of lilac and silver. One of the many gifts her brother had bestowed upon his bride had been the pleasure of completely redecorating their private quarters.

The yards and yards of sumptuous lilac and silver satin draping the large canopy bed must have cost Drake a small fortune, Imy thought. She could not help but admire her friend's taste as she stepped farther into the exquisitely appointed room.

"Celia?" Imy called, again looking around the room with a slight frown on her brow. Suddenly Dora rushed

past the duchess, knelt, and crawled under the bed. This
bizarre behavior caused Imy to lose her usual poise so
much that she stared agape at Dora's feet sticking out
from under the bed.

"What on earth?" Imy said again, as Celia emerged
from a very large dressing room situated on the other
side of the bedchamber.

"Oh, Imy! Thank God it's you," Celia said with great
relief. Imy saw that Celia was arrayed in the most beautifully designed gown Imogene had ever seen. The violet-
blue velvet seemed to deepen the emerald green flecks
in Celia's eyes.

Dora had obviously spent a considerable amount of
time on her mistress's hair arrangement, and Celia was
wearing the magnificent Severly diamonds around her
neck and wrists. Imogene thought she had never seen
Celia looking more beautiful or regal—until she looked
down and noticed that Celia's stockinged feet were
slipperless.

"Celly! Your guests are waiting. I can understand your
desire to make a grand entrance, but—"

Imy was cut off abruptly when Dora emerged from
under the bed with a cry of triumph.

"Here they are, your grace," she said with delight,
holding up a muslin bag.

"At last, Dora," Celia said, relief plainly written on
her face. "Imy, dear, I had no intention of being so late.
I just wanted to surprise Drake," she began as she moved
to sit on a beautifully upholstered settee placed in a bay
window that overlooked the formal gardens.

Dora removed a pair of violet-blue slippers from the
muslin bag and knelt to help her mistress put them on.

"Surprise Drake?" Imy asked impatiently. "Why? How?"

A smile began at the corners of Celia's mouth as she
looked up at her dearest friend.

"You see, Imy, before Drake and I were married, before I knew about the inheritance, Drake bought this
beautiful fabric because he knew I had admired it." She
looked down tenderly at the gown she wore and stroked
the fabric lovingly.

"So I sent the bolt off to Madame Triaud, without telling Drake" She continued her explanation as Dora finished tying the ribbons of her right shoe. "I wanted to have something very special for our first party. I didn't want Drake to see what Madame Triaud had created so Dora and I hid everything weeks ago. Tonight we could not find the slippers Madame Triaud had sent with the gown. Dora and I have been rushing around like mad-women trying to locate them." Celia ended her explanation on a laugh.

"I know Drake will find you a vision well worth the wait," Imy said loyally as she walked back toward the door. "But come now, before your guests think Drake's marriage is a hoax."

Celia laughed again at her friend's words as Dora finished tying the bow around her left ankle and the two friends left the room together.

"I am so pleased you, David, and the boys are staying with us," Celia said happily as they went down the stair-case arm in arm. "You are stunning this evening, Imy. I have never seen you so radiant."

"Nor I you. Marriage obviously agrees with us." Imy smiled and squeezed Celia's arm in affection. "Let me go in first, Celly, so your grand entrance won't be spoiled."

Celia hesitated on the last step, looking at Imy with a very faint frown marring her brow.

"Imy, is *she* here?"

They both knew who "she" was.

"Yes, she is," Imy said with disdain. "And so is the earl. You'll finally make his acquaintance," she said before nodding to a footman to open the door for her.

Celia stood alone for a moment outside the grand salon, listening to the loud hum of voices coming from behind the closed doors.

Tonight she really would be the Duchess of Severly, Celia thought with some trepidation.

These last four months had been the most blissful of her life. Each day she had come to know her husband better, her love had grown deeper and stronger, until she now felt as if he were a part of her and she of him. She

loved Severly Park. It already felt like home because
Drake had gone to such lengths to make her feel as if
she not only belonged at his side but that he valued her
ideas and opinions on improvements he planned for the
vast estate.

Celia adored being Drake's wife. But until now, she
had not felt like a duchess. She wanted so badly to make
him proud of her. But here she was, all flustered from
being late, she thought with some anxiety as she checked
her appearance one last time in a large hall mirror.

Madame Triaud had included a note in the parcel
when she sent the completed ensemble. The modiste
wrote that she considered the violet-blue gown her greatest creation, even more magnificent than anything in
Princess Charlotte's trousseau. Celia had to agree.

Lifting her chin, she turned back to the doors and
nodded to the liveried footmen. As the doors opened,
the merry noise coming from the mass of people seemed
to assail her senses. She hesitated slightly as the doors
closed behind her, trying to catch sight of Drake so that
he would come to her side. She saw him immediately
and, thank goodness, he was close by. She had not
wanted to cross the packed room on her own.

He was next to her instantly, his broad-shouldered
presence giving her the confidence she suddenly lacked.

Celia saw his eyes travel over her form, taking in the
beautiful gown that had been created from his gift. She
watched with shy pleasure as his slight look of surprise
changed to that look of intimate admiration that had
become so familiar to her in the last few months.

"Here you are, my love." He bowed formally over
her hand, the look on his face revealing the pride and
tenderness he felt for her.

Celia did not notice that a hush had suddenly come
over the assemblage as she smiled deeply into her husband's eyes. "Forgive my lateness, darling, but I couldn't
find my slippers."

At the absurdity of this excuse, Drake threw back his
head and laughed. Those nearest joined the duke, and
as the comment was repeated throughout the room, soon

everyone was laughing with him at the uncontrived wit of his beautiful wife.

The duke spent the next half hour introducing Celia to those in the room she had not met before. Soon, any lingering trepidation at her first social appearance as Drake's wife dissipated as everyone welcomed her warmly.

"Ho, ho, young devil, I can see why you kept this beauty hidden all this time," said the elderly Lord Layton, with a wink and a nudge to Drake's ribs.

"Why, I never thought to see young Severly so besotted with anyone, especially a wife," Lord Kerwood said to his Lady Kerwood, his voice carrying across the room due to a bit of deafness.

"Believe me, milord, neither did I," the duke said with a self-deprecating smile that caused even more comment and laughter throughout the room.

Drake continued to squire his wife among the guests, stopping here and there to chat with their guests. Celia decided she was beginning to enjoy herself, especially when she espied Corinna Sheffield and the earl of Chandley standing together on the other side of the room, deep in conversation. She had invited each of them to stay at Severly Park and was quite pleased when both accepted. Celia secretly hoped they would come to realize what she believed—that they were well matched.

Celia was pulled from the contemplation of her friends' potential romance when she heard the ever-so-slight change of tone in her husband's deep voice.

"My dear, allow me to make known to you Lord Kendall. You have met Lady Kendall, of course."

Celia paused a moment to gain her composure before turning to these guests. This was the moment she'd been dreading all day. Steeling herself for the inevitable meeting with Letty Kendall, Celia lifted her chin slightly. How like the beau monde, Celia thought with a wry smile touching her lips. It was the most urbane thing in the world to meet the husband of your husband's former mistress.

With a mental sigh, Celia knew it was best to just get

it over with; to snub the Kendalls would only give credence to any lingering gossip about Drake and Lady Kendall. Celia had hoped that they would have the good graces to send their regrets, but her hopes were dashed when the butler had brought a stack of replies for her to review over breakfast last week. At the top of the pile was a note from Lady Kendall saying that she and the earl would be delighted to attend the Duke and Duchess of Severly.

Celia hoped the smile she had so firmly planted on her lips appeared natural as she greeted Lord and Lady Kendall.

But to her surprise, the Earl of Kendall was not at all what Celia had expected. The man before her was certainly not old. He was tall, fair, and very attractive, she observed as he made an elegant leg before her.

Casting a quick look at the petite woman standing next to the earl, Celia saw that Letty Kendall looked like a porcelain doll in her pale blue gown. Except for the truculent expression marring her pretty face, Celia could not help thinking with some satisfaction.

"Welcome to Severly Park, Lord and Lady Kendall. I hope this bad weather did not make your journey a chore?" Celia said, smiling at the earl and refusing to look at Letty again unless she was forced to.

"Indeed not, your grace. Even if the weather had been far worse, it would not have stopped me from accepting an invitation to Severly Park. Everyone speaks of your grace's beauty and charm. I had a desire to see for myself if the rumors were true. I can now attest that they are," the earl drawled with what could only be characterized as an intimate smile.

Celia's beautiful eyes met Drake's in a flashing moment of shared amusement. She was hard-put not to laugh, especially when she saw the effect Lord Kendall's words had on his pouty wife. The petite woman's head whipped up to stare at her husband in annoyed surprise at this compliment.

Before another word could be spoken, Drake put his hand on Celia's elbow and said, "You must pardon us,

Lord Kendall, Lady Kendall. I see my cousin standing unattended, and he has not yet met my bride." With a slight inclination of his head, Drake drew Celia away.

As they moved across the room together, Celia tossed her husband a mock accusing look.

"I seem to recall, your grace, your describing the earl as rather old. He's only a year or two older than you if he's a day." She kept a smile on her face and her voice low.

Her husband quirked a brow and shrugged his broad shoulders. "I have no interest in Kendall's age," he stated dismissively.

But Celia was not ready to give up her tease. "He could be considered a very attractive man," she declared as they neared Imogene and David.

"Do you consider him so?" Drake's glittering hazel eyes met hers in a look of such possessive passion that her knees grew weak.

"Not really," she whispered truthfully, her eyes still locked with his.

"Good," he said huskily, allowing his fingers to trail down the inside of her arm to stroke her wrist with strong, warm fingers.

The gaiety continued well into the evening, and Celia decided that playing hostess was not so daunting after all. A smile touched her lips as she took a moment from her conversation with the Dowager Duchess of Harbrooke and Corinna Sheffield to scan the well-appointed room, making sure her guests were happy.

"You are giving a very good accounting of yourself, Celia," the dowager said fondly.

Celia gave a radiant smile to the older woman. This praise meant a great deal to Celia, for she had always admired Imy's mother-in-law. "Thank you, ma'am," Celia said as she sketched a quick curtsy. "If I have not made a goose of myself this evening, it is only because I have always tried to emulate you and dear Imogene all these years."

The dowager looked well pleased at Celia's words. Corinna gazed at her friend in admiration. She wondered once again how Letty Kendall had had the nerve to spread the rumor about Celia's being a servant when it was so well known that Celia was on intimate terms with some of the finest families in the country.

"La! This is such a delightful evening, my dear duchess."

The three ladies turned at the sound of Letty Kendall's childish voice.

Looking down at the petite woman, Celia saw the malice plainly evident in her wide blue eyes. Celia cast a quick glance at Corinna and saw her roll her eyes in distaste.

"I am pleased that you are enjoying yourself," Celia said in a neutral tone.

"Oh, la, yes," Lady Kendall tittered. "I *always* enjoy myself at Severly Park. Severly is such an attentive host."

Celia knew she was meant to catch the sly note of intimacy so obvious in the petite woman's tone. Suddenly, Celia was out of patience with the countess. It was one thing to accept the occasional social slight, but quite another to be baited in her own home, she thought in rising aggravation.

Raising one eyebrow, Celia strove to make her expression as indifferent as possible. "If you continue to make yourself tiresome Lady Kendall, this may be the last time you enjoy yourself at Severly Park," Celia said coolly.

After a moment of stunned silence, Corinna made an unintelligible sound before clamping a hand over her mouth. As Celia continued to look down at Lady Kendall, her heart racing at her own boldness, she heard the dowager duchess chuckle approvingly.

Letty sputtered her outrage. "Well! I have never—"

"Of course you have, my dear," cut in Lord Kendall silkily, stepping into their circle. Turning to Celia, the earl made a slight bow. "We have enjoyed your hospitality this eve, your grace, but alas, we must depart. Come, Leticia." There was a hard edge to his voice as he ended this pretty speech.

Letty continued to sputter her indignation as her husband led her away, with the entire room staring after them. Corinna finally pulled her hand from her mouth and allowed the barely contained laughter to escape.

Imogene, who had been standing close by with the major, leaned forward with laughter-filled eyes and said, "My dear Celia, you really are a duchess."

In the very early hours of the morning, lying together in their huge canopied bed with her head resting sleepily on her husband's shoulder, Celia felt Drake's lips against her temple.

"I love you, Celia," he said in a deep, sleep-husky voice.

Celia snuggled deeper under the sumptuous blankets, savoring the warmth of his strong arms around her.

"I love you too, darling."

She was almost asleep when a thought drifted through her mind, causing a very small chuckle.

"What amuses you at such a late hour, love?"

Raising her head slightly from his shoulder, she looked at her husband's face. She could barely make out his strong features in the darkened room. Her heart swelled with the enormity of her love for him.

"Edna would have loved this evening," she whispered with a smile.

Allison Lane

"A FORMIDABLE TALENT... MS. LANE NEVER FAILS TO DELIVER THE GOODS."
—*ROMANTIC TIMES*

THE NOTORIOUS WIDOW
0-451-20166-3

When a scoundrel tries to tarnish a young widow's reputation, a valiant Earl tries to repair the damage—and mend her broken heart as well...

BIRDS OF A FEATHER
0-451-19825-5

When a plain, bespectacled young woman keeps meeting the handsome Lord Wylie, she feels she is not up to his caliber. A great arbiter of fashion for London society, Lord Wylie was reputed to be more interseted in the cut of his clothes than the feelings of others, as the young woman bore witness to. Degraded by him in public, she could nevertheless forget his dashing demeanor. It will take a public scandal, and a private passion, to bring them together...

To order call: 1-800-788-6262

Signet Regency Romances from

BARBARA METZGER

MISS WESTLAKE'S WINDFALL
0-451-20279-1
Miss Ada Westlake has two treasures at her fingertips.
One is a cache of coins she discovered in her orchard,
and the other is her friend (and sometime suitor),
Viscount Ashmead. She has been advised to keep a
tight hold on both. But Ada must discover for herself
that the greatest gift of all is true love...

THE PAINTED LADY
0-451-20368-2
Stunned when the lovely lady he is painting suddenly
comes to life on the canvas and talks to him, the Duke
of Caswell can only conclude that his mind has finally
snapped. But when his search for help sends him to Sir
Osgood Bannister, the noted brain fever expert and
doctor to the king, he ends up in the care of the
charming, naive Miss Lilyanne Bannister, and his life
suddenly takes on a whole new dimension...

To order call: 1-800-788-6262

S435/Metzger